W9-BJP-173

DEAD IN THE WATER

DEAD IN THE WATER

Vivien Armstrong

SEVERN SH HOUSE

This first world edition published in Great Britain 1998 by
SEVERN HOUSE PUBLISHERS LTD of
9–15 High Street, Sutton, Surrey SM1 1DF.
This first world edition published in the U.S.A. 1999 by
SEVERN HOUSE PUBLISHERS INC of
595 Madison Avenue, New York, N.Y. 10022.

British Library Cataloguing in Publication Data

Armstrong, Vivien
        Dead in the water
        1. Detective and mystery stories
        I. Title
        823.9'14 [F]

        ISBN 0-7278-2229-2

Typeset by Palimpsest Book Production Ltd,
Polmont, Stirlingshire, Scotland.
Printed and bound in Great Britain by
MPG Books Ltd, Bodmin, Cornwall.

One

No one expects working for a dentist to be a barrel of laughs. And only the week before the April morning Mimsie Crane opened up the surgery to find her boss strapped in his horizontal chair with nothing but a bunch of daffodils between his crotch, Mimsie had toyed with the idea of looking for another job. Even so . . .

She stood in the doorway, holding her dripping umbrella, taking in the chaos. The surgery was in ruins: the doors of all the cabinets swinging open, instruments littering the floor, the fireplace piled with charred files. Her files. Oh my . . . And Mr Chambers always so pernickety about Mimsie's filing. Apart from the naked figure writhing on his very own torture rack, trussed up like a boiling fowl, the most arresting feature was the graffiti. The F-word was unimaginatively the central motif, but spraying those virgin walls with such explicit descriptions of the dentist's shortcomings without even the benefit of a spell-check struck Mimsie with awe and admiration.

She started to giggle, the umbrella falling to the floor as she leaned weakly against the door jamb, the gurgles rising. A dreadful ululation. Unstoppable. Worse than laughing at a funeral. A ghastly reaction causing her shoulders to shake with terrible, terrible glee.

Mr Chambers's eyes swivelled furiously like the twin barrels of a shotgun, the carefully gelled swathe of hair which normally draped his bald spot sliced off, leaving a dramatic tuft, a misplaced devil's horn projecting over one ear. His pearly dome was now, as with everything else, unveiled to common view.

Mimsie choked and with a supreme effort pulled herself together, rushing forward to rip the surgical tape from Mr

Chambers's lips. The first words were a mirror image of the fruity expletives displayed on his own surgery walls which seemed a poor response in Mimsie's view. Even so, such a natural reaction brought a grudging admiration for the man who had never hitherto presented any pretence of a 'nice side' to his receptionist.

As she smartly stripped her employer from the painful embrace of the surgical tape, her mind flipped to the arresting depiction of the flaying of Marsyas she had seen at the Academy in the summer. A satyr, bound hand and foot, waiting for the treatment, its eyes, narrowed with defiance, showed only contempt for those who had brought him to this humiliating pass.

She left the daffodils decently in place and stood back as he leaped off the couch, the yellow blooms strewing the floor. He grabbed a surgical mask from the desk in a furious attempt to drape himself, the raw stripes on his skinny shanks opening up a fascinating line of conjecture, forcing Mimsie, under the unwavering fusillade of the man's gaze, to glance away as he shoved past.

She wandered into the waiting room and listened to him stamping about in the flat above, banging doors, crashing into things, presumably creating a corresponding mayhem in his private apartment.

It was difficult to know where to start. She retrieved the flowers, arranged them in the vase on her desk, and sat waiting for Mr Chambers to reappear, vaguely scanning the appointments book. Major Fanshawe was due in under ten minutes, always insisting on being 'first to go over the top' as he called it. The continuing racket upstairs at least reassured her that the dentist was not in shock. Mimsie hesitated to cancel anything without consulting Mr Chambers, his fuse, at the best of times, being explosively short, Mimsie having been reminded on more than one occasion that, 'You are, Miss Crane, without doubt, the worst receptionist I have *ever* had!'

After a further five minutes' consideration, she shook out her umbrella, placed it tidily in the stand by the door, closed the blinds and secured the catch. Still wearing her mac, she idly stacked the magazines, wondering why whoever

2

had broken in had exclusively desecrated the surgery. A disaffected patient? A user fruitlessly searching for cocaine? An embittered dental mechanic driven whacko by Mimsie's disorganised bookkeeping? She was still turning over these interesting possibilities in her mind as Mr Chambers came downstairs.

He wore a dark suit and carried a raincoat over his arm, his flight bag packed, restored to his normal petulant self apart from the vital strand of hair which had draped his bald spot. In a nervous gesture, he stroked the place where it should have been like an amputee whose missing leg still throbbed, ghostlike and painfully insistent.

"Shall I call the police, Mr Chambers?"

"No! I have already telephoned my sister. Mrs Watson will be here very shortly. Cancel all appointments until further notice, Miss Crane."

"What shall I say?"

He sighed, the folds of his cheeks settling like the final effervescence from a dyspepsia tablet. "Say I have been taken ill. I want none of this . . ." he gestured weakly towards the door of the surgery, "to be a matter of local tittle-tattle. My sister will instruct you." He placed a cheque on the reception desk. "A month's pay in lieu of notice, Miss Crane. Your discretion—" he muttered, wincing from the sight of the daffodils in their glass vase.

Mimsie nodded, unable to tear her eyes away from the reddened flesh round his mouth where she had ripped off the surgical tape. It looked obscene. Like the guilty scrubbing at smears of lipstick acquired in a gay bar. Suddenly, she felt pity for the wretched man and moved forward, her eyes unaccountably brimming, but he pushed her aside, striding through the kitchenette and out through the back door into Yardley Street. She heard his BMW start up and when the sound of the big engine had died away she sank down, folding and refolding the cheque in her hands, waiting for Phoebe Watson, the sister, to take over.

As she pulled the appointments book forward, it occured

3

to her that Phoebe might never before have come across the lively descriptive style of the graffiti artist who had daubed the surgery walls. With luck, the dreadful old harridan might be rendered speechless.

Two

At twenty-six years of age Mimsie Crane was nobody's fool. But her hold on the job scene suffered a basic flaw: Mimsie had a congenital absence of staying power. And in the nineties, with unemployment rife, her undeniable range of experience – from fast food waitress to paid dog walker – seemed only to stack against her. On paper it looked decidedly fishy.

Nevertheless, her abrupt ejection from Mr Chambers's dental surgery with a cheque in lieu wasn't all bad news. Never one to worry about where the rent was coming from, Mimsie decided to give herself a breather. She took five weeks off and claimed a long-standing invitation to take a berth on a boat being refitted in Malta by an Aussie boyfriend, a fellow crew member she hadn't seen since her spell as a galley-dolly on a yacht in the Bahamas chartered by American tourists. Guy was a mate. No strings attached and lots of fun. Not one to take 'No' as a personal affront either which made for easy living. She returned to London looking as soft and brown as a ripe fig, her smooth legs seemingly inches longer for their Mediterranean deck sports.

The girl at the agency frowned at Mimsie's file, riffling the pages with undisguised perplexity. They were both old hands at this, Mimsie's all-too-frequent trawling of the jobs market leaving Liz Bray's professional optimism badly dented.

"What about a bit of temping?"

Mimsie's eyes rose to the ceiling in wordless prayer.

"OK. No temping. Anyway, with your speeds you're not exactly *la crème de la crème* are you? Can you dance?"

"Dance?"

"Well, wiggle about a bit. There's this PR firm takes on freelancers for press launches. Tequila girls. Passing out free

5

cigarettes at race meetings. Jiggling your tits at the Motor Show. That sort of thing . . ." Her voice trailed off as this vista of glittering opportunities passed over her client's flagging attention like an incredibly boring rerun of a Clint Eastwood video.

Mimsie leaned back in her seat, flicking a non-existent piece of fluff on her gilded knee. "I suppose it'll have to be Steve's again."

Liz lost her cool. "You've got a nerve, Mimsie. You can't take shorthand, you're always on the phone to your friends and your bookkeeping's appalling."

Mimsie laughed. "You should see Steve's payslips! Making up the wage packets on a Friday's like doling out the loaves and fishes. You need *danger money* to work in that place."

"Don't run away with the idea Steve's exactly panting to take you on again after that last time."

"That brickie you mean? The one who threatened to break his legs? It was *me* who saved Steve from GBH let me tell you. If I hadn't hid him in the girls' room and fended the guy off with my own cheque, Steve would have been in plaster up to his armpits."

"As it happens, I've already spoken to him and suggested sending you over to help out. His exact words were: 'Mimsie? You must be joking. Mimsie naked on all fours, yes please. But behind a typewriter? – give me a break'."

Mimsie burst into a chortle of delight, dispelling Liz's anger at a stroke. They giggled at the glorious mental picture of Mimsie playing doggie.

"Seriously, Mimsie, we're scraping the barrel here, but maybe I can talk him round. He was on the phone to me only this morning. Got a load of jobs on and no one to front the office. So why not? It's cash in hand."

"*When* he pays!"

"Let's face it. You've tried everything else. Shall I give him a buzz? Incidentally, what went wrong with the dentist? Did you get him to give you a reference before you went walkabout?"

"His surgery was vandalised. *And* he got mugged. Mr

6

Chambers was hardly in a position to sit down and write out a reference."

With enormous restraint Mimsie stopped herself from describing the graffiti on the surgery walls. In fact, the only person she could have shared a laugh with over this was Steve Epps, the small-time builder she worked for when all else failed.

When Mr Chambers's sister, Phoebe Watson, had bustled in to the surgery like Hurricane Hetty that morning five weeks before, Mimsie had silently applauded the woman's Oscar-winning performance. Anyone would think Phoebe faced four-letter words spelled out in day-glo spray paint every day of the week.

"We must get someone in," she muttered. "Straight away. Someone – someone – er – discreet."

"A whitewash job," Mimsie quipped.

"Absolutely. Mr Green won't do."

Mr Green was their regular painter and decorator, a local man, some sort of deacon at the Baptist Chapel. Trying to save the dentist's new receptionist from eternal damnation had practically robbed him of his faith.

"I know someone," Mimsie ventured. "I've worked for him off and on . . . Steven Epps. He does a lot of confidential work." That was putting it mildly.

Phoebe nodded, hearing Mimsie warm to her subject. She waited while Mimsie made the call, leapfrogging Steve's answer machine with some sort of password. Within the hour he arrived to measure up, promising to bring a team before lunch. They would repaint and repair the entire surgery before the weekend. His heartfelt outrage at the vandalism would have brought tears to your eyes.

Phoebe was impressed, her initial recoil at the sight of Steve's Ray Bans and designer suit mollified by the barrow-boy cockiness. Beneath the glitz Steve Epps was a type she was familiar with. They spoke the same language. Cash on the nail. No questions asked. Total confidentiality. And, Phoebe promised, if so much as a whisper about the job got out, an anonymous tip-off to the VAT inspector would be in the post with a first-class stamp.

Mimsie found herself bundled out ahead of Steve who

hoiked his foreman from the van and directed him round the back to detail the damage. He pulled Mimsie to one side while he made a couple of calls on his mobile, then gave her the full treatment, all sincerity, the rain spotting his silk lapels. He wasn't a bad looking bloke and had a gorgeous smile, she conceded. In fact, he was okay if you could take the chat. Not to mention the hassle of being the only woman in an office where the heavy tread of unpaid building labourers made working for Steve a heart-stopping adventure.

He grinned. "Thanks, Mimsie. Rush jobs always fetch a premium." He palmed a fifty-pound note from the wad in his gold money clip. "I owe you one."

Steve's entire vocabulary struggled under a burden of double meanings, and Mimsie's cheerful peck on the cheek before she dashed for her bus sealed their conspiracy of silence. It was only after she was sitting on the top deck counting the unexpected windfall the morning's work had brought that she remembered her umbrella, still in the stand by the surgery door.

It must be a sign. Time she found some sunshine? As the bus trundled past the dripping facade of the V & A, Mimsie Crane made up her mind to find out if Guy's boat was still holed up in Gozo.

Three

B ut that had been five weeks ago.

The immediate problem was the rent. There was nothing for it. She would have to pop the watch again. Mimsie's costly timepiece had been a trophy from a futures dealer to whom she had briefly been engaged. A gold Rolex seemed infinitely preferable to a diamond solitaire and her second thoughts on the 'for richer, for poorer' scenario were not burdened by the time-honoured propriety of returning the ring.

Pawning the Rolex was a wrench but there was nothing else for it. 'Uncle's' was a familiar temporary resting place for her only material asset and the pledge was always eventually redeemed. Anyway, as Liz had observed, Mimsie Crane was a lousy timekeeper even *with* a watch.

She emerged from the jeweller's pleased as a cat with a canary, her tote bag clutched to her chest. Dodging the landlord for over a week had been no joke and, in any event, if she was starting back at Steve Epps in the morning a cushion of cash in hand was a necessity. With Steve one could never tell where the next paypacket was coming from. As she was feeling in such an uncharacteristically prudent state of mind she decided to buy a new umbrella while she was about it.

Her two-roomed flat occupied the first floor front of a five-storey house in Frayne Gardens. It wasn't the worst flat she had ever had and the kitchen alcove was a distinct bonus, but the landlord was a Cypriot with a very suspicious nature. Allowing two months' arrears to accumulate had overstretched even Mimsie's ability to prevaricate and when Mr Phidias spotted her running up the front steps as he was tying up the garbage bags, the man visibly hardened his heart.

"Hey! Miss Crane!" he called, throwing down the over-flowing bin liner, empty cans and takeaway cartons spilling round his feet. He hurried up the area steps and blocked her move to put her key in the lock. He was a thickset individual with muscles which argued his claim to be a 'retired accountant'. His expression, normally sunny, set in lines of anxiety. He hated having to press his claims as landlord, the downside of what he and poor Renee had hoped would prove a quiet occupation for a mild man with a heart murmur. At least they had a place of their own and didn't have to live on the premises.

"Why, Mr Phidias! How nice! I was hoping to catch you."

He rattled off his stock diatribe about tenants who were behind with the rent and was about to launch into the full eviction preamble when the girl startlingly produced a purse visibly chock-a-block with banknotes.

"We go inside?" he muttered, motioning her to precede him down to the basement. "Girls, these days—" he grumbled, feeling wrong-footed by what seemed a premature attack on the poor little thing. Even so – eight weeks! Was that being unreasonable?

Mr Phidias carefully counted the cash the girl laid on the table and scribbled a receipt. She leaned against his sideboard, her face swimming in his myopic vision like the pale disc of a holy medal. He suggested a glass of wine, all smiles, his gold tooth gleaming in the semi-darkness behind the drawn blinds of what he termed 'the office'.

"Lovely," she said, slipping off her jacket and sinking down at the table, swivelling round to stretch long, long legs towards the electric fire. Mr P felt the cold. His 'office' was always draughty as catacombs and the air wafted a constant drift of garlic and cigarette smoke. Even so, in Mimsie's book, keeping in with the landlord was a sensible attitude and a glass of red wouldn't go amiss either. She nibbled at the salted almonds heaped in a saucer on the embroidered tablecloth, admiring the icon-like picture of the madonna gleaming above the mantleshelf.

"There was someone lookin' for you, Miss Crane. While you was on 'oliday."

Mimsie raised an eyebrow. "A man?"

"Ah, yes. Asian. Big. You know 'im?"

Mimsie shook her head. "For me? You sure?"

"Well, no exactly for you, Miss Crane. He was askin' for the dental nurse. Mr Chambers's dental nurse."

"Well, I was *never* his nurse, Mr Phidias. Anyway, Mr Chambers was taken ill. That's why I left. This man should have gone to the surgery."

"He said the place was all shut up, Miss Crane. The dentist, he gone. The cleaning lady she told 'im they both gone. Gone abroad she say."

"Mr Chambers *and* his sister?" Mimsie sat up. "And this cleaning woman, Mrs Garland I suppose, sent him here?"

The man nodded, looking worried, wishing now he had kept quiet about the fellow. Perhaps Miss Crane wasn't as sweetly innocent as she seemed. Maybe this bloke lookin' for 'er was a policeman?

Mimsie grinned. "Well, *I* don't know where old Chambers is. Perhaps he went off with his sister while the place was being redecorated. Still, he must be back by now. It's been over a month . . . When was this man here?"

"Called *several* times, Miss Crane. Wouldn't take no. His English was bad," he said with all the contempt of a full British citizen. "'e wanted an address of you. I *told* him you was on a boat. Gone on your 'olidays I said. He was very angry. A guy with toothache, eh?"

Mimsie rose, frowning at the bowl of nuts, suddenly chilled at the thought of one of Chambers's patients on the prowl. She gathered up her coat and bag and despite a further flurry of questions got nothing more from Mr P, not even a name.

He was flummoxed by her swift change of mood and wished he had forgotten all about the persistent fellow. It was his rule *never* to take messages for the tenants. Never. Only that Miss Crane could have upset his house rule and what thanks did he get?

Mimsie let herself out, patting his arm abstractedly before bounding up the steps.

She ran a bath, lying in the scented water admiring her

11

tan, mentally fingering her options. Working for Steve wasn't so terrible – at least he was always cheerful, never crusty like old Chambers. Steve Epps was more of an entrepreneur really. Instead of juggling his chorus line of chippies and plasterers he should have been managing a rock band or running a circus. Whenever things got really sticky Steve broke into a tap-dance routine and clattered round the filing cabinets crooning 'Singing in the Rain'.

She grinned, wondering if Eva, Steve's current live-in girlfriend got first call on the wage bill for the housekeeping. Mimsie rather doubted it. Eva's command of English was as bad as Mr Phidias's and a neat turn of phrase was the very minimum requirement for any sort of toe-to-toe with Steve over money.

Now Phoebe, Chambers's sister, was a match for Steve all right. Though, knowing him, it wouldn't surprise her if a little extra unitemised bartering was added to the bill for that cosmetic job on the surgery walls. Hollywood style bridgework on Eva's teeth for instance? Or what about a nice clean-up on the terrible gnashers of that guard dog of his, Havoc? That was the trouble with invoices from Epps Building Services. There were always loads of hidden extras.

She climbed out of the tub, frowning at the recollection of her last day at the dental surgery. Fancy the place still being closed? Old Phidias must have got it wrong, the man trying to track down Mr Chambers's dental assistant was probably an old flame of Lynne Peters, the nurse who got the heave-ho from the dentist the week Mimsie herself started work in reception.

It was never quite clear what the row had been about. Lynne had just stalked out slamming the door behind her, leaving a waiting room full of bug-eyed patients. Old Chambers had had to get his sister to come over. After that he relied on agency nurses most of the week or, when really pushed, Phoebe Watson would stand in. He had never asked Mimsie to help out even in an emergency . . .

Having wasted not a single thought on poor old Chambers

for the past month, Mimsie found herself intrigued. Was the surgery really still closed?

She decided to take an evening stroll through Kensington Gardens and suss it out for herself.

Four

S teve Epps's builders' yard and office occupied a corner
site just beyond Chiswick Bridge. The ugly sixties
warehouse building had seen service as a trade showroom,
a block of cooperative craftworkers' workshops and, more
recently, a gym club. When the gym folded with the arrival
of a smarter outfit only half a mile away, Steve made a deal
with the new owner: free rental including the use of the car
park as a storage yard in exchange for a special price on the
refurbishment of the club into office units. When the final
unit was let, Steve would move on.

Naturally, the job proceded slowly and even the developer,
a formerly patient man called Jerry Logan, started lying
awake at night mulling over the pros and cons of this
peculiar arrangement with Epps Building Services. Trouble
was, Steve's boys were good. The units Epps *had* done
over were first class and whenever Jerry Logan tried to
pin him down to some notion of timescale, the man's
naked enthusiasm for the Pollard Place Project bemused
him with mingled hope and terror. Even the bank manager
was mollified.

In the meantime, the yard was constantly in use and
Steve's nightwatchman, aided by Havoc, the rottweiler,
erased any anxieties Logan and the insurance company had
about security.

Mimsie took a taxi to work next day feeling temporarily
flush – never an enthusiast for public transport first thing in
the morning. Pollard Place was now surrounded by a high
fence topped by razor wire, and an old character actor called
Austen Malone, who was 'resting', kept surveillance over
the single entrance by day with the acidity of Cerberus at
the gate.

Mimsie and Austen were old pals, Austen's patchwork career – like Mimsie's – dovetailing nicely with spasmodic stints with Epps Building Services. Mimsie dropped in for a chat, raising Austen's woozy libido with a glimpse of sun-kissed thigh as she wiggled onto the high stool at his bench inside the hut. Havoc lumbered in, jaws drooling, recognising the voice of the passing angel whose pockets generally produced a Rollo or two at the very least.

Austen perched on a shot-off tennis umpire's chair which raised his massive bulk to regal enthronement. He wore a cream flannel shirt with a yellow silk cravat, an oddly reassuring image for a security guard. The chair afforded the same false impression as lift shoes might have done, for in truth the man was not hewn on an heroic scale, but merely comported himself like a king. He kept a reptilian eye on the comings and goings of Steve's itinerent workforce jotting details in a pad at his elbow of any unusual transport of timber and supplies both in and out. His most valuable activity was via the direct line on the mobile phone with which he alerted Steve of any unheralded arrival of Jerry Logan, clients or stern-faced strangers. Austen had a special gift for this, a sort of sixth sense which made his rare appearances on the boards a serious drawback to Steve's line of business.

Mimsie patted Havoc, resting her elbows on the bench and scanning the row of vehicles in the yard. Morning mist off the river swirled round the car park in a desultory half-promise of better things to come, the sky pearly and indeterminate as only English summer skies can be. Steve's red Volvo was yet to put in an appearance.

"Well, what's new, Austen?"

"Not much. Logan's on the prowl. He managed to rent out two top-floor units to a firm of sports promoters and kicked Steve's outfit downstairs last week. Churned him up no end – he'll have to get going on the next stage now."

"How many units to go?"

"Three – no, four. But, knowing Steve, that'll take some time." Austen roared with laughter, a full-throated bellow perfected with his best Shakespearean role, a run at Stratford with Falstaff in the seventies.

"What about the shower block?"

15

"Still there. Steve reckons he needs special lifting gear before he can tackle it. Twenty bloody cubicles all set in concrete. Jesus!"

"And the swimming pool?"

"Logan's biding his time on that one. Hopes to wangle it in with the basement let. Some sort of colonic irrigation clinic on the hook last time I heard."

"A what? No, don't tell me. It's too early in the day. My stomach couldn't stand it." She glanced at the alarm clock on Austen's bench, doing time with all his other little necessities: the kettle, the copy of *The Stage*, the spilled bag of crisps, the ciggies and a half bottle of gin.

She sighed, slipping off the stool like a seal sliding into low tide.

"Must go. Which floor did you say?"

"Second. No one in yet except Bobby."

"The 'Varlet'! What's he this time? Cleaner? Gofer? Or Steve's Man Friday?" 'Varlet' was Steve's little witticism. Bobby Clark was a teenage would-be actor who followed Austen from pub to pub, touching the hem of his garment, convinced that the old has-been was the key to the stage doors of every theatre from Leicester Square to Hammersmith.

"Assistant floor manager he calls himself now," he said with a grimace worthy of Dr Frankenstein contemplating his regrettable invention.

She grabbed the bag of crisps and sketched a gesture of goodbye before jogging across the yard and upstairs.

Steve's new office was pretty much the same as the previous one on the top floor but the paintwork was scuffed and flecked with what looked like old bloodstains and the entire place was still redolent of sweat and heavy-duty machine oil. Relics of the gym club in the form of framed grainy black and white blow-ups of gleaming pecs surmounted by the totally committed manic gaze of an assortment of health freaks competed for her undivided attention. A final clatter in the back room announced Bobby's cleaning stint was in its death throes and Mimsie sighed, delaying the moment when raising the boy's diminishing self-confidence must clank into play.

Steve's attitude didn't help. His persistent ribbing of the wretched kid would have bruised the ego of de Niro himself.

16

Austen had somehow attracted this weedy youth like fluff
under the bed, Bobby's stage-struck innocence now firmly
hitched to that flickering star, Austen Malone, whose name
still rang bells in theatrical agents' outer offices.

Mimsie flopped down at the receptionist's desk, a grand
affair topped by smoked glass and fronting a small area
bounded by three leather sofas. Steve's movable outer office
kit. A coffee table stacked with current issues of *The World
of Interiors* and *Country Life* augmented the style which
Epps Building Services cultivated, the counter manned by
whichever Temp of the Week was in situ. The reception
area was, in fact, a drawbridge. It cut off Steve from the
first assault via the front steps and gave him time to slip
down the fire exit from his office at the back if Austen's
signal should warrant it.

Mimsie settled at the computer thankful that it was only
Wednesday – two days before the painful business of explaining away Steve's absence came into operation. Fridays were,
without a doubt, a pill and even the temps, blinded by
Steve's undoubted charm and spasmodic generosity, could
never stand the strain of any permanent employment. Even
so these girls were a limited edition of some distinction. All
pretty. All smart as paint and all, with practice, as smooth
tongued as the job demanded. But Mimsie was Steve's
favourite. Despite her obvious professional shortcomings,
Mimsie Crane definitely had something. Tall, slim – verging
on the thin – straightbacked, long legged and with an air of
the country girl about her which must have arisen because
of her colouring as she was, most certainly, a city girl at
heart. A brunette with creamy skin and wide blue eyes. Sort
of classic Irish.

Bobby's head shot round the door, his shock of carroty
hair contrasting cruelly with the acid-green tee shirt.

"Hey, Mimsie! Didn't know you were coming back. Where've
you been?"

"On holiday. Before that working for a dentist."

"Ouch!"

Mimsie nodded, sifting through the pile of unopened mail.
"You said it. He even had me dressing up in this nurse's
outfit like some old rerun of 'Emergency'. But don't tell

17

Steve – I'll never hear the end of it. Who was here last week? Nobody's touched the post for days."

"That girl Priscilla – you know, the debby one. She came in for a couple of days but Steve's been strapped for weeks. Even got Eva in for a bit last month but her accent on the phone was so thick poor old Logan thought he'd got the wrong number. Thought it was some massage parlour on the line."

He rewound the vacuum cleaner cord, mesmerised by Mimsie's air of detachment as she flicked through the post, sorting invoices from the painfully handwritten worksheets, stacking them into separate piles, running her fingers down Steve's diary entries for the day. It was if she had never been away. She smiled, giving Bobby her full attention at last.

"Well, everything looks okay to me. Plenty of work, no final demands in the pipeline. How's life with you?"

He was just getting into his stride with a description of an audition for the chorus in the new Lloyd Webber when the doors flung open and Steve blew in.

He wore a pale grey suit and aquamarine tie, the snaffles on his Gucci loafers sparkling like something Aladdin had rubbed up with his magic lamp.

"Hiya, doll! Great to have you back. Bring those lovely legs of yours out from behind the bleeding desk and give these poor old peepers an eyeful to start the day."

Five

M imsie followed him into the back office with the appointments diary. Steve's chat-up lines were invariably sexist and utterly harmless. Whatever he *said* Steve Epps never laid a finger on employees and his bawdy allusions were soon – once she had recovered from the initial outrage – discounted by even the thinnest-skinned temp. Mimsie hardly noticed this macho style any more and would have been astonished if any eavesdropper had suggested his conversational approach was insulting if not actually actionable.

Steve's new HQ was spartan by comparison to the penthouse unit from which he had been so recently ejected by Logan. He caught her eye as she completed a recce of the room and launched into a detailed specification of the proposed restyling of his current suite of offices. Mimsie could well believe it. Steve would pull whoever he needed off any job to make his own stage set client friendly. Her heart sank at the prospect of the entire premises being in a state of flux for a week at least while the makeover took shape.

"First things first, popsie. Get Bobby to cart them poncy cheesecake pictures down to the skip. And make a list of any toilet stuff we need for the boys' room. I've got a contract on the brink for a boutique on Sloane Street. The bloke in charge fancies himself and if he comes up here to see Charlie's paint finishes he might want to powder his nose."

"Look here, Steve, I'm not sharing a loo with all you lot!"

"Big girl like you? About time you could go on your own."

"You know what I mean. Is the water on in the basement? I'd rather hike down two flights and have somewhere private."

He frowned. "It's pretty crappy down there, doll. You sure? Suppose I could get Bobby to run a distemper brush over it seeing as you've got so exclusive. Talking about a whitewash job, what about that bloody dentist's?" He punched the air with a flourish, grinning like a champ. "Who d'ya think done it?"

"Heaven knows. If it had been your place I'd guess the unpaid workforce," she said grimly. "But Mr Chambers? Never owed a penny. Could have been a secret gambler p'raps, but can't see it myself."

"No husband out for his blood?"

She choked with laughter. "Mr Chambers? You've clearly never set eyes on the old coot. Anyway, he's not the sort."

"Gay? Given one of his patients hepatitis or something worse?"

"Of course not! Honestly, Steve, the man's so boringly normal it'd make you weep. You saw the sister. Two of a kind."

"Must make a nice change working for yours truly then," he quipped.

"If you say so."

Steve never gave up, convinced she was just putting up a smokescreen, reining herself in. Eventually even Mimsie must succomb to his lovely ways.

"Incidentally," she said, "Did Phoebe Watson say where they were moving to?"

"Moving? Why? There wasn't no structural damage to speak of." He paused, then tried a shot in the dark. "Was the poor bugger seriously done over then?"

"The mugging you mean? Did Phoebe tell you? I thought we weren't supposed to mention it."

He shrugged. "She dropped a word in my ear. On the QT of course."

Mimsie relaxed. "No blood or anything. Just stripped and tied to his dentist's couch while they daubed the walls. Perhaps he walked in and caught them at it . . ." She described her discovery of Chambers that Monday morning, giggling when she got to the bit about the daffodils. Steve kept a straight face, letting her run on, agreeing that no breath of the wretched business must leak out to Charlie and the chain gang.

He said, "Chambers knew the guys what did it?"

"I didn't get the chance to ask him. He wasn't exactly in a chatty mood last time we had words. What worries me is the place is still shut up. The patients have been referred to other practices. I phoned the NHS people to check."

"Lucky I got my money up front then."

"Did Charlie say anything about a man looking for Chambers's nurse while he was there?"

"You'll have to ask him yourself. I only popped my head round the door just to make sure it was going okay. We were in and out of the place in days. Wish I had more jobs like it. Causing trouble is he, this nursie fan?"

"No – well, I'm not sure. He got sent on to me. God knows why. That old bag Mrs Garland gave him my address – must have thought he was a boyfriend of mine or something."

"Ask Charlie. If this guy gets to be a nuisance, give me the nod. I'll get Glen to sort him out. You haven't seen Glen, have you? New fitter I pinched off that firm what advertises in all the estate agents' freebies – Classic Conservatories. Glen's magic with extensions, sunrooms, you name it. And quick! That boy can slice patio doors into a wall while you're brewing up. But expensive." He waved his hand as if his fingers had been singed, his ruby-eyed cufflinks winking like traffic lights. "Built like an ox. Six foot four and all muscle. You wait – he'll be in at the end of the week."

"I'm breathless." The irony was lost on Steve who, without pause, launched into a run-through of the jobs in hand, handed over a bundle of scribbled estimates for typing and listed those persons whose telephone calls were *not* to be put through to him till at least Tuesday. "Say I've taken Eva to Paris for a long weekend."

Mimsie settled back at her reception desk and after sending Bobby for a takeaway cappucino from the Italian cafe round the corner, got into the rhythm of keeping all the Epps Building Services' balls in the air.

In fact, working for Steve made a pleasant change from the tense atmosphere of the dentist's waiting room. Apart from a few straightforward decorating jobs, Steve had two big contracts on the go: refurbishing a restaurant in the Kings Road due to open in ten days, and what he termed 'the hospital job' – a long-term project for a Prince Abdullah's Regents Park mansion, a project which had already trailed on for months, the team pulled to cover more urgent work at least once every few days and only reinstalled when the importunate secretary started to panic.

She even got a bonus at the end of the month. And everything was going smoothly until she got home after midnight one stifling evening in August and found a figure slumped on her doorstep. He was decently turned out and fully alert – certainly no homeless glue sniffer.

"Miss Crane!" he said, scrambling up.

Mimsie shook her head, muttering denials but the man was not to be fobbed off.

"Don't make excuses. I've been following you for three days. You're working at Chiswick, for that company that cleaned up the surgery." He sprang forward, gripping her arm, unfazed by Mimsie's frantic attempts to shake him off. He hung on, his fingers digging through her cotton sleeve, his dark complexion suddenly exposed in the lamplight as they wheeled round. The street was empty and it flashed through Mimsie's mind Mr Phidias would already be back in his own home half a mile away, tucked up with his roly-poly wife, dreaming of his sunkissed homeland. Oh, sod it.

She tried a conciliatory line. "Look, you're mistaken. I don't know *anything* about the nurse. I only worked at the surgery for a couple of months or so. Anyway, Mr Chambers has gone away so—"

"I *know* all that! And the other woman. The sister. Both bolted. Where to?" His voice thinned dangerously as if Mimsie's mild protestations merely fuelled his impatience.

"He owes you money?" After a stint in Steve's employ, the assumption that every threat involved unpaid bills was automatic.

"Chambers owes me more than that!" The man was no more than thirty and slim as a whippet; even in the darkness it was clear he was well dressed in a conventional, if rather old-fashioned style. He could be a bank clerk or even a junior doctor. But the bloodshot eyes burned with emotion, his grip on her arm intensifying as he repeated his demands – he was clearly not the sort to waste time on social niceties.

"There's some mistake, Mr – er –? You see I know no more than you and—"

"Khan. There's no mistake, miss. You are in big trouble. You and that Chambers. I'd kill that man for it and you kid me you're not in it with him!"

"In it?" Mimsie croaked. "In what?"

A car entered the cul-de-sac and lit up the touching scene of the couple on the doorstep locked in an apparent embrace. Mimsie struggled, now seriously alarmed. This freaker was obviously unhinged, another of the thousands of nutters loose on the streets.

"Look here, if you don't leave me alone, I'll scream my head off. I'll bloody well have you arrested. I don't know *why* you think I'm in on some scam with Chambers but, believe me, you've got the wrong girl."

"Where is Chambers?" he said quietly, intensifying the painful grasp on her arm. "I won't ask you again."

"What is it with you? I tell you, I *don't* know anything. If you've got a beef with Chambers or his bloody nurse, go to the medical council or the dental board or whatever. Tell them about it." She kicked out at his shin, landing a lucky blow which carried all the pent-up fear and anger the desperate encounter had whirled her into.

He reeled back, hopping about in pain. "I'm not a *patient* of his, you fool."

The car had parked a few yards down the road. A woman got out and waited for the driver to join her, watching the scuffle on Mr Phidias's doorstep.

She called out in the ringing tones of a long-established Neighbourhood Watch supporter. "I say there. Are you all right?"

Khan broke away, limping along the pavement to his motorbike parked in the shadows between a line of cars.

Mimsie fumbled for her keys, waving wordlessly at the woman whose husband was already trying to pull her away from what was shaping up to be an embarrassing public fracas.

Safe inside the hall, Mimsie leaned against the door, taking shallow panicky breaths, confused by the venom of this stranger, a man she had honestly never before encountered, not even as a patient in the waiting room it seemed. But whatever war of attrition Khan was waging, he was clearly not averse to taking innocent hostages.

She crawled into bed, chilled to the bone, wishing to hell she'd never come back to London.

Six

O ver the next few days Mimsie grew increasingly para-
noid, expecting Khan to jump out at her at every corner.
Despite growing fears, she said nothing to Steve, hoping the
nutter was, in fact, harmless and had either been reclaimed by
his therapist or had moved on to a different target. Lately he
had contented himself with shoving anonymous notes through
the door at Frayne Gardens and had got a flea in his ear
from Mr Phideas who had no qualms about calling a spade
a bloody shovel.

She did confide in Austen, however, whose fatherly concern would not involve a night-club bouncer brought in to
protect her as Steve might well do.

"Look, Austen. Just keep an eye out, will you? I don't
want a fuss but if anyone's hanging about let me know. It'll
probably blow over in a couple of days – he's clearly fixated
on the wrong girl. He thinks I was Chambers's nurse – she
probably gave him short shift on the phone or something.
That's the trouble – you don't have to have a logical reason
if you're bonkers."

"It's the uniform that does it, Mims. Black stockings are
a terrific turn-on," Bobby smirked.

"Black stockings?" Austen bellowed. "What's the stupid
boy on about?"

"Shush! For heaven's sake. I don't want Steve hearing about
this. You know how he always exaggerates everything."

"She had to dress up at her last job," Bobby whispered.
"Pretend to be Nursie."

Austen winced, sipping his coffee, eyeing the girl with
weary disapproval.

"I was working for a *dentist*, Austen. Honestly, Bobby,
you make it sound like some sort of porno movie."

25

Austen roared with laughter. "Your Wonderbra wouldn't do you much good there, darling. Dress up? Are you serious? NHS dental surgery complete with a professional comforter? I would happily endure full extraction if I might flap my toothless gums over a handmaiden in starched white linen."

"It wasn't *only* NHS. Mr Chambers had private patients too," Mimsie protested. "Actually, he was a very good dentist."

"Sexy? Like Doctor Kildare in the old TV series?" Bobby needled.

Mimsie peeled herself from the huddle in the night-watchman's hut with a sigh of resignation. "You're not taking me seriously, are you? This guy with a thing about nurses is watching my house at night, for God's sake. Leaves notes through my letterbox. All I'm asking is, *please* don't let him through the gate. I feel safer here," she admitted, glancing at the Colditz security fence Steve had installed.

"Why don't you report it?"

"To the police? Are you kidding? Say I've got this black guy giving me the eye? Hasn't actually raped me, officer, but you know how it is, they're all the same. 'Little Red Riding Hood sees Wolfie behind every tree' they'd file on the report. They wouldn't *do* anything. Women get beaten senseless by their husbands every night of the week and the coppers write it off as 'domestic'."

She emerged from Austen's hut more depressed than ever, burdened by the additional prospect of it being Friday, the day the work teams descended on Steve's office for their pay cheques. If Steve didn't owe her so much back pay she'd push off back to Gozo and spend the rest of the summer on the boat with Guy.

But there was the Rolex. She still hadn't managed to scrape enough together to get the watch out of hock. No doubt about it, Mimsie would have to shake Steve down and get herself some cash before she could clear out of London.

Over the past few weeks, Steve had sugared the pill of Fridays by taking her out to lunch at a quiet Italian place at the unfashionable end of Kings Road. They had a regular corner table where Steve could bicker with Mimsie about the payslips without being overheard. Being at the receiving end of the workforce's rancour – Steve was invariably out 'doing an estimate' on Friday afternoons – Mimsie felt he at least owed her some say in the payout. She rooted for Glen who towered over her desk, seemingly indifferent to her wide-eyed innocence, regarding the deficiency of the cheque, not to mention the 'bung' in cash which healthily bulked out the envelope. Charlie, the foreman, was always given priority, even Steve admitting the necessity of having at least one regular employee. Kenny, the electrician, came near the top of the list mainly because faulty wiring was a sure-fire method of retribution.

The others took their chances. The twins, Kay and Karen – also resting actors like Austen – freelanced with their special paint effects: stippling, marbling, stencilling, they even proved to be dab hands with a full-size mural so long as lions and tigers did not feature. Somehow their wildlife always took on a pussy-cat cosiness which no amount of nudging from Steve with books of Rousseau illustrations from the library fierced up. They got a poor run of it on Fridays and Mimsie felt a sisterly affection for Kay and Karen who took Steve's tardiness in good part and gave as good as they got when it came to ribald back-chat from the builders. They were known as The Special Ks.

"Whoa! Get a load of them Earthas, Glen!"

"How about shagging them Barbies for Father's Day, Charlie? Better than a new pair of socks, eh?"

"On video! Yeah! We could run it every Friday on that fucking jumbo telly Steve's rigged up on his wall. Extra wedgie."

"Get Mimsie on for an encore. Trios! And for afters we could—"

The unimaginative scenario the lot of them shared struck Mimsie as an insight into the limited sexual fantasies of the average man in the street. She'd heard it all before. Like what they would do with the money when they won the rollover jackpot in the lottery. It reminded her of the graffiti on poor old Chambers's walls. Nothing remotely witty or even original. It was all a bit sad.

She got on with her work, fielding a number of tradesmen

and suppliers in pursuit of Steve, typing a priority list for the restaurant job where a multitude of finicking minor faults had really got up the proprietor's nose. Mimsie oozed sympathy down the phone, promising that Charlie plus a chippie would be back on Monday *without fail*, oiling the poor punter with heartfelt reassurance, on the verge of confessing that yes, honestly, she *did* understand his problem but they were all in the same boat. Even Steve. The nineties had hit him in the crotch just like poor old Chambers. Interest rates had eaten away the margins and Steve's insistence that 'I'm making *nothing* out of this job, mate! On my mother's eyes, I'm doing it AT COST,' was almost true.

They settled at Cosmo's corner table, the one he normally reserved for lovers, Cosmo having a marshmallow centre when it came to romance. Cosmo's had seen better days, attracting a clutch of media types until the dealers had muscled in. Now any heart-to-heart over the check tablecloths was invariably about deals, deals of all sorts, and Steve snuggled into this clandestine environment like a maggot in an over-ripe peach.

Today, Mimsie admitted, he looked the goods, his cream linen suit and open-necked silk shirt setting off the all-the-year tan which she guessed could only be won under a sun lamp, Steve having to her sure knowledge rarely stopped grafting since Black Monday hit the money market between the eyes, leaving most of his regulars running to their laundry baskets with as much undeclared loot as it was feasable to hide from the taxman. Forget the relandscaping of the backyard, forget the little French *gîte* needing a sympathetically rustic extension, forget Epps Building Services for the duration. RIP.

But if Steve mistrusted foreign travel he lapped up home comforts, and eating in all the best places and being seen at the classiest night spots was, as he explained, necessary for business. Epps Building Services kept its head above water only by paddling furiously below the waterline and it had to be admitted Steve's own personality was a powerful rudder.

"That restaurant bloke, Rizzoli, was on to me again this

morning, Steve. I pencilled in Charlie on Monday. He'll need a chippie but he can make good himself. Okay?"

"Don't break a leg for Rizzoli, babe. He still owes on the variations."

"What 'variations'?"

"Long-established clients," he said, po-faced and utterly sincere, "get extras at cost."

Mimsie choked on her Perrier, grinning from ear to ear, feeling herself redden with the effort of keeping a straight face.

"Blimey, you got hot flushes already, Mimsie? You should see your face. Time marches on, sweetheart. Told you it was about time you got yourself some little sprogs, didn't I? I'm always ready to oblige, you know that."

"Get in the queue, Steve. I've already had one offer from Kenny today."

"Kenny? You don't want any short circuits from a bleeding sparks, my girl. What about it? Seriously. I'll bounce Eva. Just say the word."

This little proposition came up at least once a week and Mimsie shrugged, their long-standing relationship untrammeled by any deeper involvement. Mimsie sometimes wondered what Steve would say if she took him up on it. Run a mile probably.

When the coffee arrived she laid out the dozen or so empty paypackets on the cloth and brought out her list. They negotiated like hardened delegates at a UN summit, batting claims and counter claims back and forth in urgent undertones, Steve slapping banknotes on the table and writing cheques as each case was eventually proved. Cosmo knew the score but other diners regarded the glittery couple in the corner with awed fascination, cash passing from Steve to Mimsie before disappearing again into her tote bag.

At the finish, Mimsie reckoned she had won on points and Steve called for the bill. He never actually *paid* Cosmo. Like all his other fiddles, he and the restaurateur had a private deal which notionally evened up when Steve's gang moved in during August to splash a bit of paint about and render the kitchen roach-free in time for the health inspector.

"Steve, there is one thing." She paused, letting the ripples

29

subside before throwing another pebble. He looked up, all smiles.

"Could you let me have an advance?" she whispered.

"No sweat. How much? Didn't I just say we could come to a nice little arrangement and—"

"A thousand." There, she'd said it. Just like that. Whew.

"A long 'un," he croaked, knocking over his glass as his hand flew out. The waiter hovered with the bill, sliding the account on the table and, seemingly in the same deft movement, produced a fresh glass.

"A loan. I'll pay you back out of my cheque each month."

"You mean like HP? You'd be drawing your old-age pension before you paid me back. Be cheaper to keep you at home with Eva. A nice double act."

Mimsie sighed. What was it with men? Always wanting second helpings of everything. A tear glittered and Steve instantly dropped the comedy turn.

"You need an abortion or something, Mimsie? Tried the quack? You can get that stuff for free if you play your cards right." He wasn't joking. There were some things Steve held sacred and a cash loan was one of them.

She shook her head. "It's my Rolex. If I don't redeem it this weekend, it must go. I haven't been able to keep up the interest," she lied. "It's all I've got, Steve."

Letting a shylock get away with your gold Rolex was a tragedy Steven Epps could relate to. It touched his heart in a way an unwanted pregnancy never could. He turned aside, peeling off a bundle of notes under the table and flapping them against her trembling knee. Her hand closed over the money as his slid up her thigh and as if to save the moment, the waiter returned. Steve signed the bill, laid a fiver on the plate and they both rose, Steve strolling over to chat to another couple while Mimsie, heart thumping, made her way to the door.

Now she was free to take off *any time she liked*. If Khan continued to badger her she could catch a plane this very weekend if she felt like it. First thing in the morning she would get the Rolex out of hock. She hailed a taxi.

In fact, as soon as she got back to the office she knew

not only was she not going back to Gozo, she wasn't even going back to her flat that night.

There was a message on the answerphone. It was Khan's unmistakable voice, no intro needed.

"I thought you'd like to know Chambers is dead, Miss Crane. Good night."

It was the 'goodnight', spoken slowly with unspecified menace which froze her blood. Chambers dead? Really dead? Murdered? Was 'goodnight' some sort of threat? She felt faint and, telling Bobby to watch the pay cheque envelopes in her bag, tottered down to the basement. The empty pool area echoed with the clatter of her slingbacks as she teetered across the tiled floor and locked herself in the loo.

Seven

She stayed in the dank basement for nearly an hour, surfacing only to distribute the pay cheques. Bobby eyed her warily and must have warned off the others, their usual banter diluted, even Glen's reception of Steve's idea of a weekly wage reduced to a muttered, "Ta, gel. I s'pose it's no good asking when Steve's coming in?"

"Not before Monday, Glen. Sorry. He's gone down to Esher to collect on that Greek thing."

"The temple?"

Mimsie nodded, lowering her puffy eyelids. The 'doric temple' was a standing joke at Pollard Place. An old client of Steve's, now retired, had employed Epps Building Services to put together a grecian-style construction – complete with stone pillars and mini dome – from an architectural kit, erecting it in the middle of the client's suburban lawn. Steve had taken snapshots of it at various stages and the final effect was surprisingly graceful, albeit a trifle cramped. To offset this expensive garden folly, Steve had persuaded Old Man Quinn to let him build a curved wall on the boundary which afforded the tempetto a backdrop. It was a strange idea for such a situation but from the photographs it had dignity, being in no way 'over the top'. It had to be admitted that despite Steve's personal style, his intuitive taste was impeccable.

Bobby sidled up to her desk with a mug of tea.

"It's five o'clock, Mimsie. Why don't you pack it in? Steve won't be back till Monday. We can switch on the answerphone."

She smiled, wiping a thin line of sweat from her upper lip. Being the only girl working here is, she thought, like being Snow White with the seven dwarfs. "You're an angel, Bobby Boy. But I'm miles behind. I'd better finish. You go—"

"Well . . . if you're sure? I've got a date tonight."

"Terrific! Anyone I know?"

He rattled on, filling in the details. It was like painting by numbers. A smashing girl had picked him up at the bus stop. They were going to see that new Swartzenegger film in Fulham Road, then go for a curry. She didn't believe a word of it, but so what? Bobby had this compulsion to brag about his weekends which Mimsie had started to question in her mind weeks ago. It had probably kicked off in an effort to keep his end up with the savages who descended on the office for their pay packets each week. Why shouldn't Bobby have his little fantasies like everyone else? At least his 'dates' with the dream girls didn't involve the usual tits and bums embellishments of the builders.

"Actually, you could do me a favour before you go, Bobby. If you're not in a hurry or anything?"

"Yeah? What can I get you?"

She fished out her purse and passed over a note. "Could you buy some things from the corner shop?" She scribbled a short list. "In case I don't get away before they close. And tell Austen I'll be working late. He can warn the nightwatchman – Ben Bailey, isn't it? – the lights'll be on."

It was after eight before she finished the letters Steve had left on tape for her. The Friday lunches were fun in a way but took a big chunk out of the day, especially when Steve expected everything to be lined up for Monday morning. She checked the worksheets and scrawled a memo in the appointments book about Rizzoli's priority list.

Finally, she switched off the machine and flexed stiff shoulders, sandbagged with the brute misery of typing for a living. After an anxious contemplation of her own dismal prospects for the weekend she drifted into Bobby's cubbyhole and made herself some coffee. Now the place was empty, she had a chance to appreciate Steve's makeover of the second floor. It was very stylish. Moving premises so frequently allowed Steve to try out the newest trends he latched onto from the glossies, the foul-mouthed gang he had working for him doing the rest.

The walls had been resprayed to a shimmery silver beige, misty under the cunning lighting effects. The reception desk and leather sofas remained as did Steve's state-of-the-art oak slab which constituted his own work surface in the back room. Simple white blinds blurred the evening sky, lending the functional interior a rosy warmth. Mimsie's little touch of luxury, a bunch of florist's flowers fresh each Monday morning, glowed in the slanting rays of the sunset as if spotlit for a fashion shoot. The cost was squeezed in under various spurious headings on the expense sheets and this week's best buy, yellow sunflowers, still smiling through, suddenly stabbed a flashback of the daffodils with which poor old Chambers had been decked.

That had been a wretched business. Looking back on it, Mimsie could almost accept the wrecking of the surgery for whatever twisted reason Khan's bully boys had justified themselves. Vandalism comes cheap. But the gratuitous humiliation of a middle-aged dentist trying to earn a decent living was something she couldn't understand. She shivered, then purposefully thrusting the nightmare from her mind, got on with the job in hand.

She fetched a car rug from Steve's office and spread it on the sofa in Reception, bunching up some scatter cushions at one end. She had just begun to unpack the shopping – butter, eggs, bread, salad, two chicken breasts, a toothbrush and a jar of honey – when she heard the lift start up below. Swiftly shoving the things back in the carrier, she tensed, stiff with fright. But hearing the unmistakable pant and patter of Havoc accompanying the squeaking footfalls of Bailey making his rounds in his rubber-soled bovver boots, she relaxed.

He peered round the door, his bobble hat, cheerful as a tea cosy, topping the grinning black face.

"Hi there, darlin'? You okay, Mimsie? Long time, no see." He eyed the home comforts strewn on the sofa.

"Sure. Come in, Ben – want a cuppa?"

"Not now. Later maybe. Steve makes me fill out this little timesheet do dah every two hours."

"Well, it's nice to see you. Look, Ben, could you keep quiet about this?" She made a vague gesture at the rug and cushions. "Steve would have a fit if he found out. I've got to crash out here for the weekend. My landlord's kicked me out."

34

"Jesus, Mimsie! You can't sleep in dat ol' chair. You welcome my place any time till you find somewhere. Here, I'll ring Tish right this very minute and—"

"No, really, Ben! I'm absolutely fine. Honest. I'll be like a bug in a rug on the sofa. It's a hot night and I've got everything I need. Look." She showed him the shopping. "I can use Bobby's microwave and Steve's new boys' room is like something at the Hilton. By Monday I'll have sorted something out. It's just for the weekend," she wheedled, her hands opening in a gesture of appeal.

Havoc lumbered over, slobbering into her carrier bag and wriggling what went for a tail in the stubby version of pure amiability all rottweilers perfect for special friends.

"You sure?" Ben Bailey looked worried, fretting at the additional responsibility of a pretty girl to watch over. "Right. See you later then . . . I won't bang about if your light's out. The TV's workin' in Steve's room."

"Really? That's a brilliant idea. Night, Ben."

When he clocked in on his third round, she was still wide awake and lay, fully dressed plus one of Steve's sweaters, watching the midnight movie from the sofa in his office.

"Okay there, girl?" he called as the lift doors opened.

"Ben! Do you think I could keep Havoc up here? Just for company?"

The dog padded in and, climbing up beside her, licked her face. She grinned, waving Ben away, the poor devil now thoroughly confused.

"Sure," he mumbled, backing out.

"I'll be fine now. Thanks."

She stroked the rippling muscles on the dog's back, determined to feel more relaxed in the big empty building with Havoc to hand.

Refolding the tartan car rug, she tried to settle down, pushing the dog off the couch but too jumpy to douse the TV. It flickered in the semi-gloom, company of sorts, but the nagging fear about her stupid situation loomed as the hours ticked by, expanding in her mind like shadows on the wall.

Khan *must* have been the wrecker. Who else would pursue Chambers to the grave like that? And Lynne Peters? Where did she fit in? Had she totally misread Khan's demands? Or had the man never actually set eyes on Chambers's ex-nurse? Was that the reason he was dogging *her* footsteps, hounding her with telephone threats and anonymous notes? Did he really think she had been in cahoots with Chambers over something? And even if that was so, wasn't ruining the man's surgery revenge enough? Why this manic pursuit of 'the nurse'. Had someone given her name to Khan by mistake? Good heavens, she didn't even *look* like Lynne Peters! On second thoughts, perhaps there was a passing resemblance . . .

It seemed best to lie low here, well away from her flat or the night pavements where anything could happen. She must get hold of a newspaper somehow, see if Chambers's murder had been reported. For all she knew the body hadn't even been found yet. And then, of course, the whole thing could have been a big lie, scare tactics on Khan's part to frighten her into giving him more information. Trouble was, she didn't know anything. By God, if she *knew* where Lynne Peters hung out she'd have no qualms about passing on her address to the damned nutter. Give him another innocent victim to terrorise.

Her head ached abominably and the conundrum swelled and twisted in her exhausted brain making sleep impossible. And there was her bloody Rolex, as if there wasn't enough complication without that. If she was going to take off back to Gozo she *must* first get her stuff from the flat and reclaim the watch from Uncle's. The problem was Mimsie was terrified of finding Khan camped on her doorstep. If he *had* finally flipped and killed the dentist, was Chambers's supposed nurse, Mimsie Crane, next on the blood list?

It took her addled wits another hour and a half to hit on the obvious solution. She would borrow the van, take Havoc with her to Frayne Gardens and fill her suitcases while Khan was off base. Even *he* had to sleep *some time*. Havoc in Work Mode would be a frightener even to a homicidal maniac.

She flipped through Steve's filing cabinet, located the keys of the van and whistled up Havoc to follow. She flew across the yard to Ben's hut and whispered her plan to whip her stuff from the flat from under the nose of her landlord while he wasn't looking. Ben nodded enthusiastically, always a ready conspirator in the anti-landlord war.

It was a piece of cake. Quite exciting in fact. And Havoc took to this pseudo burglary with alacrity, whooshing up the stairs at Frayne Gardens like a greyhound. The house was quiet as a graveyard, the air heavy with the fetid atmosphere of double glazing and security-locked apartments. When she eventually drew up outside Pollard Place and Ben opened the gates to let her drive back in, dawn was breaking.

He helped her stow the suitcases in the basement and they celebrated her successful raid with a double tot of rum from his personal first-aid box.

Havoc and Mimsie slumped exhausted on Steve's sofa when they got back to the office, crashed out like recidivists happy to be back inside, safe from the big bad world.

It had been something of a thrill stealing her own belongings from her own flat in the dead of night. Was there a glamour in crime she hadn't rumbled in her blameless life? Her heart thumped at the memory of the silent house in Frayne Gardens and its snoring occupants. Creeping up the stairs, restraining Havoc's natural exuberance, pausing on the landing and holding her breath, it all recalled the mixed terror and sly audacity of that childhood party game, 'What's the Time, Mr Wolf?'

'Dinnertime!'

Agh . . . grr . . . grr . . .

Eight

S he woke at daybreak to the sound of the dog snarling at the lift doors, braced for attack. The electric hum of the cage rose to the second floor, the indicator winking its progress, the everyday sound suddenly menacing. Mimsie leapt off the couch and crouched behind the door, her knees trembling as she waited for the intruder to pounce. Havoc skittered in the narrow passage, growling and barking in the approved guard-dog manner detailed in the rottweilers' handbook, then became quiet. She peered round the door, now horribly afraid as the clack and scrabble of claws on floor tiling now formed a tattoo to cheerful yelps of welcome. Had the bloody animal changed sides?

But it was only Ben Bailey signing off his security monitor to end the night shift. Mimsie emerged, feeling a fool, still clutching the car rug to her shoulders, her face white and strained.

"Hi there, Mimsie! You okay? Did I wake you?"

"Ah, Ben . . . Sorry . . . I'm, er, not really sparkling first thing. What's the time, Mr Wolf?"

He laughed, shaking his fist in mock attack. "Just on six-thirty. I'll be off now. Anything I can get you?"

"No . . ." then urgently, "except a paper maybe. As many as you can get. Anything will do. The shop on the corner—?"

She scrabbled through the desk, passing over the loose change in the stamp box. "Would you mind? I'd rather no one knew I was here."

"Sure. I'll put Havoc in the yard."

Mimsie tidied herself in Steve's cloakroom, now rigged up like an hotel barber shop, every designer smelly in the trade ranged on the smoked glass shelving. A real poofters' parlour. If she didn't know different . . .

Ben was back in a trice, dumping a huge pile of newsprint on her desk without so much as a quibble. He rattled on about the big story splashed over most of the front pages: a fresh royal scandal of miniscule proportions, blown up to bulk out the news like a fart in an empty cinema. Ben shifted awkwardly, refusing a mug of coffee, obviously ill at ease.

"You don't have to worry about me, Ben. I'm perfectly fine here." She grinned, patting the sleeve of his donkey jacket. "Till tonight?"

"That's the trouble, Mimsie. I ain't here weekends."

She blanched. "Someone else does nights?"

"No. That's not the problem. No one will find out about you bein' here, Mimsie. My lips is sealed, girl." He hesitated, still frowning. "See here. It's like this, honey. Steve, he don't pay weekend rates so Saturdays and Sundays we sets all the security alarms direct to the nick."

"That's okay, Ben. Leave Havoc and only secure the outside doors and gates. I'm not going anywhere."

He looked doubtful. "Yeah, well, normally I could, though Havoc has to have a leak some time, you know." He shuffled about, rubbing his chin like a man worried about stubble trouble. "Truth is, every weekend I take the animal to my house. Gives the poor mutt a break. Me and the missus take him to the park with the kids – muzzled up, of course! – and Havoc he really loves my kids. He's a pussy cat at home with us but don't you go gabbing all this to Steve. He knows I take the dog off the premises when it's unmanned but 'don't you go turning him into a bloody lapdog' he says. I tell Steve I lock the poor crapper up in my shed, no messing."

He smiled and she guessed her secret had a counterpoint in this little confidence of Ben's. She glanced out of the window where the dog ranged round the parked cars, sniffing between the piles of bricks and roof tiles like a bloodhound.

"Oh, yes – I see." The response was flat, her mind running over the prospect of being entirely alone for forty-eight hours.

Ben stumbled on, encouraged by her meek acceptance. "Trouble is, Mimsie, it's my youngest's birthday on Sunday. We can't have a dog of our own, see. Too expensive. But

Havoc, he deserves a bit of time away from work," he said, this added justification firm as any shop steward's. "I promised my boy Tyler, like." Mimsie frowned, thinking Ben was making a big deal of all this. With a rush, the nightwatchman decided to come clean.

"His teacher complained about him skiving off, getting into trouble, 'losing' his dinner money and all that sort of stuff. We couldn't get nothing out of him – and before all this started he was always such a quiet boy. We only found out when he came home with his head busted and admitted he'd been pushed in the road at the bus stop – he was nearly under a lorry, Mimsie. Crying like a babe, he was, a big boy of twelve. That's no way to go on, is it? Tish, she was all for goin' up to the school and tearing into them bullies herself – it'd been going on for months – but Tyler, he begged her off. And I could see it would only be worse for the boy. That weekened we took Havoc out to the park with us. He'd been coming home weekends for quite a while and was used to the kids but we never took him to any public places till then. Tyler took him on the choke chain and just walked round the park on his own, saying nothing to this mob from the school who was hanging round, badmouthing the kid, threatening to put the boot in next time they got him on his own, Tyler told us. We watched from the road, keeping our distance and even from the fence you could sense the respect. No one would dare handle Havoc the way our Tyler does. After that there was no more trouble . . . You know . . . kids!" He shrugged, inviting her connivance. "If I don't take Havoc *this* weekend, my Tyler'll be gutted. And Steve says we're not supposed to leave a guard dog loose in the yard with no handler, Mimsie," he added. "See what I'm up against?"

"Ben, of course I do. Don't give it a thought. Poor old Havoc's earned his weekends off. It's very kind of you and Tish to take him on. Very brave, in fact. Dogs like that sometimes make people hostile."

"Oh, that Havoc, he gives no trouble. And Tyler, he just *loves* that ole cur."

When Ben eventually signed off he left a full set of instructions about the security system and keys for her to come and go as she pleased. In fact, without Havoc, Mimsie was determined to go *nowhere*. On Monday she would get the Rolex and skidaddle.

She spent hours that Saturday poring over the newspapers searching every page, even the supplements. She caught each news item on the radio and watched the abbreviated weekend telly coverage. Nothing. Not a word about Mr Chambers's body being found. Not even an *unidentified* corpse. She telephoned the vacant surgery but there was no answer and even rang Phoebe Watson's home number. She tried several times, hearing the mocking tone cheeping away in presumably yet another empty house. No answerphone.

It occurred to Mimsie she might be holing herself up in this empty office block for nothing. Had she scrambled into this dugout to escape non-existent gunfire? She tried to see the funny side of it but the icy tone of Khan's final message rang horribly true. Chambers *was* dead. In their limited contacts Khan had never struck her as being the sort for party games. Was she next?

Mimsie made herself a fresh coffee, her hands trembling, and tried to rationalise her fears. She stood at the window cradling her mug, and watched the traffic through the side of the closed blind, pulling back when a motorbike parked across the security gates. She had an urgent desire to bolt. But, having lugged all her wordly goods over here, it seemed crazy to risk another encounter with Khan when she was within an ace of being right out of this ridiculous mess.

She must stay put for another couple of nights. Play safe. Let *him* make the next move. On Monday she would redeem the Rolex and book a flight out that night.

The day dragged by, leavened by the television set Steve had seemed unable to live without even in the office. "For the Budget" he once explained, verbally embroidering a whole line of bunting with reasons for the necessity of telecommunication of some sort for every waking moment. In fact, golf coverage from the American Open got a look in as did race meetings when the ebb and flow of clients' accounts became desperate.

By Saturday evening she was at her wits' end, fluttering about like a caged linnet, yet terrified of moving outside and setting off every alarm in the building. The news programmes reported nothing about a murdered dentist but then even international calamities got short shrift on the weekend's scrappy reporting. Why should poor old Chambers hit the headlines? He wasn't exactly a drugs baron. Was he?

By ten o'clock she had calmed down, lulled into resignation by the total non-happening in Pollard Place. It was as if she had been shipwrecked on a desert island or the sole survivor in a city hit by Armageddon. Having only experienced weekdays at Steve's HQ when it resembled nothing less than Pandemonium, the utter stillness of a weekend in a shuttered office block was almost miraculous. Perhaps Steve could make a turn on all this peace and quiet. Rent out Pollard Place as a weekend retreat from the world, a backwater in which 'to seek one's inner being'.

Mimsie giggled, finding something to laugh at at last, knowing herself to be truly scraping the barrel if the company of a rottweiler on a Saturday night had become her most fervent desire. She stood in the men's room taking stock of the face in the mirror, the tousled head of dark hair falling round her shoulders, the fading tan, and eyes wide with tension. Too much caffeine, that's the problem, she decided. And another sleepless night loomed. Remembering Steve's client-basting kit she searched the bank of filing cabinets until she found the bottle of whisky. A nightcap. Only two more nights on the sofa and then freedom.

She swigged straight from the bottle and carried it through to the main office still littered with copies of Saturday's newspapers and several unwashed mugs and plates. She decided to leave the chores till Monday and put through a call to Ben Bailey's home, just to hear a friendly voice. His treacle-dark assurances smoothed the raw edges and eventually she dozed off, wryly conscious that Khan had made a monkey out of her, terrified the socks off a stupid girl by the merest hint of a threat. Chambers dead? Who was he kidding? In a boozy act of bravado she switched off all the lights and slumped on the sofa.

She awoke with a start, hearing the lift doors jangle. She ran blindly into the corridor, drawn by the flickering indicator, the only point of light in the utter blackness.

Someone was in the basement. She could almost smell the whiff of chlorine just thinking about the cavern of the swimming pool area echoing with the merest squeak of a rubber sole on slimy tiles.

She fell back, her pulse racing, mesmerised by the illuminated arrow on the call button. He was coming UP! Where could she go? Unbolt the fire exit in Steve's room and run down the outside stairs? The violation of the security system would set off every alarm in the building and frighten him off. Or would it? Hadn't Ben said something about direct wiring to the nick? But if Khan *had* followed her here, his break-in would have already set off bells somewhere, wouldn't it? Even if it was rigged to buzz only at the station? Oh, what the hell! Either way, bursting out via the emergency exit would give her a head start.

She flew through the back office, throwing off any semblance of logical thought, frantic to be in the open air. Fumbling in the total darkness, she released the bolts and was about to scuttle down the fire escape when the man grabbed her from behind, bringing her crashing to the ground, her forehead smashing into the iron railings of the stairway.

They plunged down the steps locked together, dropping heavily like a bale of hemp rolling off the dockside.

Mercifully, she passed out.

Nine

When she came round she instinctively knew herself to be slumped on Steve's sofa, her assailant drubbing her forehead with what felt like a sock full of nuts and bolts. She flinched, keeping her eyes tight shut, waiting for the final curtain. But this ineffective assault seemed a silly way to polish anyone off. Carefully, she opened one eye, shielding it from the glare of the clutch of ceiling spotlights.

"Steve!" she gasped, grasping his sleeve. "You saved me. That stalker . . . he broke in . . . Tried to kill me!"

Steve Epps was white as a sheet, his ebullient self knocked overboard by the sight of Mimsie's bloodsoaked tee shirt and the rapidly swelling egg perched on her right eyebrow.

"Christ Almighty! What you talking about? What bleeding 'stalker'? You been shoving stuff up your nose or something?"

She struggled to sit up, her head reverberating like Big Ben at midnight. His face swung into focus, his anxiety transformed into taciturnity as she incoherently mumbled meaningless phrases about a black guy shadowing her, making threatening phone calls, leaving notes through her door.

"And you reckon he was *here*?"

"He broke in, Steve. Tried to beat me up. We fell down the fire escape. Did he get away?" She gripped his lapels, screwing the life out of the sharp tailoring.

He dropped the roughly knotted handkerchief, and ice cubes skittered across the floor forming wet pools as the two of them bickered, trying to get on the same wavelength.

"Just shut up for a minute, Mimsie! There ain't no one here. I thought *you* was the bloody burglar. It was pitch dark," he protested, his temper melting like the pebbles of ice littering the polished floor. "I'll make some char and get you sorted. Then," he said, glancing at his watch. "I'll have to split. I only came back for some extra cash."

"It's still Saturday night, isn't it?"

"Sunday morning – two-thirty there about. I was in the middle of a poker game at Tony's place. Got cleaned out. I've got to get back or they'll send the heavy mob out looking."

Mimsie lay back, reeling from the tangle which her aching head seemed incapable of unravelling. "Poker? You mean *you* threw me down the fire escape?"

He nodded, detailing the sequence of events as he moved across the room into Bobby's cubby hole to brew up.

"You ran out of cash? And came *here* for more stake money?" she repeated.

He proffered a mug of steaming tea, black like it had been made with Oxo cubes, sugar silting the bottom in a slug of shock absorber. Steve squatted on the edge of the sofa as she sipped the tea, his mind already fizzing elsewhere as he turned aside to check the bundle of notes in his back pocket.

"Tell me again," she said, gingerly exploring her bruised scalp. The blood seemed to stem from a single slit along her eyebrow, the swelling already closing her eye.

"I got in over my head," he admitted, "and if I want to pick up the game tomorrow night, I had to settle up PDQ. I keep a little nestegg in a floor safe down in the basement – that's strictly between you and me, Mimsie. For emergencies—"

"Emergency bets, you mean! How about emergency pay packets?" She was feeling better already.

He ignored this. "I spotted these suitcases stowed in one of the cubicles and when I tested the lift I found that stupid bastard, Bailey, had forgotten to shut off the lights on the first floor. I heard some scuffling and got up here damn quick. When I saw someone trying to charge out the back through my office I thought it was some kid after me telly and stuff. It was only when I got the lights on, I sussed it was *you*, you silly tart. What you doing here at two in the morning?"

"I got thrown out of my digs."

"Them bags in the basement yours?"

"I couldn't pay the rent."

His eyes narrowed. "Pull the other one, doll. What happened to the long'un I lent you to bail out the Rolex?"

Mimsie faltered and started extemporising about her Barclaycard, an elaboration which sloshed over Steve's credulity without leaving any backwash whatsoever.

"Oh yeah?" He strolled over to his desk and lit a cigarette, facing her. "And what about this bruiser you 'ave nightmares about? A bit of rough that turned nasty on you, Mimsie?"

She started to weep, her swollen eye obligingly squeezing out a tear. Steve stared at his watch, steeling himself against this ultimate weapon of hers. Steve Epps was bulletproof to most appeals but Mimsie's waterworks always scuppered him.

"Okay. Tell Uncle all about it. You double-crossed this black guy and now he's on the beat?" He unknotted his sodden handkerchief and draped it over the big framed snapshot of Havoc, the rottweiler, propped on his desk.

"It goes back to that business at the dentist's. The mugging."

"Chambers?"

Mimsie nodded, wiping her nose on her sleeve. "This bloke's been dogging me for weeks, seems to think I know where Chambers is hiding out."

"Hiding out? Why should he do that?"

"Don't ask me! Khan says I was in on some sort of scam with Mr Chambers. He's mixing me up with a previous girl who worked there, I think. Someone called Lynne Peters. Khan found out where I live – he rings me up when I'm at work – leaves messages on the answerphone! I got frightened. He says Chambers has been murdered, Steve!"

"Dead? Straight up?"

"I don't know what's going on. Mr Chambers's sister's vanished, the surgery's closed . . . I thought if I hid here for the weekend, he would push off."

"You want me to sort him out?"

"No! Just let me stay here till Monday. Then I can get my watch back from the pawnshop and run."

"You leaving me in the lurch, girl?"

"Can you blame me? Would you hang about if the boys from the poker school were after you?"

46

This last retort seemed to shoot the man into instant reverse. "Yeah, well . . . I've got to get back to Tony's, Mimsie. I'll lock up. You're safe as houses here, babe. Stay put and I'll sort you out in the morning. I'll find out about Chambers – I've a mate at the Chelsea nick. He'll know. About eleven? I'll take you out to breakfast – there's a place in Brompton Road. You all right? Want a doctor to stitch up your eye?"

She started up. "Is it that bad?"

"No way. Just a scratch. Looks worse than it is," he swiftly assured her. "Okay then? I'll bring you some plasters, Dettol or something . . . Got any sunglasses? Eva's off for the weekend. On some sort of Polish jump-up in Bognor. I've got a job on at Esher tomorrow but that can wait."

He rose, smoothing his crumpled lapels, anxiously dabbing at a smear of blood on his cuff. He patted her shoulder and hurried out, waving briefly before closing the lift doors. She waited to hear the Volvo starting up in the yard but there was no further sound. Steve must have parked in a side street and come in through the back.

Mimsie lurched into the cloakroom and washed her face. She stared at the white mask which gazed back at her in the mirror, black hair tangled around her thin shoulders, her right eye almost closed, the slashed brow already blackening like the careless twirl of an eyeliner. Genuine tears ran down her chin as she tried to pull herself together. Oh sod it. Life was turning out to be a real bugger and no mistake.

Ten

To her surprise she slept like the dead after the disasterous episode with Steve Epps. Only *Mimsie* could be reassured by hurtling down a metal stairway at two in the morning with an unknown assailant. Truth was, despite Steve's worst efforts, Mimsie continued to regard him as being on her side, his sharing the problem of the mysterious stalker being an enormous relief. It was as if she was caught on a merrie-go-round, a racketty circuit getting nowhere. At least Steve, with all his faults, was a solid focus on this whirling ride and, with no one else to turn to, a 'fixer' was just what she needed.

She woke late, stiff and thirsty, her throat dry as if she'd been snoring all night long. Stretching out on Steve's office sofa, she tested her bruised eyelids, experimentally rolling her eyeballs, running her fingers over the jagged surface of her cuts. While freshening up in the new men's room, she carefully avoided the mirror until after she had steadied her nerves with a mug of strong coffee. It was already ten-thirty. He said he'd be here by eleven. But Steve Epps was, like his cheques, always late.

Counting her blessings, the prospect of brunch in Brompton Road was a bonus. She took her bag back into the cloakroom and made a start on her image. The cut above her brow had knitted beautifully but the black eye flowered in startling hues of mauve with a nasty magenta penumbra. Her fair skin accentuated the problem and the frame of dark hair did nothing to help. Where had her tan suddenly gone to? She made up her face, blending in a honey camouflage to minimise the pallor. Better. But obviously false. She combed her hair from a side parting to form a curtain brushing her cheek but it didn't really help. In desperation Mimsie got out her nail scissors and chopped a swathe through the peek-a-boo effect, producing a heavy fringe which would have disguised a labotomy. Not perfect but at least she wouldn't be continually twitching at her hair to drape the worst of it.

She could do nothing about the bloodstained tee shirt until Steve arrived, not daring to raid her suitcases in the basement in case he had reset the alarms. A police posse was the last thing she wanted. So much to explain . . . and Steve wouldn't thank her for drawing attention to any dodgy goings-on at Pollard Place. She stood at the window watching the yard, picturing Steve the night before kneeling in the dark in the swimming pool area, counting his 'funny money' then discovering – shock, horror! – he was not alone in the building. No wonder he had rugby-tackled her on the fire escape like a pro. Nothing fired up poor Steve like the prospect of a thief on the premises. She laughed aloud, imagining regaling Glen and the Chain Gang with the story of The Night Steve Gave Me the Black Eye. This wicked bit of fantasy kept her smiling while she tidied up the office.

The lift whirred in the shaft and she picked up her shoulder bag.

"Hi there, popsie. Hey, you look great! All set?"

Mimsie grinned, relishing the sight of Steve looking far from wonderful himself after a night paying out to Tony and the poker school. He wore baggy denims, a sweatshirt and trainers – presumably his idea of Leisure Man. But the informality didn't gel. He looked dreadful. She sensed a whiff of panic about him which was entirely new. He took off his Ray Bans and scrutinised the new hair-do.

"Suits you."

"Slimy toad. It's perfectly horrible. But I'm hungry. I need that breakfast you promised me. At the Boulangerie you said."

"Oh yeah. Yeah, sure." He passed over his sunglasses. "Here. Try these. Once you cover up that tee shirt I could take you anywhere. Got a jumper or something?"

"In my case. In the basement. I could change in one of the cubicles."

He grabbed her arm and they took the lift. Her luggage had been restacked in full view at the poolside and Steve stood over her while she unlocked it and riffled through her hastily packed belongings, unashamedly gawping at her frillies, some sports gear and a hundred pairs of odd socks. She pounced on a skinny-rib sweater and fresh jeans and shut herself in a shower booth to change, leaving Steve to juggle with the locks on the overstuffed bags. When she emerged he was grinning from ear to ear, holding up the creased white nurse's overall and perky cap.

"Fancy dress, Mims?"

She snatched it from him, stuffing it in the case, snapping the locks, furious at leaving herself wide open to old Hawk Eye.

"Chambers's office gear," she snarled. "Right, Steve. Had a good laugh? Can we go now?"

He chuckled in the murky darkness, humping the cases ahead of her.

"Where are you taking them to? Can't they stay down here till Monday?"

"No way. Just stop gabbing on, woman. You can't spend another night here. You're coming back to my place tonight then we'll find you another pad. But first, we've got to stop off at Esher. That little job I mentioned won't wait. Then we'll fetch Eva and get her to rustle up some red-hot goulash for Sunday night supper."

He shoved aside a toolbox, stowed her cases in the boot of his car and steered her to the passenger's door.

"Hey! What about breakfast? You said—"

The Volvo roared into life and after negotiating the steel gates they were soon established in the Brompton Road bistro where the Chelsea set spent their Sunday mornings ironing out the effects of Saturday night. Steve visibly blossomed in this heady atmosphere, waving to a couple of single guys across the room and abruptly leaving Mimsie with a plate of scrambled eggs and smoked salmon before her to greet an unsmiling lady sitting alone near the pastry trolley.

"Who was that?" Mimsie murmured, dreamily contemplating the fragrant croissants.

"Oh her? Mrs Mountfield. She's a physio at the Harrington Clinic. I help her out sometimes. Got a face like a bag of chisels but she looks better in the uniform. Bet you could send a man nuts in yours," he quipped.

"Is she the one Glen tells me you help out on the fourth floor of the Harbour car park?" she flicked back.

Steve grinned, unabashed. "Yeah, well . . . tit for tat. Never know when my poor old back'll start playing up again."

They dawdled in the cafe, ordering fresh coffee, poring over the Sunday papers, bickering over the headlines like an old married couple. By the time they were back on the road, it was getting on for three.

"Why Esher? And why you?" she persisted. "I thought you never did any jobs yourself."

"It's that bleeding doric temple. Glen trimmed it off last month, laid down the hard landscaping, the lot. Sent in my bill and blow me down, the silly old geezer *then* says he wants one of the pavers heaved up and a load of mementoes cemented down under it."

"Oh, we did something like that when I was at school. A biscuit tin full of stuff for people to dig up in a hundred years' time. Pictures, newspaper clippings, school reports—"

"'Mimsie Crane must try harder' you mean? I'll drink to that."

"Will it take long?"

"Half-hour at most. But the Captain's an old customer and a quick payer. Well caked up. Bit gaga now but 'worth a detour' as they say."

"Why not send Glen back to finish it?"

"Quinn doesn't want anyone else to know about it except Yours Truly. Very hush hush. Don't go blabbing about it to Glen."

"Is this client of yours a train robber or something? One of your poker playing pals?"

"Our Captain Birdseye?" He roared with laughter, causing Mimsie to draw away, jarred by Steve's uncharacteristic see-saw mood this weekend. First he's jumpy as a cat, now crazily hilarious. Steve recovered himself.

"Don't worry, doll. I'll make sure he ain't burying no gold bricks." He gabbled an explanation, putting the poor client's biography into bite-size portions.

"Quinn used to captain a very de luxe cruise liner out

of Florida. Must have been a handsome bloke in his day. Married a famous model in the eighties. Nina something or other. She died at Easter. Fairly broke the old guy up. Aged overnight. He left the shipping line to look after her at home. I've always done the maintenance work on the place, redecorating, you name it. A regular moneyspinner but nothing big. No extensions or conservatories for instance. You could have knocked me down with a feather when he got me to estimate for that crappy garden folly."

"I've seen pictures of it in the office. It looks lovely, Steve. Perhaps he's into gardening now he's got nothing else to do."

"Waste of money, if you ask me. Once the old guy croaks the neice'll clear the site. Three acres of prime building land. Worth a mint! She's all but signed on the line to say when it comes to it Jerry Logan'll have first bid. Still that's all pie in the sky with dykes like Rio Rita. D'you know, Jerry bought a house on St George's Hill only last Christmas for over seven hundred grand just to knock it down and clear the site? When Quinn rung me up to give an estimate on this temple lark, who am I to tell him to put his money back in his pocket? This wife of his must have been dead set on the idea. Saw one like it at the Chelsea Flower Show before she got ill, he said. I s'pose he promised he'd get it done and now she's gone he's put it in anyway. Felt guilty she never saw it finished most likely, the poor old sod."

They drove through an impressive archway leading to a network of winding roads and hidden residences. Grange Park. 'Private' the board read. An estate agents' dreamworld.

She gripped his arm. "Isn't this where that TV star lives? Jess O'Darrell?"

"Ritzy suburbia. One of the Beatles used to have a place here once but I don't reckon much to it meself. Why pay a couple of million for a pile of bricks in upmarket Cheam? Give me Chelsea Square any time."

"Nice for families though. Safe."

Huge houses surrounded by tasteful boscage slid past. There were no walkers and no parked cars at the kerb. In fact, even for a Sunday afternoon, the estate had an uninhabited look, several homes secured from the next with mounted security cameras, high walls and lower windows barred with fancy wrought iron grilles.

Mimsie fell silent. It was the sort of environment entirely unfamiliar to her, a beautiful ghetto, inward looking, glossy as a time-share promotional video. But dead. Quite, quite dead.

On this sombre note they drew up outside The Willows, an older property than its neighbours, mock Tudor, gabled, the rosy brickwork strung about with plump roses and yellowing leaves of wisteria. While they waited for the electronic gates to open up for them, an urgent question shot to the surface.

"Steve. Before we go in, did you get any information about Mr Chambers from your police contact?"

He glanced at the girl sitting beside him, weighing up how much the shock factor would aggravate her present edgy state of mind.

"Yeah . . . Well, the gist of it anyhow. I'll know more next week. Norry tells me your informant got it right. Poor old Chambers went missing a few weeks after we did up his surgery. Phoebe reported it to the police and his car turned up dumped behind a quiet beach with a bundle of clothing. Bognor or somewhere along the coast there. A suicide note was—"

"He drowned himself? Weeks ago?" she whispered.

"Possibly." He patted her knee. "Don't take on. Crafty old sod probably tried to frame the insurance company if you ask me."

"Then he's *not* dead?"

"Well, he *might* be. No body's been washed up so far." Steve chose his words carefully. "But one night last week they dragged a bloke out of a crashed car outside Birmingham. Practically burnt to a cinder, poor devil. But from certain items found on the body it's bound to be Chambers. Phoebe's identifying the stiff one way or another this week. If it's Chambers, he'd been lying low. There was another guy in the car."

"Mr Chambers was *with* someone?"

"Apparently. A witness said another man, presumably the driver, legged it just before the car exploded. The police never traced him though."

53

"Whose car was it?"

"Stolen vehicle. Chambers might have been hitching a lift. The hospital think the dead man had been living rough for some time. Hiding out p'raps? Don't ask me. I only got the bones of the story from Norry this morning but the police are sure it's their man. They're definitely closing their file on Chambers. Phoebe's been renting a house in Sussex for weeks, by the way. I've got her address if you like."

"Khan was right."

"Khan?"

"My stalker. He *said* Mr Chambers was dead."

"*You* told me 'murdered', Mimsie. This guy croaked in a car accident. Forget it. Phoebe told the police Chambers had been a patient at some private nuthouse in Eastbourne prior to his disappearance. That mugging at the surgery shot him straight off his trolley by all accounts. He either drowned himself and is still sloshing around in the Channel or he went AWOL and was keeping his head down till the insurance paid out."

"Why hitch a lift from a joyrider?"

"Who knows? Who cares?" Steve snapped. He had enough worries of his own without mixing himself up with a possible insurance fraud.

The gates swung open and the Volvo cruised up the drive.

Mimsie sat stiff with fright, all the fun of a day off her crazy carousel entirely dissipated. Mr Chambers *was* dead one way or another. And Khan knew, possibly before anyone else, that the dentist had died. Had Khan rigged the car crash? Was he the driver who had vanished from the scene before the car burst into flames?

Eleven

S teve pulled up by the front door and took his toolbox from the boot.

"Why don't you come in and meet the old guy?" he said. "He likes pretty girls. Very charming, makes all the right moves. Don't worry about the black eye. His sight's terrible – and he's much too polite to mention it anyway."

Mimsie frowned at her reflection in the visor mirror but decided to go for it, curious to see the inside of a house reputably worth all of half a million just to knock down to rubble.

Steve patiently waited while the doorbell rang and rang. "He's none too quick on his feet but he knows we're here – he opened up the gates for us."

"He lives alone?"

"Only Sundays. There's a daily and a gardener-cum-odd-job-man who hang about midweek."

"Still a big house for one person, isn't it?"

Steve rattled the knocker and peered through the stained glass in the panels of the door, seeing a shadowy figure approaching at last. The door opened six inches and a woman's head popped round. She addressed Mimsie, ignoring Steve.

"Miss Quinn?"

"No, she's not. Who are you?"

"Doctor King. I was expecting the Captain's neice."

"He's waiting for *me*, not Rita," Steve retorted. "We've got an appointment."

"Just wait there. I'll check." She slammed the door and Steve started to stamp about, his macho sensibilities on a short fuse when it came to professional women. He dropped the toolbox at his feet and it crashed down like a box of ammunition.

"Shall I sit in the car?" Mimsie ventured.

"No! You stay here. I don't want any nasty stories getting about. These bossy cows are all the same – get the hots for builders and either think you're out to rape them or shout blue murder if you don't. I 'avn't come all this way on a Sunday to be shunted off the step like a double-glazing salesman."

They stood in silence, the atmosphere growing increasingly raw, the effects of a bad weekend vibrating between them. Mimsie adjusted the sunglasses, feeling distinctly 'piggy in the middle'.

Eventually the woman's footsteps echoed through the hall and she opened up, ushering them in and closing the door but barring their way ahead. The house smelt of beeswax and of the pot pourri filling a Chinese bowl on the hall table. She addressed Steve briskly.

"Before you speak to Captain Quinn, may I suggest you keep your visit short? He's had a fall and is still a bit groggy. I've telephoned his niece and she can stay until nine this evening but I am far from happy. He shouldn't be alone here at night. He tells me you have been engaged on a private matter this afternoon, Mr Epps. And your friend?"

Steve stiffened, refusing to explain Mimsie's role in all this. The girl shrank back, perfectly certain that her battered appearance might escape the notice of a short-sighted old man but the rainbow hues of her forehead were doubtless all too apparent to any lynx-eyed practitioner.

She was a stocky female, no more than thirty-five and attractive in a tweedy sort of way, her freckled face framed by a gingerish bob, her blue gaze icy.

Steve pushed past, clearly familiar with the layout of the house and Mimsie trotted behind, closely followed by the doughty doctor. The three entered a room which overlooked the garden, a study of sorts, the wood panelling closely hung with prints of sailing ships, a modern portrait of a lady in evening dress taking pride of place over the mantel, and several battered leather chairs crowding the room. An elderly man in a dingy sweater and flannels hastily rose to his feet, holding out both hands to Steve in a gesture reminiscent of a missionary approaching the natives with both pleasure and trepidation. He was over six feet tall and held himself stiffly, every inch an officer and a gentleman.

"This is my friend, Steve Epps, I told you about, Doctor King. And this must be—?" he murmured, smiling at Mimsie.

"Mimsie Crane," Steve replied. "My former assistant. She does agency work but sometimes manages to fit me in. On rush jobs," he enigmatically added, brushing aside Mimsie's blank response and diverting Quinn's questions with a flurry of queries about the temple. The doorbell rang again and the Captain pressed his finger to his lips, winking at Steve as the doctor hurried off once again.

"That'll be Rita. You remember my niece, of course. The doctor insisted I had someone here and phoned my 'next-of-kin' in Brighton without so much as a by your leave." The man's confidence faded as he drew Steve aside. "The wretched woman's gone mad. Fancy bringing Rita into it? Really!"

"What about this fall?"

Quinn shrugged, his temper overriding an obvious disquiet at the trouble he had accidentally brought upon himself.

"It was nothing. Absolutely nothing. I was fetching a bottle of sherry from the cellar and slipped down the last few steps. I crawled back up here and couldn't find my pills. Angina, you know . . . I rang the doctor and she's been behaving like a wretched social worker. Private medicine's not what it was."

"And she phoned Rita?"

"Insisted on it. Said I could either spend a few days in Hollyberry House – a retirement home in Guildford she's always trying to interest me in – or I must have a live-in attendant of some sort. It would be 'unethical' she said to leave a patient alone after an emergency call-out. I ask you!" he fumed.

The two men huddled in mutual irritation, Steve, for his own purposes, as determined as his client that the old fellow should remain independent. Steve had grappled with Rita Quinn on previous visits and fighting over the control of their precious benefactor was a set piece.

"Leave it to me," he said, standing shoulder to shoulder

57

with the beleaguered Captain as the doctor led two more women into the room. The first, clearly the niece, was built on Junoesque proportions and looked decidedly beefy in a red anorak, her steps dogged by a pallid creature decked out in the all-weather garments of an animal rights supporter.

"Oh, Christ," Steve chuckled, "Butch *and* Cassidy!"

"Cassie," Rita's sidekick remonstrated wearily, having heard his joke before.

"And who's this?" The niece jerked her thumb at Mimsie after taking in her uncle's apparently swift recovery at a glance.

"Nurse Crane," Steve snapped. Mimsie looked the woman in the eye, her practised sang froid in the face of Steve's raging creditors coming up trumps. Doctor King's jaw dropped.

"Toby and I," Steve continued, nodding at their bemused host, "decided the time had come to take the doctor's orders to heart. Nurse Crane will undertake all night duties and the day staff will be here at all other times. She will also supervise Captain Quinn's diet, act as his driver and fully cooperate with Doctor King here."

The niece pushed forward, attempting to intervene but the old man stepped in, augmenting this little fairy tale with admirable aplomb. As a double act Quinn & Epps could pull the crowds at an end-of-the-pier concert party. Mimsie made herself scarce, choking back the giggles, seeking out the kitchen to make some tea. After a further twenty minutes' argy-bargy, the combatants called a truce, the two women subsiding on the leather sofa, Steve and the doctor unexpectedly drawing together as a support team either side of the poor patient.

Mimsie re-entered the room, pushing a creaking tea trolley, the sunglasses adding a bizarre touch to her hostessy bit part in this little drama.

"I expect you would like some tea before you go," she said, handing a cup to Rita. She poured from a silver teapot, passing sugar lumps to the men without so much as a blink. Steve glowed, feeling like a man who had produced a royal flush from what had, at first, seemed a terrible hand.

The doctor declined Mimsie's proffered cup with a smile

and left them to it, banging the front door behind her. Steve steered the conversation into calmer waters and the Captain played out his role.

The 'two harpies' as Steve referred to them, marched off before six, promising to call back the following Sunday afternoon. Mimsie groaned, aware that Steve's impromptu solutions never worked long term. Shaking off the old boy's next-of-kin *and* his doctor in one fell swoop was all very well but where did she fit in in all this?

As Mimsie washed up, she gazed out at the garden where Steve and the Captain were already at work on the doric temple, prizing up a section of paving. In the fading sunset, the long shadows cast by Quinn's folly struck a sepulchral note and Mimsie's thoughts swam back to the weird disappearance of her former employer, poor Mr Chambers. *Was* she safe now the man was dead? Khan was supposed only to be trailing her in an effort to find the guy. Wasn't he?

Twelve

The evening was drawing in before the two men finished their clandestine operation on the base of the temple and the garden view from Toby Quinn's study had simplified into a monochrome grid of clipped hedges and dense evergreens.

Mimsie sat in one of the leather chairs wishing there was a telly she could switch on. The library shelves sported few books but one of the deep alcoves accommodated piles of old records, mostly Victor Sylvester, whoever *he* was, and a wind-up gramophone. So much for mod cons. Toby Quinn's tastes were evidently limited. There were stacks of lavishly illustrated car magazines and a brand-new radio, but little other evidence of how he spent his time.

The door swung open and Steve held it for the Captain who seemed extraordinarily perky in view of Doctor King's strictures on her patient's ability to cope alone in the big house. Mimsie jumped up, ready to go. She held out her hand to Quinn, trotting out the usual polite phrases prior to departure.

Steve butted in. "Hang about, Mims. You got a train to catch or something?"

She pouted, wishing now she had kept out of Steve's current little excursion and stayed on at Pollard Place. "What about Eva? Won't she be waiting for you to pick her up?"

"Yeah, well, she's not exactly standing at the bus stop, is she?"

"Let's have a drink," Quinn put in, pouring oil on what was likely to be troubled waters.

"Why not?" Steve threw himself into a chair and Mimsie temporarily subsided. The men nattered on and after a mutually congratulatory summing-up of their work in the garden, the subject of Mimsie's predicament floated to the surface. It was immediately apparent that they had already explored the subject fairly exhaustively and Mimsie perched on the edge of her chair, clutching a glass of gin and tonic while Steve elaborated on his latest brainwave.

"Look here, Mimsie. You and the Captain are both in a jam. You need somewhere to stay and Toby has to fend off Rio Rita and that new doctor of his. Why not give it a go for a week or two? Just till things quieten down."

He continued embroidering the pros and rubbishing the cons of the job on offer. Mimsie wondered how far the Captain had been enlightened when it came to her flight from Khan and whether the Chambers connection had been fairly described. Murky . . . Trouble was, Steve's interpretation of the truth was inevitably subject to 'variations' and Mimsie was terrified of becoming embroiled, yet again, in unorthodox employment. It smelt suspiciously of jumping from the frying pan into the fire. She decided to ignore Steve's version which was never without hidden extras and plunged in, turning to face the old man with fierce determination.

"Look, Captain Quinn, let's not beat about the bush. I'm no nurse. What possible use could I be here? At best I'm no more than an au pair who can type your letters for you. Why don't you get a proper nurse from an agency? Someone qualified."

"My dear, I know what I need. And it's not a bossy Florence Nightingale. That would be almost as bad as moving in with Rita and Cassie. If I have *someone* in the house, that's all I need. Please reconsider. Steve here has explained everything. I can afford to be generous. A young assistant like yourself is all I require and I promise I am in no way a dirty old man." This last remark made him grin and Mimsie's heart lurched, just a fraction. She could see what Steve meant when he said the Captain must have been a handsome guy in his heyday. She started to speak but he held up his hand.

"I'm far from decrepit, whatever they say. Rather poor sighted, I admit, but plugged into medication which keeps me reasonably agile. The duties here would be minimal I assure you and it would be wonderful to have someone in the house on whom I could occasionally call to drive me about in the evenings. The Rover would be exclusively at your disposal, of course, and you would only be needed here from six in the evening until Aileen came next morning. Your days would be entirely free. Saturdays, Frank – my gardener – is generally about so you see the burden would be far from heavy. A friend of mine, George Sutton, would be happy to join me on your nights off."

"I can't cook."

"Aileen does all that. I have a hot lunch and a snack at suppertime which she leaves in the fridge. My housekeeper is a cheerful soul. I'm sure you'll find her so, but she is determined to stay in her own home and who am I to quarrel with that?"

"But 'Night Nurse'? It sounds, well, sort of – serious."

He laughed. "A label only. Think about it. Come back tomorrow if you prefer."

"That doctor said she'd phone back tonight," Steve warned.

Quinn laughed. "Doesn't trust me, old man." He quoted a generous salary and sketched out a possible schedule of duties which to Mimsie's ears sounded the nearest to a sinecure she had ever encountered.

"And that's *it*?"

"Let me show you the accommodation."

Steve excused himself to make a couple of calls while Mimsie followed the Captain upstairs. One part of the house was locked. Storerooms, he said.

The self-contained suite he showed her was frankly luxurious, comprising a sort of boudoir with a sofa and television set, a dressing room and a newly installed bathroom. In her brief tour of the rooms downstairs Mimsie had the impression that this part of the house was the only area which had been redesigned, the rest being rather old-fashioned. Elegant and spotlessly clean but nevertheless giving off a whiff of having seen better days. It suddenly struck her what it was. The house and its furnishings were, apart from the apartment he intimated could be hers, like a cruise liner: a bit dated, rigorously tidy, the sort of ambiance, now she came to think about it, all to familiar to a man who had spent his life at sea.

As they came back downstairs, Steve was coming through the front door toting Mimsie's suitcases, never a man to let the grass grow under his feet.

"Upstairs?"

Mimsie shrugged. "Just for now. Just until I get my Rolex," she added with a grim smile. "Oh, and another thing, Steve. You said you had Phoebe Watson's address in Sussex. Mr Chambers's sister. I'd like to go down and see her – condolences and all that . . . Would you?"

He looked doubtful but scribbled a note on the back of an envelope and passed it over. "I'd better get my skates on, kid." He saluted the Captain and patted his back pocket. "Thanks for the cheque, Toby. See you."

He was off before either of them could say another word and the mismatched couple left standing in the hall found the sudden silence pressing. He made the first move, offering his arm as if to invite her to take a turn on the terrace, and lead them into his snuggery.

"Don't look so worried, my dear. Worse things happen at sea!"

She giggled, realising at last that if The Willows was not exactly a desert island, being marooned in this barely inhabited ghetto known as Grange Park wasn't really such a lousy port of call. 'Worth a detour' as Steve would say.

She made some sandwiches and a pot of coffee and the Captain persuaded her to join him in a game of chess. They were evenly matched which came as a surprise to Quinn whose lack of familiarity with girls in jeans had led him to assume all beautiful women were decently shortchanged in the brains department, a delusion probably fostered by his wife's girlfriends in the rag trade.

Photographs of the dead woman were scattered throughout the house, her dark hair mostly drawn back in a chignon or smoothly coiffed in styles requiring much lacquer and fixings. The face of Nina Quinn had a haunting loveliness, almost timeless, certainly not easy to pin down. Despite the disparity in their ages, and it would seem Toby Quinn had won a wife much younger than himself, Mimsie guessed that Nina's career on the catwalk had been curtailed long before her illness set in.

Romance was something Mimsie rarely encountered in real life, the men of the nineties who swanned about her little pool being more concerned with their own image, 'scoring' being the key word when it came to relationships. Toby Quinn was clearly still in love with his wife and his constant affectionate references to her brought a hidden presence into the house which, once Mimsie got used to it, made her feel at ease in a way she had never felt before in her racketty progress since leaving home.

"Where did you learn to play, Mimsie?"

"Chess? Oh, at school. My mother's always worked. She liked me to stay late so I had to join all sorts of clubs, even ones I wasn't particularly interested in. The Chess Club was on Wednesdays. The Music Club was much more popular because it was on Fridays and alternated with the boys' school which meant there was a waiting list. I filled in the other nights doing weird stuff like Greek dancing and netball."

"Bridge?"

"I've never been any good at cards."

"Pity. You could have made up a foursome occasionally. A group of us meet several evenings a week for a rubber or two, mostly here because of my difficulties with transport since the doctor refuses to allow me to drive any more." He leaned across the low table, charming in that matinee-idol manner Mimsie had only before seen in old black and white movies.

"You being able to drive me about in the evenings opens up all sorts of possibilities for me. I am quite excited at the prospect, my dear. Tomorrow, shall we give the Rover a spin? After six, of course, whenever it suits you."

Later they left the crocks in the sink for Aileen to deal with next morning, there being no dishwasher and, as far as Mimsie could judge, a central heating system out of the ark. One thing which *was* thoroughly up to date was the burglar alarm system which he painstakingly explained to her.

"The insurance people insisted upon it. Trouble is, I don't always remember to set it before I drop off so if you could keep an eye on it before you turn in I'd be enormously grateful. One irritating effect of all this security nonsense is that once one is settled for the night, the upper landing is alarmed which may trouble you at first."

"I'm used to it. At the office."

"I sleep badly and have never been able to shake off a lifetime's habit of early rising so I'm always downstairs before six to unscramble the system – well before breakfast so you need have no fears on that score, Mimsie. By the way, please feel free to entertain your friends here at any time. I miss having company and a house of this size needs young people."

Their conversation was broken by the shrill insistence of the telephone in the hall.

"I'll get it."

It was Doctor King. She seemed taken aback when the girl answered.

"Ah, Nurse – er – Crane? How is our patient?"

Mimsie muttered brief assurances and the woman sharply made her point. "I shall be calling in in the morning. About eleven. Just to check the Captain's blood pressure and so on. But I must have a word with you about his medication. You will, of course, be supervising his health programme."

"I hardly think Captain Quinn incapable of handling his own affairs *just* yet, Doctor," Mimsie retorted. "I may not always be here in the day, of course, but so there are no misunderstandings, I am happy to discuss the case with you tomorrow if the Captain is agreeable."

Mimsie congratulated herself on this smooth performance, surprised by the protective reflex which snapped into play in her reaction to – as Steve would have it – the 'harpies'.

Whether she would be around long enough to save Toby Quinn from Rita and the doctor in this dogfight over his valuable person was something else. But since she had already accepted a generous cheque to cover a month's salary in advance, the poor man was going to get his money's worth, if only until she had tied up the loose ends with Phoebe Watson regarding the astonishingly elusive dentist.

Thirteen

M imsie spent the next few days getting to know Toby Quinn and Aileen, the woman without whom the whole shaky edifice would falter. Quinn's housekeeper was a gem and, what was more, a gem with irrepressible sparkle. The noble ship's captain obviously had an eye for *people*, unerringly choosing a daily woman and an odd-job man who, between them, kept him afloat. Introducing a 'slip of a girl', as he proudly described Mimsie Crane, into this *ménage a trois* was a feat of high diplomacy but luckily, with an unbelievable range of employment behind her, fitting in at The Willows was, for Mimsie, a piece of cake.

Aileen was a Yorkshirewoman, forty-five and of indefatigable energy. She lived on the outskirts of town, arriving promptly at nine each morning in her Ford Escort, bringing the Captain's supplies aboard. After a run at the housework, Aileen prepared lunch for the three of them.

Toby insisted they all sat down together in the kitchen and at first Mimsie was happy to play along. For one thing she was waiting for her black eye to pink out and, for another, wishing to bide her time before drifting back to Steve's office, just in case Khan was still on the loose. Her phone calls to her landlord threw no further light on the matter, Mr Phideas having no more hand-delivered hate mail awaiting her. She sent him a month's rent just to keep her toe in the door and began to breath easily, confidence blooming with the fading of the bruises. But, as her courage revived, a growing curiosity also burgeoned. What had *really* happened to the dentist?

She telephoned the number on the back of the envelope Steve had left with her, hoping to catch Phoebe Watson at home. During her short stint at the surgery, Mimsie's run-ins with Chambers's sister had been legendary but, she reasoned, Phoebe certainly owed her some sort of explanation. Why else would a girl like Mimsie be holed up in the gin and Jaguar belt with a pensioner and his two middle-aged retainers?

On Friday afternoon, hearing the gramophone scratching away in the rarely-used drawing room, Mimsie pushed open the door expecting to find Toby relaxing after lunch with a little light music. The sight which confronted her made her whoop with pleasure. The rugs had been rolled back and, oblivious of the interruption, Aileen relaxed in the formal embrace of her employer as they twirled to a foxtrot rhythm. Quinn, gay as a hussar, started to sing along to the strict-ballroom orchestration.

"R-Rio Rita. Life is sweeter, rrRita . . . When you are near," he warbled.

Catching sight of Mimsie in the doorway, Aileen stumbled, laughing her head off. Toby rewound the gramophone and, pushing Mimsie onto the sofa, the two executed an encore, a mind-boggling complexity of footwork which Aileen breathily dubbed 'a quickstep' just to keep Mimsie in the picture.

Next morning, harking back to this delicious little vignette as she drove to Pevensey. Mimsie grinned to herself, accelerating into the fast lane, feeling the surge of power as the Rover swept towards the coast. She had finally caught Phoebe Watson and, surprise, surprise, the old bag was desperately anxious to see her, refusing to elaborate on the telephone, the mere mention of 'Khan' an open sesame.

The house the dentist and his sister had rented proved to be a nasty bungalow backing onto the sea. Mimsie parked in the drive and, in a half-glance at the number above the porch, saw the net curtains twitch. The door opened as she cut across the grass and Phoebe Watson stood grim-faced in the doorway, pulling the girl quickly inside as if they could be watched.

The bungalow smelt musty, the wallpaper marked with what might have been ancient tidemarks from flooding or rising damp. Mimsie was shocked, not only by the clear descent from grace of this woman, but the ravages her obvious misery had wreaked. They moved into a small living room where a gas fire hissed, giving off the stale scent of bad times. In less than a week at The Willows, Mimsie had unconsciously absorbed the comforts of a warm, cared-for home and this awful place of habitation could never, by any feat of imagination, have ever been a 'home'.

Phoebe had lost weight, the strong personality having perceptably faded in the months since Mimsie had walked away from the ruined surgery. Even her Jaeger suit looked careworn, the lapels flapping sadly across a grubby pink blouse. Her face softened, her greeting warm once they were safely inside, a welcome which left Mimsie more than a little confused.

She touched Mimsie's hand in a gesture of reassurance. "I'll make some coffee," she said, leaving the girl bleakly surveying the scruffy furnishings.

The coffee seemed to revive her and she listened with interest to Mimsie's prattle about the new job, neither of them touching on the real purpose of the visit. After twenty minutes, Phoebe produced a bottle of sherry and Mimsie ventured to mention Mr Chambers.

"I was so sorry to her of your loss," she murmured, trying to smooth the inadequacies of her mini skirt over her knees. "Steve Epps mentioned—"

"My loss?" Phoebe barked. "What loss?"

"Er – your brother – ah, wasn't he – Mr Chambers. I thought he had been killed – in an accident?"

"Dead? Certainly not. Whatever Steve Epps told you is a pack of lies. That – that *person* in the car crash was a common tramp. A thief presumably."

"It wasn't Mr Chambers?"

"Absolutely not! I went to Birmingham on Saturday. The police think I am deluding myself but I can certainly recognise my own flesh and blood, even on a slab in the morgue. No. My brother is certainly not dead. Of course not!" These last words sounded as if she were repeating a mantra, a private incantation warding off bad omens. Phoebe's temporary flare-up fizzled out and the poor woman subsided, seemingly crushed to the bone by months of anxiety.

"No, Mimsie, Mr Chambers has not been found. Not yet. But he will be. I am sure of it. He must have lost his memory, poor darling. Confused by the sheer trauma of all this hounding by that wicked man Khan."

"He's still missing?"

"I had to view this cadaver they produced, the accident victim. Clearly unrecognisable in their terms but I *knew*, I knew at a glance it was never Edward."

"Why did they think it was? Steve said the police were quite convinced. Had closed the file—"

"There were items seeming to identify the man. Credit cards, a wallet, an engraved watch I had given to Edward myself, years ago."

"*His* things?"

"Oh yes. I don't deny it. And because the face was so cruelly burned it was impossible to make much of any scientific comparisons. Also," she admitted, "there were no teeth."

"Toothless?"

She nodded. "Regrettably Edward also wore dentures. The pathologist had remarked on this. An affliction my brother was obviously not proud of, not these days. A dentist with dentures? Most embarrassing."

Mimsie sipped her coffee, amazed at the fragments of hope which Phoebe clung to in what was obviously an enduring nightmare.

"Is there anything I can do? Would you like to talk about it?"

Phoebe shuffled round the overcrowded little room, searching for something, scrabbling amongst papers spread across a desk piled with correspondence, eventually surfacing with her enormous battered handbag which she found behind the sofa. This monumental handbag was an item which had occasioned cruel conjecture from Steve Epps who maintained Phoebe kept a dead baby in it. She extracted a pack of cigarillos and, after Mimsie's open-mouthed refusal, lit up, exhaling clouds of smoke which, it must be admitted, improved the fetid atmosphere. Fortified, Phoebe broached the painful subject from another angle.

"You said that creature Khan had been troubling you. I

70

wonder why that was? You never had any dealings with that horrible man, did you, Mimsie?"

"Of course not! I'm totally baffled, Mrs Watson."

"Phoebe. Call me Phoebe. It's far too late for insincerities."

"I thought *you* could tell me why Khan was following me? He *frightened* me, you know. I was too scared to go back to my digs. That's really why I took this job at Esher. Being a 'minder' is not really my sort of thing."

Mimsie paused, sensing the sherry had loosened Phoebe's reserve, and plunged in. Nothing ventured . . . "Tell me, Phoebe, was Lynne Peters *involved* with Mr Chambers?"

The heavy-lidded eyes shifted obliquely like the reptilian glance of a chameleon.

"What do you know about the woman? Has she been to the Press?"

"The newspapers?" Mimsie squeaked. "Well, no, not as far as I know. It's just that Khan seems to assume I know more than I do about Mr Chambers and it occured to me he had confused me with the nurse who worked at the surgery before."

"Lynne Peters should have been dealt with right at the start. I *told* Edward! I *told* him to cut her off."

Mimsie recoiled, sensing things were getting out of hand. The woman had obviously suffered dreadfully in the past weeks and the threat which had tipped the balance of the brother's sanity was clearly now hanging over *her*. Forced to view the body of an unrecognisable accident victim wouldn't have steadied her nerves either . . . Mimsie changed tack, dropping such an emotive line.

"Do you like it here?" she said brightly. "Lots of sea air, of course. Very bracing."

Phoebe glanced around the room as if she saw it for the first time. "This place? It's cheap. And when Edward entered the clinic – as a voluntary patient you understand – it seemed convenient. For visiting. His treatment was an enormous drain on our resources. You knew he had suffered a minor breakdown? That frightful vandalism of the surgery hit him right between the eyes."

"I can imagine!" Not only between the eyes, Mimsie reflected.

"He will never practise again. *Never*," she repeated, focussing on Mimsie with fervour. In view of the fact that the missing dentist was probably still sloshing round one of the busiest sea lanes in the world seemed a mere detail to Phoebe Watson. Practise again? Chambers would be lucky to paddle ashore.

"Why are you waiting here, Phoebe? Wouldn't you be more comfortable at home? Or with friends," she suggested, now frankly alarmed by the woman's manner, and incredulous at the implosion of such a powerful persona in a matter of a few months. Phoebe flushed, her crêpy cheeks taking on a hectic glow.

"Friends? Edward and I are private people. Inseparable, especially after the failure of my marriage, which was hardly a union made in heaven and lasted barely a year." Phoebe leaned forward, spilling ash on her skirt, her lips trembling. "I *must* stay here. Edward knows I would never abandon him. He didn't say goodbye, you see."

"Before his suicide you mean?"

"Exactly. The police are unimpressed by my insistence that he is *not* dead. They keep telling me people drowned along that stretch of coast are sometimes *never* recovered. The strong currents . . . Even his doctor supports their assumptions. But I have *one* ally from an unlikely quarter. An investigator from the insurance company also has faith in Edward's survival. Mr Miller. He's been to see me several times and is as convinced as I Edward didn't drown. Mind you, it suits his purposes, of course. If no body is produced, insurance companies can withold payment for seven years. But I'm on Mr Miller's side. What joy would there be for me in living off Edward's corpse?" She shuddered. "Edward was born with a cawl about his head, you know."

"A what?"

"People born in such circumstances can *never* drown."

Mimsie drew back, but Phoebe continued, warming to her subject.

"Fire, yes. When the police informed me about the car accident, I had a moment of despair I must admit. But when

72

I viewed the body in the morgue I felt *nothing*. Nothing! Mr Miller was very surprised. He very kindly explained to me, you see, that I could apply for a court order overriding the delay in repayment even if my dear brother's body is never recovered. The police were more than anxious to shut their files on Edward's disappearance and my refusing to accept all the evidence that that man killed in the car accident *was* him was, in their view, and to Mr Miller, foolish of me. He is sympathetic to my predicament, you see. A very decent man, unused to honest claiments I suspect."

"How much money is involved?"

"Oh, a tidy sum. A fortune, in fact. More than enough for my lifetime."

"And this life policy was new?"

"Dear me, no. That might have seemed odd, of course. As a family we have always been prudent. We both placed insurance premiums high on our financial priorities. Edward's cover was taken out as soon as he qualified. I am his only kin, of course. He never married."

She refilled their sherry glasses and Mimsie's stomach growled. She wondered if there was anything to eat in this spartan set-up. Phoebe started scrabbling in her bag again, finally producing a snapshot which she handed over. It showed Edward Chambers standing in the sunshine in front of a sea view, the bald head suntanned but his expression as severe as ever.

"This was taken in May. Just before he disappeared."

"Here? In the garden?"

"No, in Eastbourne, in the grounds at the clinic. He was progressing very well. In fact, Doctor Wellington was talking of his returning home only the week before he tried to leave us. Abandoning the car and his clothes like that didn't seem like Edward. So melodramatic."

"But the suicide note?"

Phoebe shrugged, dismissive, irrationally unimpressed by such evidence. There must be something else, Mimsie reasoned, some pact between the two of them which Phoebe refused to relinquish.

Mimsie wondered how far she dare draw Phoebe out. She *must* be holding something back, presumably the reason

73

the insurance inspector was keeping his eye on her. Steve Epps might be right: the missing dentist was biding his time, waiting for the big payout. Chambers the insurance fraudster? That must be the 'scam' Khan mentioned. In it with Peters perhaps? But even as this notion took shape she didn't really believe it. Phoebe's trust seemed transparently sincere. And if it *was* true, how could Chambers collect? Would he move in on Phoebe once the dust had settled and shock her into ditching her moral scruples? Even so, with Phoebe clinging to the wreckage, that could take seven years! And if the insurance company did pay out, how would Chambers *dispose of* his sister before he could walk away with the money? From what she had seen of Lynne Peters she was hardly the sort to be patient. But then Chambers was hardly Don Juan, was he? Mimsie felt the whole thing impossible.

Phoebe was still waiting for Mimsie's response, her eagerness that of a True Believer whose trust in the power of love laid her middle-aged heart open to every kind of treachery.

"But if Mr Chambers was feeling so much better, what finally tipped him over the edge like that?"

Phoebe withdrew a grubby envelope from her bag and held it at arm's length, inviting Mimsie's curiosity.

"You must swear to keep this private between us. Nobody else knows – not even Edward's psychiatrist. Edward made me solomnly vow not to tell *anyone* but I can't bear keeping it to myself any longer." She passed the letter to Mimsie, nodding in an abstracted way. It crossed the girl's mind that maybe it was Chambers's *sister* who now needed professional counselling.

"This letter was forwarded here with our other mail from the surgery."

Mimsie skimmed the brief note.

"Twenty thousand pounds! Mr Chambers was being *blackmailed*?"

Fourteen

The postmark was 28 May and it had been mailed from London SW1. The letter was handwritten in block capitals on cheap lined paper and the message was unnervingly brisk.

"I opened it myself," Phoebe said, "with all the other letters for Edward. Since his illness I have dealt with all the correspondence. There was quite a lot of office work connected with the closure of the surgery and I had my own bills to deal with of course." She jabbed at the flimsy notepaper Mimsie held in her hand, her bloodshot eyes wide with apprehension.

"And you showed it to Mr Chambers before going to the police?"

Phoebe nodded. "I could see no other way round it. I almost tore the thing up and resolved to say nothing about it to Edward but, in the end, I felt it best to consult him."

"What did you tell the police?"

"The police? Oh no, I couldn't possibly discuss it with them. Edward agreed with me. 'Pay it' he said. 'Pay it, Phoebe.' Can you believe it? I wish now I had followed my first thoughts and put the nasty thing in the dustbin. But he became quite frantic, insisted I followed the instructions to the letter. I suppose, you see, he wanted to escape any further embarrassment after that appalling attack in the surgery. We'd planned to live abroad when everything was settled but since undertaking therapy with Dr Wellington, Edward's attitude changed. He was terrified by this despicable demand. Perhaps it was the drugs."

"But the letter doesn't mention *why* your brother should pay this money. Are you sure it wasn't just a private debt?

It says nothing about any problem which could embarrass Mr Chambers, does it?"

"It was Khan, of course. A continuation of the vandalism at the surgery."

"Mr Chambers *knew* Khan had done it?"

Phoebe nodded, wiping away a tear, screwing the rag of a handkerchief between her fingers. "He wanted no police involvement. Insisted on it. There was nothing I could do. He wouldn't even discuss it."

"And you paid Khan this huge sum in *cash*?"

"I followed the directions in the note. Took the money to a supermarket cafeteria in Brighton almost at closing time on the following Wednesday and left it under the corner table at the back near the exit."

"And this was your own money? Your savings, Phoebe?"

"No. Edward had a safe in the flat above the surgery where he kept drugs and valuable items. He told me the combination. He kept a cash float there."

"Some float!" What was it with these people and their little nesteggs? Mr Chambers was regarded as a model citizen but, in fact, he was no better than Steve.

Phoebe struggled to continue, blowing her nose with determination. "I went to the cafeteria and ordered a coffee, and made sure I sat at the right table. Then I put the plastic bag under the seat, out of sight. The place was almost empty. I left straight away and drove back here."

"You didn't wait to see who came?"

"No! I had already fiercely quarrelled with Edward because he would not allow me to report it and I was anxious not to project him into any sort of relapse if things went wrong. He was so near to being discharged. We really could not afford any further private treatment at the Greenwood Clinic and Edward refused to expose himself to a NHS psychiatrist again. He had been sick before, you see. Chronic depression. Two years ago." She plunged on, dismayed by Mimsie's look of disbelief that a woman of her intelligence could be bamboozled by such an amateur con trick. A pity she hadn't confided in Steve Epps – Glen would have made mincemeat of any little twister like that battening on the stupid pair, Phoebe and her less than stable brother.

"Dentistry is a very stressful occupation, my dear. And some patients are so vindictive if there is a mistake. His reputation was at stake."

"There was trouble at the surgery? Previous threats?"

"Oh no and *nothing* like that criminal vandalism. But a foreign girl, a Filipina, a maid working in one of those diplomatic households in Kensington, had hysterics in the chair and her employer blamed him and threatened to report it. Lynne visited the girl several times and smoothed things over but after that Edward was aghast at the possibility of any criticism reaching the authorities."

Mimsie felt herself out of her depth, wishing Phoebe would come clean but the woman was obviously very protective of the wretched man and her anxiety to please had evidently short-circuited any misgivings. She probably hid her head in the sand, not wishing to know the exact details. A malpractice suit would certainly tip the balance with a depressive like Mr Chambers.

"But why didn't your brother handle the matter himself?"

"How could the poor man traipse to a Brighton super-market with a bag of money? He was an in-patient at the Greenwood, Mimsie! His health wasn't up to it even if he could walk out without explaining his absence. Dr Wellington was very strict about the terms of treatment. Even visitors were vetted – I was the only one Edward was allowed to see. They were anxious to avoid any disruption of the cure. Such as it was," she added tartly. "As a matter of fact they keep writing to me about the final account which I can't possibly pay until the insurance question is settled. I *know* they have a business to run but Dr Wellington's demands are becoming increasingly curt and he's even ceased to sugar the pill by promising to hand over a parcel of the few possessions Edward left in his room when I call in. I shan't go, of course. I'm damned if I will be dunned while my brother's things are held to ransom! And such people say *Edward* was the one lacking professional ethics!" This sudden glimpse of the former Dragon Queen persona heartened Mimsie to probe further.

"How did he lay up all this cash?"

"Ah. Well, that was another thing. A little dishonesty

I only discovered when Edward confessed his misgivings about fighting the blackmail. Edward had another source of income, you see. Private patients, apart from his regular list, mostly Arab families to whom he had been introduced when working in Dubai some years ago. He had an arrangement with a colleague in Bayswater and on occasions rented the other surgery at weekends. He was paid in cash. A private matter, he said. So that we would never be dependent on the State in our old age."

"And he never informed the taxman?"

Mimsie relaxed. Things were starting to look more normal. Having worked for Steve Epps the acclaimed high morality of the dentist and his sister had *seemed* too good to be true. The way things were shaping up, Mr Chambers had not only conducted a tête-à-tête with Lynne Peters, his dental nurse, but had submitted false tax returns and might even be involved in insurance fraud. Mimsie wondered if Lynne assisted him when he operated at the Bayswater place.

"But where does Khan fit in? Did he find out about the moonlighting?"

Phoebe flinched at this vulgar interpretation of Edward's 'overtime' but soldiered on, anxious not to lose the sympathy of her sole confidante. "When Khan and his brother attacked Edward in the surgery that night and tied him up while they vandalised everything, he said they insisted Edward *ceased* practising."

"But if Khan was trying to blackmail your brother, why should he threaten his only means of making money? And the vandalism was weeks before you got the blackmail letter. You still think the cash you left in the cafeteria was destined for Khan?"

"Of course it was. Edward thought that would be the last of him, silly man. Just as if one can ever shake off a parasite by nurturing it! Between you and me, Mimsie, I believe Edward had paid Khan before. I just hadn't got to hear of it. Shameful. But Edward insisted that because his current whereabouts were unknown to Khan – the letter had been sent on by the Post Office, you see – he was safe."

"Couldn't you just ignore it? Spin things out until you

resettled abroad? You said Mr Chambers was almost better, about to be discharged from the clinic."

"Settling our affairs might have taken months, years even, and we needed the money from the sale of my house to finance any move. If Khan carried out his threat to report him to the General Council about that old trouble with Maria, the Filipina, his work at the other surgery might have come out. The complications could have cost a fortune in legal fees at the very least. We'd already paid for the girl to go home – her employers said she was too nervous to work in London – and—"

A ring at the doorbell caught them both unawares and Phoebe leapt up, pulling back the curtain to see who was at the door.

"Good God! It's Mr Miller."

"The insurance inspector?"

"I shall have to let him in. Don't say anything about our conversation, I beg you."

"I must go. My boss is having a bridge party this evening."

"You will come again, won't you, Mimsie? You're the only one I can talk to. I'm really at the end of my tether with all this and the bank manager is starting to fuss. I relied on Edward's income and—"

The bell pealed again, impossible to ignore.

Phoebe hurried from the room and Mimsie gathered up her things, hiding the blackmail letter in her bag as she wildly glanced around. Did this complicity with Phoebe Watson make her an accomplice to whatever fraud Mr Chambers had been involved in? And how had Khan found out about the Filipina maid? Who was the link in all this?

She riffled through the mass of papers on Phoebe's desk and came up with an address book. She could hear muffled voices on the doorstep, Miller evidently refusing to go away. Mimsie found the list of entries under 'Staff' neatly penned in Phoebe's forceful handwriting. Lynne Peters. An address in Fulham. Mimsie made a note on the back of a gas bill and hurried to the door, almost colliding with Phoebe entering the living room with a sharp-featured young man in a grey suit.

79

"Mr Miller," she explained, whey-faced, her eyes signalling impotently to the girl as she edged past them into the hall.

"I'll call you, Phoebe. Must dash. Nice to meet you, Mr Miller," she added, letting herself out.

The day had deteriorated since she had left Esher that morning, the sky filled with billowing rain clouds blowing in from the sea. All the way back she puzzled over Phoebe's garbled account of the blackmail payment. What *was* the woman playing at? The windscreen wiper squeaked like a manic metronome and Mimsie's thoughts skittered back and forth as she tried to make sense of it all. Steve would know what to do. The traffic began to seize up and Mimsie anxiously estimated the time she had left before being due back on duty at The Willows. There was no time to contact Steve, to ask his advice. Did Steve think she was still Khan's only link with the missing dentist?

Her excuses to Phoebe were, in fact, true. Toby Quinn had invited his friends to the house for the evening and she had promised Aileen she would do the coffee and serve a cold buffet to the Saga Set between rubbers.

The clock on the dashboard was defunct and her notion of time hazy. She glanced at her reflection in the rear-view mirror. The black eye was barely a shadow. On Monday she would *definitely* redeem her Rolex. And tomorrow she would track down Lynne Peters. She wondered if the blackmailer wasn't Khan at all. From the notes she herself had received from Khan, his handwriting was much more angular, the style almost italic. Still, a blackmailer would obviously try to disguise things, wouldn't he? But her direct confrontations with the man had never indicated much subtlety, had they? He had seemed *driven*, certainly, but not devious. Khan had not disguised himself to Mr Chambers when he and his brother had vandalised the surgery after all. Surely, it would be more logical to assume it was Lynne who had put the bite on her vulnerable employer . . .

But even if Khan *had* written the blackmail note and his instructions had been carried out to the letter as Phoebe swore they had, why would he need to track down the missing dentist through Mimsie? The blackmailer had already established an indirect line with his victim three months earlier and all he needed to do, after collecting the payoff, was to trail Phoebe back home. Any sort of amateur sleuth could work that one out. She couldn't recognise her follower. She would suspect nothing. And if she made the £20,000 drop in May, why was Khan not seeking Chambers till August? He would have known that the man had topped himself months before. If he knew about Mr Chambers's dicey practices, his informant would certainly have filled him in about the suicide.

Mimsie's estimation of Mr Chambers drilled from rock bottom to sub-zero as she considered the man's cavalier treatment of his only relative. Having lumbered Phoebe with the job of paying off his blackmailer without even explaining the *real* reason why he had been victimised, Chambers — whether alive or dead — had baled out, leaving his sister to agonise over secrets which she had promised never to divulge. It was monstrous.

In Phoebe's shoes, Mimsie knew what she would have done: emptied the safe of the dentist's undeclared earnings, officially identified the unknown body on the mortuary slab as her brother, claimed the insurance money and gone to California. And why not?

Fifteen

M imsie had arranged with Toby Quinn to be on hand every evening from six and take Mondays and Tuesdays off. On these days he would – to placate his doctor – accept the offer of his friend George to stay over at The Willows after Aileen departed or to spend the night with one of his other chums. The older folk accepted Mimsie's so-called professional status at face value and Aileen turned a blind eye. "Ask no questions and you'll be told no lies" as she put it. If Toby was to keep his home intact and his niece at bay, he must be seen to fit in with the doctor's orders and if Mimsie Crane was billed as his 'nurse', the Saga Set was happy to oblige.

The bridge foursome met at least two evenings a week and were far from gaga. Boy Levinson and his wife Pat, and Sally Bowker-Smith lived within a mile of Grange Park and proved a lively bunch, a surprise for Mimsie who had little experience of elderly people apart from oddballs like Steve's bloke on the gate at Pollard Place, Austen Malone. Toby was clearly better off financially than the other three whose conversation frequently hung on problems with pensions or diminishing savings. On the nights when he played bridge away from home, Mimsie drove him there in the Rover and occupied herself in another room either watching TV or surfing the piles of back numbers of *Vogue* and *Harpers* she had discovered in the woodshed at The Willows.

The old glossies had obviously belonged to Toby's wife and Mimsie was soon able to pick out the classic features of poor Nina who, as Aileen confirmed, had been a top model. Mimsie asked her about Nina's final illness but there wasn't much to tell. "The end was quick. Too quick for him to take in, if you ask me. He locked all her things in the two spare rooms at the back. Won't let anyone in there, not even me. Morbid! Can't bring himself to throw them out, poor soul."

This temporary job of Mimsie's had turned out to be a lot less boring than she had feared and the 'duties' as such were embarrassingly minimal. Quinn's doctor took her aside on one of her unannounced visits, explaining in detail the medication by which Toby's dicky heart regulated itself.

"He's a lot sicker than he looks, so watch out! He had a bad setback when his wife died, a coronary problem which gave us all a fright. He also suffers from the onset of Macular degeneration, the loss of central vision," she patiently explained, "for which, as you know, there is no treatment. Try to persuade him to wear his shaded spectacles when he goes out, especially in strong sunlight. It does help."

Mimsie listened intently, saying little, a response Doctor King took in at a glance. "You're not an agency nurse, are you, Mimsie? Toby hasn't trusted me with his little secret but I'm no fool. Obviously, his main concern is to avoid Rita's plans to prize him away from here, to live near them in Brighton, I gather. Incidentally, Cassie, her partner, *is* an SRN so don't try to be clever. As far as I'm concerned, my first consideration is the Captain's peace of mind and it seems to me you're doing a better job than Rita could ever hope to do. He becomes visibly agitated as soon as she presses the doorbell."

"They don't get on?"

Mandy King grinned as she packed up her medical bag. "Just keep up the good work, phone me day or night if my patient is in any sort of distress and make sure he keeps Taking the Pills. Apart from that—" she shrugged and quickly departed via the back door, leaving Mimsie more relaxed since the day she was first catapulted into this job by Steve's fancy footwork. It looked as if keeping Rita and Cassie at arm's length was her real purpose in being here. For the time being she would play their game – she had already fallen for Toby Quinn's gentlemanly ways – and the rest of them seemed determined to be kind to her on his account.

Aileen had left some cold chicken and salad in the fridge the night before, together with sandwiches and a large Dundee cake for Toby and the gardener who spent Saturdays at The Willows. After a cup of tea with her new boss, she helped him set up the bridge table in the drawing room and laid out napkins and silver in the dining room. From her experience of the two social evenings to which she had already accompanied him that week, the expectations of the Saga Set were not onerous: plenty of booze, a bucket of ice and the central heating turned up.

The evening cast a golden haze over the tempetto in the garden and as Mimsie washed the salad at the sink her thoughts drifted back to the strange meeting with Phoebe Watson. For unequal chances in life, Phoebe and Nina Quinn were worlds apart. Before her trip to Pevensey that day, Mimsie had never wasted a moment's thought on the meagre emotional range afforded to the dentist's sister: a failed marriage followed by a spinsterish existence devoted to that shit Chambers. Whereas Nina . . . Oh, Nina had had a short life but what gifts had been heaped upon her! Beauty, wealth, success and, to cap it all, a husband who still adored her. Mimsie thrust aside the gremlin which nudged this train of thought. Mimsie's own aborted relationship with the city trader had been no love affair and her 'Brilliant Career' was yet to happen. Nevertheless, she still had her looks as Steve was only too frequently reminding her and there was always, God bless it, the Rolex.

Halfway through the bridge evening, Sally Bowker-Smith rapped on the kitchen door to remind Mimsie to put on the coffee and to help carry the food through. She was a lively spark, at least seventy, but with a witty sense of humour which kept her little circle constantly amused. The woman was a natural gossip, filling in Mimsie's understanding of the Quinn set-up and waxing eloquent on the subject of Toby's saintly devotion to Nina in the last months of her illness. The subject changed as they set out the cups in the dining room, the old girl's latest bone of contention being her dwindling capital.

"It's all the Government's fault, of course. People like us fall between two stools, Mimsie. We're too comfortably off to claim one of those nice flats in council sheltered accommodation yet can't afford to employ extra help at home. In extremis we dare not enter a private nursing home or throw ourselves on the mercies of our grasping relatives. But I've thought of a way out." She chuckled, gripping Mimsie's arm in her claw-like fingers. "I saw it on the news. They've built this new prison exclusively for geriatric criminals. Wonderful place! Better than any old folks' home."

"A prison?"

"That's the only difficulty. We were laughing about it just now. Boy Levinson says it wouldn't work but I've thought up this great wheeze. All we have to do is act together as a gang."

"Doing what? Robbing banks?"

Mrs Bowker-Smith clapped her hands in delight.

"Oh, you are so *quick*, Mimsie. That's *it*, don't you see? One of us is the lookout, setting up a timetable so we know when the security van arrives. Boy and Pat go inside and hold up the clerk and I drive the getaway car. Of course we would each need a balaclava or something. A disguise."

"Then you are not necessarily banking on being caught? But if you *were* arrested you intend to be put away for the rest of your days in this cosy jail. All together. The four of you?"

"Exactly! Either we get away with a million pounds or so and live in comfort like the train robbers or they lock us up and we have no more worries about providing for our old age."

Mimsie giggled, moving back to the kitchen to brew the coffee. The woman followed, warming to her subject.

"Trouble is we would need a weapon. We don't want some silly old judge feeling sorry for us. Giving us community service or worse, put a probation officer on to us for the rest of time. Ugh! We must have a gun – just to make the charge really serious."

"No trouble there. Toby's got a gun."

"Has he?"

"Oh, yes. I found it when I was checking his pills in his bedside drawer."

"A revolver? He didn't tell us, the old sly boots."

"Frightfully lethal looking. Scare the pants off any burglar."

Hearing the others in the dining room, Mimsie hurried through with the coffee pot and then left them all to it, listening to their loud guffaws as she beat it back to her room upstairs to catch the start of the late-night movie.

Much later, Toby Quinn tapped on her door to wish her goodnight, finding Mimsie sprawled on the floor in front of the TV. She touched on Sally Bowker-Smith's crazy master plan to net a million in a geriatric bank bust. He roared with laughter.

"She's potty, of course. But it *could* work, you know. Who would suspect a quartet of oldies? I'll have to research it for her. Incidentally, Mimsie, may I ask a special favour of you? Rita's coming to tea tomorrow. She likes to check up on her inheritance – make sure I'm not flinging my money away on floosies or the betting shop."

"I'll be here, Toby. No problem. I can handle Rita and Cassie. In fact, Aileen and I have already set the scene. She starched my uniform for me."

"Uniform?"

"My nurse's white overall. I had it for a previous job with a dentist. Aileen thought Cassie would be impressed if I dressed up a bit – looked more the part, she said."

"Would you? Would you really? I'd be most awfully grateful. Rita never used to bob up like this but since Nina's gone the wretched gal haunts me. Wants me out of here. Thinks I'm mad staying on – would have me locked up if she could. I'll never leave here. Never!"

"It's a big house, Toby. And I'm only temporary, you know. Just till you decide what's best."

"I would die rather than go from here, my dear. I could not abandon Nina, you see."

Mimsie gaped. "You mean she haunts the house?"

He laughed. "No, of course not! No. Nina and I had a pact. I promised her I would never leave her all alone in some miserable churchyard. When I go we shall be together, naturally. Interred side by side. I've the plot already reserved. But in the meantime—"

He turned away, blowing a kiss from the doorway, and closed the door.

Mimsie sat back on her heels, feeling a shiver run down her spine like an icy finger.

"Jeepers! Maybe the man keeps an embalmed body here in the house."

Sixteen

As soon as Aileen arrived on Monday morning, Mimsie set off back to London for a couple of days. She tried to ring Steve's office from the station but Eva picked up the phone, "Apes' Services" it sounded like, her husky accent sexy as a men's deodorant ad. No wonder Jerry Logan thought he had hit on a massage parlour by mistake when Eva had been drafted in to man the reception desk before.

Mimsie replaced the receiver without speaking, knowing full well that any messages left with Steve's Polish live-in lover were doomed from the start. He must really be strapped, dragging Eva in again. She *looked* wonderful, of course, darkly mysterious and all Slavic cheekbones but her sheer incompetence cut no ice with Steve's suppliers and even the Chain Gang soon tired of it. Mimsie decided to try again later. While she still had her purse in her hand she phoned Lynne Peters on the off chance, but wasn't surprised to get no joy there either. The girl was probably at work. The third item on her tick list could wait.

'Uncle' was unimpressed by her cash settlement for the Rolex – the pledge had been 'his' and 'hers' so often he regarded it in the same bracket as the time-share apartment he kept in Benidorm. Mimsie danced out of the pawnbroker's on air, feeling the firm pressure of the gold strap on her wrist like a lover's caress. She even went to the bank and paid off her credit card and then, feeling wantonly solvent, splurged on a flouncy skirt she had spotted in a shop window in the Kings Road.

She caught a bus back to Frayne Gardens to be greeted by the wide grin of Mr Phidias who was busy washing dogs' shit off his steps.

"Hey, Miss Crane! You bin away? More 'olidays?"

"You got my cheque, didn't you?"

"Yeah, sure. No problem. You lookin' nice today, Miss Crane. You stoppin'?"

"Only tonight. I've got a new job – just temping but it's live-in." She edged past his bucket, making for the stairs, unwilling to be pinned to the wall and questioned about her night-nursie duties.

"See you later, alligator," he trilled after her, tickled pink with his command of the jazz talk of these young girls. Mimsie winced, but obligingly responded: "In a while, crocodile!" Where did Mr Phidias *get* all this olde-worlde stuff from – some second-hand phrase book he'd picked up in the market?

She unpacked her overnight bag and after redoing her face, pirouetted in front of the wardrobe mirror, admiring the swirl of the new little pleated number which rippled enticingly about her thighs like an ice skater's pelmet. Thank goodness she had left all her bedding behind on that last lightning raid on Frayne Gardens with Havoc.

For the first time ever, the bedsit felt like home. The luxurious appointments of the accommodation Toby Quinn had assigned to her were all very well but her lungs only expanded in the exhaust fumes of the city. Also, since Toby's little aside about his late wife's temporary resting place at The Willows, Mimsie felt very uncomfortable, especially since it was distinctly possible that the bed she occupied was probably the one in which Nina Quinn had breathed her last. Mimsie dare not question Aileen about it, baulking at the truth, but the elegantly decorated suite of rooms was just the style the poor woman would have chosen.

After a snack in a pizza place in Earls Court Road and an hour of bliss getting her chewed-looking fringe put to rights with a cut and blow-dry in Harvey Nichols, she bussed it back to Pollard Place.

Austen Malone was away. "Rehearsing," Bobby informed her, goggle-eyed at the mere mention of such a glamorous alternative to being Steve's gatekeeper. "*Two Gentlemen of Verona.*"

"The RSC?"

Bobby grinned. "Not exactly. A modern-dress version for a fringe outfit they're hoping to book into some drama festival. Pre-run premiere tonight at the community centre at World's End. He left all these tickets for the blokes here but nobody wants to go."

"You got a date tonight, Bobby?"

"Nah, no such luck."

"We'll go together then, shall we? We needn't see it all through but we could pop round the stage door and wish Austen good luck."

Bobby visibly expanded, promising to meet Mimsie there half an hour before curtain up.

"Right, you're on, Bobby boy. Don't you dare stand me up! Now ring through to Steve on his mobile, will you? Tell him I'll wait out here. Saves any explanations to Eva."

Steve's girlfriend was notoriously suspicious and Mimsie had in the past been whipped down to the basement when Eva turned up at the office. "Have you made up some stupid stuff about me, Steve?" Mimsie had raged. "Told Eva some lies just to make her jump?"

"Now *would* I, babe? Trust me. You know how that green-eyed Polack is. I just told her you was old and ugly, that's all." Working for Epps Building Services was never dull.

After a decent interval, Steve emerged from the building and a maroon BMW pulled out and purred to a halt by the gate, allowing Mimsie to slide into the passenger's seat like silk.

"New car, Steve?"

"Courtesy vehicle," he snapped, refusing to elaborate. He seemed very tense. "I can't stop. I've got to see this woman in Gloucester Terrace straight off. About some variations. It's urgent. How about lunch tomorrow? Cosmo's do you?"

"Great. But can't I come along for the ride? There are a couple of things I want to ask you before tomorrow."

"Oh, I don't know, Mimsie. It's business." He glanced at her smooth legs and new hairdo and reluctantly agreed. "Okay. Take notes and don't, for Gawd's sake, laugh."

"Laugh? At what?"

"Glen played a right blinder this morning. I'd had to let him go on Friday."

"I thought Glen was your star turn."

"Yeah, well . . . The bank got moody and I had to shortchange the wages. On top of that Glen's pay cheque had bounced the previous week. I *told* him it was just a question of representing it in a couple of days, but he went ballistic. After we finished sparring on the phone first thing, that effing jerk went straight back to the job we'd just finished in Gloucester Terrace – a first floor conservatory, smashing piece of work – and told the woman he'd come back to pick up his tools. And do you know what that bleeder did to me?"

Mimsie shrugged, nervously watching the traffic lights as Steve cannonballed through every amber along the Fulham Road.

"Took a hammer to practically every pane in the place! Coolly told her it was sub-standard glass and walked out, leaving the woman in hysterics, broken glass everywhere! I've been on the phone to her lawyer for an hour trying to calm him down. I'm bringing Charlie in on overtime to make good."

"On second thoughts, Steve, I'll leave it if you don't mind." She jumped out at the next set of lights and called out to him as she reached the kerb. "See you tomorrow. One o'clock at Cosmo's?"

He nodded, unsmiling, his tanned features yellow with apprehension. The BMW roared off, as bad luck would have it, just as it started to rain. Mimsie dived into the nearest tobacconist's, bought herself a couple of magazines and, on impulse, an 'A to Z Street Guide.' Lynne Peters's place was somewhere near. She could call in later and catch her after work.

Her Shakespearean evening with Bobby was a mixed blessing, the production being under-rehearsed and the ticket holders ribald in response. Looking around, the audience seemed entirely composed of young hopefuls like Bobby, presumably all admitted on concessionary rates of one sort or another, either drama students, old ladies, or UB40 holders sheltering from the rain.

The best part was seeing Austen Malone in his element at last, his fruity delivery filling the public hall with all the right vibrations, his appearance which included the partnership of a trained mongrel being by far the most entertaining scene in the entire play though, as Bobby pointed out, the jazz trio which enlivened certain key episodes was a touch of magic which kept the audience awake right through to the curtain calls. Afterwards, they joined Austen's little coterie in the pub next door and Mimsie had to admit an evening with the luvvies made a rollicking alternative to one of Toby's bridge parties.

Steve was already seated at their usual table in Cosmo's when she arrived next day, a bottle of champagne on ice at his elbow. The waiter greeted Mimsie like a visiting angel from heaven, pulling out her chair with a flourish, mesmerised by the new flirty skirt and her long, long legs as she strode across the room.

"Celebration?" she said, flouncing into her seat, grinning from ear to ear. "I thought you were in Mudsville with that poor woman in Gloucester Terrace. What did she say?"

He rolled his eyes, holding up both hands in mock surrender. "*You* know Steve. I let her bawl herself hoarse for ten minutes, patted her arm and got her to listen in on her bedroom extension while I confirmed delivery of a new set of panes *within the hour*. I explained that Glen had, in his way, been right. We had heard that the original glass was liable to shatter in high winds and decided AT NO EXTRA COST to replace it with specially toughened, extra-thick panes. Glen had just got too previous that was all."

"And she bought it?"

"Why not? All the poor cow wanted was her nice new conservatory back in business. Why sue me? We was just like this, Mrs Grabski and me," he said, crossing two fingers, "by the time I left."

"You're a slimy toad, Steve. I bet she's even grateful."

"Course she is. Got herself a better deal all round in the end. Screwed a new contract out of it – I'm doing up her spare room. Silk wallpaper, tented ceiling. Blimey, the woman'll have the place in *House & Garden* before she's finished.

Anyway, enough shop talk. What's new in the suburbs, doll?" Steve ordered for them both and poured the bubbly, giving her the full megawatts of his attention.

She told him about her first week at Quinn's and he questioned her closely about Rita's reaction to the new 'night nurse'. "You keep on the right side of Rio Rita, babe. She's a real snake in the grass. If she can wangle control of the old guy she'll sell that site over our heads and poke him in some lousy retirement home, given half the chance. Bloody Gaga-land."

"Talking of nuthouses, Steve, did you know that the dentist – remember Mr Chambers, my old boss? – absconded from a private clinic and apparently committed suicide a few weeks after that vandalism at the surgery? That mugging drove him right over the edge. Literally." She laughed nervously. "Off a cliff or as good as."

Steve choked, taken entirely off balance. "He drowned? Four *months* ago?"

"Well, yes and no. Your police chum who told you Mr Chambers had been killed in a car smash recently *may* have been right but his sister couldn't identify the body so it's still unclaimed. The police think this person had been living rough and thumbed a lift or something. The car was stolen and the driver got away. I visited Phoebe Watson at the weekend. You remember Phoebe?"

He nodded, looking thoughtful. "She'd rather have it Chambers drowned 'while his mind was disturbed' as they say. Bumming around for months sounds a lot less hygienic. He was in the middle of some psycho treatment when this happened?"

"Yes. But he was almost better, about to be discharged, in fact. Occasionally let out to stay with Phoebe at weekends I imagine. You thought he *staged* something, didn't you? Fake suicide for the insurance? A provision for Phoebe who had relied on his income apparently. So that she wouldn't be hard up in her old age."

"You born yesterday, Mimsie? From what I heard that creep never struck me as having a heart of gold. If he was faking any fuckin' suicide it was for his own benefit not for that horse-faced sister of his."

Mimsie struggled to see Steve's point of view and conceded

that the insurance inspector, Miller, was sceptical. "Anyway, they're not paying out and Phoebe's not helping. She won't believe he's dead, though with blackmail to add to his worries I would have thought Phoebe would be the first to guess why the man wanted to end it all."

"Blackmail? You're kidding me, Mims! You mean that bloke Khan who was stalking you was trying to catch up with Chambers so that he could put the bite on?"

"Oh, I don't know . . . Khan didn't strike me as a blackmailer." She explained the complications of the time factor. "The vandalism took place on April the twenty-second just before I took off to Gozo and was definitely carried out by Khan and his brother because Mr Chambers admitted that to Phoebe himself. And she says he then went straight to a hotel in Brighton and sought counselling from some doctor he knew while his sister sorted out all the details of shutting down the practice. Then, almost immediately, he admitted himself to the clinic and Phoebe rented this awful bungalow on the coast to be on hand for visiting."

"When did the blackmail start?"

"Phoebe's not sure. The first she heard of it was in May but she thinks her brother may have been paying up before this. While he was in the clinic she opened the demand note and eventually was bullied into taking the money to the drop as Mr Chambers insisted. Steve, Phoebe put twenty thousand in a plastic carrier bag and left it under a table in a supermarket cafe!"

He roared with laughter, causing the waiter to sidle up, hoping to catch the joke. Steve waved him away and leaned across the table, egging her on. "How did you hear all this?"

She described her visit to Pevensey and produced the dog-eared note from her bag. He handled it gingerly as if it was the blue touch paper of a skyrocket. "And the police know nothing about this? Even after he threw himself in the sea?"

"No way. She promised him she'd keep the blackmail quiet. Phoebe doesn't want any scandal, especially while the insurance people are so fidgety. I suppose she thinks he will turn up and they can get on with their lives as before. Attempted suicide's not a crime, is it?"

"What did Chambers do to attract this pinch?"

"Phoebe wouldn't say exactly. But there was trouble a couple of years ago. A foreign maid went bananas in the surgery. It was all hushed up. And on top of all this, there was the funny money in his safe. Undisclosed earnings – private patients on the side."

Steve leaned back, expansive with pleasure.

"Oh, my. This gets better and better. You mean that crooked wanker got himself in the treacle with the Inland Revenue as well as touching up the patients? Unprofessional conduct." He shook his head, mentally calculating the possible worth of such a bag of scorpions. "Big trouble with the Chief Tooth Fairy at the Dental Association, babe."

"Shush, not so loud! We don't *know* what happened with the girl. Lots of people get panic attacks at the dentist's. The nurse, Lynne Peters dealt with all the fuss and there was some sort of settlement so she could fly home. I thought I would try and locate her while I'm here. After all, it seems likely Khan was only harassing *me* because he thought I was the dental nurse at the time. Perhaps the Filipina was a girlfriend of his. He got mad and decided to go for Mr Chambers's surgery – accidentally got the man himself as well, though that doesn't explain the two-year interval, does it? Unless Mr Chambers has been regularly paying out to the girl and got behind with the payments. Or even," she said brightly, "he was the victim of some sort of protection racket, eh Steve? Say the lump sum Phoebe left at the supermarket was supposed to be a final payment. Even so, I don't see Khan as an extortionist. He's too violent for that. If he had a beef with Mr Chambers he'd more likely shove him off a cliff himself than shake out his pockets. Nothing was stolen when he attacked the surgery – Phoebe would have said."

"Well, you've certainly been chewing at it, kid."

She was surpised by the way he was taking her seriously – normally Steve would have laughed himself silly at Mimsie's half-baked theories. "Still, I may be wrong. Anyway, I tried to catch this Lynne Peters at her house last night but she wasn't there. I left a note through the door. She may ring me when I get back to Esher."

He returned the letter to its tattered envelope and pushed it across the table, looking grave. "You keep out of it, Mimsie. Let Phoebe sort out her own troubles. It's a rough old world out there." He quickly changed the subject, asking her about Toby Quinn.

"And that's another fine mess you got me into," she muttered. "That man keeps his wife's body in the *house*."

Steve relaxed, laughter flickering behind his eyes like the first ominous crackle of a fire underground. She slapped her hand on the table, her temper flaring.

"It's not *funny*, Steve! The whole set-up gives me the creeps."

He struggled to keep a straight face. "And you've seen this mummy in the cupboard then?"

"No, of course I haven't. He keeps the room locked." Tears welled up, temper giving way to real misery. Steve relented, patting her hand.

"Believe me, you've got it all wrong. The poor old sod keeps her ashes in a box under the paving of that temple place in the garden. I cemented it down myself. Honest to God, Mimsie, it's just his little fancy. There's not an ounce of mystery in the guy; it's just he didn't want anyone else to know about it. He kept the urn in his bedroom for months then got worried in case Rita made him take it to the crematorium or bury it in a proper cemetery or something. That's why he built the bloody temple in the first place. He can't let go, don't you see? Needs to have her somewhere close. He didn't want Rita to put her spoke in so I promised to keep it secret. Blimey, Mimsie, what's got into you? Spooks round every corner. And I thought you was a bright girl."

"It's this business with Chambers." She sniffled, taking a sip of champagne. "It's so – so – crazy! My imagination's been in overdrive ever since that man Khan started pestering me."

"Well, don't start thinking Toby's got himself a private mausoleum, darlin'. It's no big deal. Just a temporary thing. I swore I'd rebury the ashes with his before Jerry Logan cleared the site. He's getting it fixed up with his solicitor, adding the instructions in the will. All expenses up front."

"You're a scheming devil, Steve. You're only concerned

96

about Toby because you've got some rotten deal lined up with that developer."

He grinned. "Toby trusts me, Mimsie. All he's interested in is someone doing the job right. Who *else* in the building trade could bring it off?"

Mimsie sighed, relieved to be shot of her latest nightmare: the Body in the Locked Room. Even so, if Steve was her appointed guardian angel Paradise must be short of staff.

"I see you've got the Rolex back," he quipped. "Don't forget you still owe me, doll."

Seventeen

W hen Mimsie got back to Esher on Wednesday morning Toby was tucked up with his solicitor in the study. Aileen looked worried and sat down at the kitchen table to share a pot of coffee with her.

"He's like a dog with two tails, all excited like. I 'aven't seen him so pleased with hisself since before poor Nina died. I can't *think* what he's up to," she said. "I hope it's not going to cause trouble with Rita. He wants us to witness a new will."

"Really? That sounds fun. I've never done that before."

"He said he'd call us when they've read it through. It's the second time Mr Blair's been here this week. What do you think, Mimsie?"

She shrugged. "Old men with money like to twitch the reins now and then. I expect he's just fiddling with the details to put Rita on the rack."

Aileen moved to the Aga and checked the roast. "Mr Blair's staying for lunch. I've put out all the best silver. He said I was to lay an extra place for you in the dining room when you got back."

Mimsie groaned. "Oh no. Not on my own. Aren't you sitting down with us? These dried-up old lawyers give me the pip. I won't know what to say."

Aileen curled her lip. "You'd better change," she said, eyeing the new mini skirt, and turned away to busy herself with the vegetables. Mimsie took the hint and ran upstairs, reappearing ten minutes later in a pair of narrow black linen pants and a yellow Argyll patterned sweater.

Aileen nodded and started fussing with a cream trifle dotted with angelica and glacé cherries. Toby's door squeaked and he called along the passage, urging the two women to join them. Aileen brushed her hands across her apron and pushed Mimsie along ahead of her, making the girl stumble into the room, feeling like a schoolgirl propelled into the headmaster's study.

Toby rose from his desk, expansive as ever, and prodded the man confronting him who turned hastily, dropping his pen as he swivelled to face the two witnesses who had been dragooned into service. He unscrambled long legs to swoop to retrieve his pen before standing stiffly to attention, apparently as unsure of the niceties of will-signing sessions as the rest of them.

Mimsie stared, visibly stunned by the personable young solicitor staring at her. He brushed aside a floppy forelock and held out his hand. The two men were both tall and the four of them certainly overfilled Toby's den, crowded as it already was with too much furniture. Mimsie stepped forward to shake hands, saying nothing, smiling inanely at Toby's elaborations on her role in the household. Fortunately he did not embarrass her in front of Alex Blair by placing her duties in any sort of medical context, but leaving out this aspect of the job specification meant that the rest of it sounded pretty thin and Toby's rounded phrases extolling her driving, her expertise with the alarm system and, not least, her enjoyment of his bridge evenings rang hollow as a cracked bell. Aileen saved the day by brusquely insisting in her blunt Yorkshire way that "I 'aven't got all day, Toby. There's this duck glazing in the top oven and it'll crisp to a cinder while we're chit-chatting here."

The lawyer fumbled with the papers on Toby's desk and, his client conversing unconcernedly while scribbling his name on the dotted line, Alex Blair then indicated the place for Aileen to sign.

"Mimsie?" he queried after the daily had finished.

"Miriam," she said flatly, printing her full name underneath her signature so that there would be no mistake. She tried to catch a glimpse of the closely typed pages but Blair deftly held a blotting sheet to mask the details. Aileen scuttled out leaving Mimsie to provide the small talk.

"Well, that's that," he said, stuffing the papers in his briefcase.

Toby rubbed his hands. "How about a drink? Gin and tonic? Some sherry?"

"Nothing for me, thank you, sir. I've a meeting this afternoon."

"But you will have a glass of wine with lunch, won't you?" Toby was disappointed by his refusal, clearly in the mood to party. But Mimsie played along, toying with a g and t, answering Toby's polite enquiries about her shopping expedition to London. "I see you got a Rolex," he said, twinkling.

Mimsie blushed, wondering if Steve had been indiscreet about the new minder's chronic cash problems.

"It's been repaired," she mumbled, feeling the wink and glow of the costly timepiece to which all eyes were now riveted as if she had been caught trying on Nina's jewellery. Alex Blair looked sombre, suddenly every inch the lawyer in his dark suit and rugby club tie. Mimsie felt an irrational urge to explain herself, to dispel any lurking suspicion this po-faced legal eagle might have that she was just another bimbo, battening on to the susceptibilities of a wealthy old man.

Lunch proved a stilted affair, Toby's efforts to lighten the atmosphere tumbling about his ears. He felt cheated, being a romantic old salt at heart, and his flat-footed efforts to introduce some company of her own age into Mimsie's embroilment in the Saga Set obviously failing dismally. Alex Blair excused himself as Aileen brought in coffee, whizzing off down the drive in his rattling two-seater as if lunch with the firm's favoured client was one of the deadliest parts of the job.

Later, over a quiet cuppa with Aileen, when Toby had gone upstairs "to close my eyes for ten minutes", Mimsie caught up with the news.

"He's been out both mornings you were in London," she confided, "doing goodness knows what in Kingston. I heard him ordering a taxi both days. Gone all hours he was and *Kingston* of all places! He hates the place as a rule. Pity you wasn't here, Mimsie. You could have driven him in the Rover and seen what he was up to."

"Well, Kingston's not exactly Soho, Aileen. I don't think there's much scope for naughties there."

"Little do you know, Miss Cleverclogs. Men of his age get strange ideas. Misses Nina, that's his trouble. You don't think he's meeting any of these women who advertise in the weekend papers, do you?"

"Singles? Looking for 'mature man with sense of humour who likes foreign travel'. That sort of thing? He's a bit past it, Aileen. Getting married again in your dotage takes a bit of courage." She laughed. "Shall we split on him? Ring up Rita?"

Aileen slapped her wrist, not a bit amused. "You may laugh, my girl, but there's many a slip. And another strange thing. He's turning out the spare room."

Mimsie frowned. "Clearing out all Nina's things?"

Aileen nodded. "That friend of his, Mrs Bowker-Smith's been helping him. Took a carload off to some charity shop she runs in the village. Dresses, coats, lovely things. Some of them hardly worn. Funny sizes though. Would fit you all right, you being so skinny and Nina *was* very tall. Come to think of it, you look a bit like her. Ever thought of being a model?"

It was Friday before she got a return call from Lynne Peters by which time Mimsie had almost forgotten what a nervous state she had got herself into over Khan and the missing dentist. She sounded quite businesslike on the telephone, curious to know Mimsie's angle after all these months. Mimsie said nothing of her trouble with the stalker or of the latest complications surrounding the disappearance of their former employer, the, in all probability, late Edward Chambers. She merely said enough to whet Lynne's curiosity by describing her visit to Phoebe and after a brief exchange – Lynne was using the phone at work – they agreed to meet at her house in Fulham on Saturday morning.

"Not too early, Mimsie. I like a bit of a lie-in at weekends. How about eleven o'clock?"

Eighteen

As soon as she walked into Lynne Peters's house Mimsie *knew* this woman wasn't the blackmailer. Twenty thousand pounds in used notes had *never* passed over this scruffy threshold in Fulham and the woman herself looked exhausted after yet another week's hard graft as a dentist's handmaiden.

"I remember you now," she said, closing the front door. "You took over in Reception the week I walked out." She giggled. "I've never done that before – anyone would think I didn't need the money! It's not as if jobs are easy to come by these days."

Mimsie's quarry was a tall dark girl in her late thirties at a guess, her hair recently cut in a neat bob but the initial impact of her sagging posture one of chronic tiredness, a woman worn down by routine. She wore a mauve tracksuit which did little for her complexion but her expression was cheerful and she seemed a thoroughly nice person, the sort who gives up her seat in the bus.

The house was gloomy despite the September sunshine trying to break in through the closed windows and the thick net curtains which also served to block out the rattle of Saturday morning traffic.

"Coffee?"

"Great!" Mimsie followed her into the kitchen and they waited for the kettle to boil.

"You still working as a receptionist?"

"Not just now. I'm sort of between jobs. Killing time."

"Poor you. I was left this house by my aunt last year and as soon as the market perks up I'd like to sell. It's really more than I need and by the time I've settled all the bills I'm no better off than when I was paying a landlord."

"You're here alone?"

"That's the trouble. There's a lodger and I don't like to chuck him out. My aunt let him have the rooms upstairs for years and charged peanuts. He's not a sitting tenant but I'd feel rotten pitching him out on the street. He's over eighty."

"He'd probably be offered a place in a council home if you insisted."

"Yeah, well, maybe I'll get round to it. He's company of a sort. Deaf as a post so I can bang about as much as I like, he'd never complain."

"Is that his radio on now?"

Lynne Peters laughed as she poured hot water into two mugs. "The old lad *loves* his Classic FM. First thing in the morning till last thing at night. You'd think I kept the Royal Philharmonic up there sometimes. Thank God it's not rock and roll. Do you know what? My aunt used to say he was an unfrocked priest. He's never mentioned it to me but he and Maggie got on like a house on fire."

They settled in the living room and Mimsie wondered how to broach the problem on her mind. In fact, it was Lynne who kicked off, curious to hear the latest about Phoebe Watson and her missing brother.

"You knew he had apparently committed suicide? Jumped into the sea near Eastbourne in May?"

Lynne nodded. "I bumped into Mrs Garland a few weeks ago. Do you remember her? The cleaning woman at the surgery? She gave me all the grisly details though the old witch said she wouldn't believe he was really dead till they found the body. She *disliked* the man well enough but not sufficiently to wish him dead, I suppose. But then old Ma Garland was always ready to spread the muck about. She also told me the surgery had closed down – not before time if you ask me."

"Oh? Why do you say that?"

"Come off it, Mimsie. You must have guessed what was going on."

"I was only there a short while. It all seemed perfectly normal right up to the mugging."

"What mugging?"

"It was supposed to be a secret but after all that's gone on

103

since, I can't see Phoebe keeping the lid on everything." She described the vandalism of the surgery that Monday morning in April, regaling his former nurse with the Strip and Strap Story of Edward Chambers tied to his own dentist's chair. Lynne's eyes grew round and she didn't laugh which only proved to Mimsie that her own hilarious response to the poor man's predicament had been heartless in the extreme. And yet it *had* seemed funny at the time. Hadn't it?

"And then he committed suicide right after?"

"No. Not for another month. He went off to the south coast and got himself into a clinic. The Greenwood. Have you heard of it?"

"Yes! It's *very* pricy. A patient was warbling on about it only last week. Her teenage daughter had gone there with some eating disorder and it cost the *earth* she said. I'm surprised old Chambers could afford it."

Mimsie didn't mention the private work he had allegedly undertaken at weekends and let this go by. "Lynne, you said you'd bumped into Mrs Garland, the cleaning woman. She was the one who dropped me right in it."

"A proper old blabbermouth that one. What did she say?"

"Only told a perfect stranger where I lived, didn't she. Gave him my home address and, in fact, I don't think he was looking for me at all. It was someone called Khan, a friend of yours, wasn't he?"

She shook her head, puzzled. "Khan? A patient?"

"He said not. Don't you remember him at all?"

Lynne giggled, slopping her coffee. "Khan's as common as Smith these days. Don't you remember the number of times Khan cropped up in the bookings?"

"This bloke positively *haunts* me. Follows me home. Rings me at my office. Puts notes through the door. Scares the pants off me if you want to know."

"He's got a crush on you?"

"Hardly! He just wanted me to point him to Mr Chambers. Or Phoebe. Absolutely obsessed."

"Why not go to the police?"

"Once I'd been told Mr Chambers had died in the car crash I thought that would be the end of it."

104

"You said he drowned."

"It's a toss up either way if you ask me and, frankly, I don't really *care*. Listen." Mimsie ran through the facts she had gleaned from Phoebe Watson and described the woman's horrible situation, holed up in a damp bungalow waiting for news.

Lynne nervously paced the room, chewing her thumbnail. "And this man Khan is *still* after Chambers, you say?"

"Probably. Who knows? No body's yet been identified and the insurance people seem to be dragging their feet. I'm living in a sort of limbo just now and I don't want to move back to my old haunts until I'm sure I'm off the hook with this stalker. Are you certain you don't remember the man, Lynne? It was the *nurse* he was looking for. He didn't seem to cotton on to the fact I was the receptionist. It was those awful nursy outfits he made us wear."

The woman suddenly flopped onto the sofa, white as a sheet.

"Ah yes. I remember him now. You're right. He wasn't a patient."

"Tell me what happened. If we share what we know I could go to the police and they could stop him. He's already forced Mr Chambers out of business and possibly driven him to suicide. And then there's the blackmail."

"Blackmail?"

"Yes, that was what got to poor old Phoebe in the end. She's a different woman, Lynne. You'd never recognise her – all that bossiness blown away by this awful thing." She produced the demand note, the letter now looking distinctly shopsoiled by so much handling.

"And Phoebe gave you this?"

"Not exactly. But the drop was effected in May – months ago. She hasn't had another demand so we can assume the blackmailer knows Mr Chambers really is dead. Khan told me so when he phoned the last time but that was only recently and I have a gut feeling this man is after blood not money. He won't give up even if Mr Chambers *is* dead. The blackmail had been going on long before Khan started following *me*. Phoebe mentioned that about two years ago you were a sort of go-between with a Filipina and Mr Chambers.

Do you think the girl has been getting money from him all this time?"

Lynne Peters looked stunned, struggling to sort things out in her mind. She levered herself from the threadbare sofa and took an envelope from a bundle of letters propped behind a clock on the mantelshelf. It contained a garish card hand sewn with sequins plus a snapshot of a pretty Asian girl holding a child by the hand. The little boy was European and dressed in what appeared to be a brand-new school uniform, the photograph presumably a memento of his first day at school.

"That's Maria. She's got a new job with a family in Kuwait. She was out of work for over a year; couldn't bring herself to go abroad again. She sends me a postcard now and then."

"You befriended her?"

"Not really. I just felt sorry for her and said if ever she was in London again to get in touch. It was a terrible thing to happen to a girl like that. She was so innocent – unused to our rough ways," she added with a bitter smile.

"You arranged for her flight home, Phoebe said."

"I covered up for *him* she means. Whatever she may have said to you, Phoebe Watson knew what her brother had done. I left Chambers's money with Maria and calmed down her employers. They didn't want any trouble and poor Maria's English evaporates with any panic."

"What happened to her?"

"Hang on. I'll make some camomile tea – it'll settle my nerves. Just *thinking* about it makes my blood boil. Can I get you something?"

Mimsie waited in the living room enduring the roar of Tchaikovsky's 1812 booming through the ceiling from the flat upstairs. The whole place was something of a shambles and Lynne Peters had clearly had neither the money nor the time to redecorate: even the wallpaper was Festival of Britain geometrics. She returned with a tray of tea and toast and they settled in front of the blank television set.

"Mr Chambers sometimes fitted in late appointments in emergencies and Maria's employer brought her in about five one afternoon with a broken tooth. She was a pitiful looking kid, all skin and bone – looked about fifteen though in fact she was twenty-two. It was her first job abroad and she was very shy. I think the Arab lady who brought her was a bit of a bully, at any rate she was pretty fed up with Maria for causing all this bother and insisted the girl be dealt with pronto. Privately. There was to be no hassle about treating Maria on the NHS and naturally old Chambers bent over backwards to accommodate these embassy people."

"She was in pain?"

"Probably but didn't complain at all. Just sat hunched in the corner of Reception waiting her turn."

"Her employer just went?"

"Sure. Couldn't hang about she said. Had guests that evening. She left some money on the desk for me to call a taxi for Maria afterwards. The receptionist had gone too by then and Maria was the last patient."

"Phoebe wasn't around?"

"No. She only filled in if I called in sick or the girl on the desk was on holiday. I attended in the surgery while he gave her a preliminary examination but he said he needed some sedatives from the safe upstairs in his flat. When I came down he shoved me out of the surgery telling me to push off home, he wouldn't need any help as he was only doing a temporary filling and would complete the treatment when he had more time."

"But the girl was all right?"

"Sure. But she was such a bird-like little thing, all eyes. I don't think she had ever sat in a dentist's chair before and first time is pretty scary, all those lights and instruments. I left him to it while I sorted out the supplies in the spare medical cabinet in his office upstairs and then decided I might as well wait and see the girl into a cab, her English was terrible and I thought she might make a hash of getting home."

Lynne chewed her toast and when she spoke it was as if she was thinking aloud, wearily putting a commentary to a bit of old video film which was all too familiar.

"When the surgery door reopened, the girl seemed incapable of moving. Transfixed with fright I thought. She had been in there ages and made no sound. Mr Chambers was shocked to see me standing there – he thought I'd already left. I fetched a warm drink for Maria and she quickly recovered. Then before we could stop her she started to yell like a scalded cat and bolted out of the place into a taxi that had just pulled up at the corner."

"And you both just let her go?"

"I was *worried*, of course I was, but she had obviously just panicked in the chair. It was only the next day when the Arab woman came busting in and the fat was in the fire."

"She accused *you*?"

"Indirectly, yes, she did. She said I had been in cahoots with him. *Me*! We bundled her into his private office upstairs and he told the receptionist to cancel the next three appointments before lunch. He tried to cut me out but I insisted on hearing her accusations about me face to face."

"What did she say had happened?"

"Maria had arrived home in tears and at first wouldn't say anything at all, just ran up to the room she shared with another girl. Then she asked this girl to fetch the priest from the church round the corner and get him in through the back without telling Madame. Another member of staff noticed the man leaving and when he tackled the poor kid about it, Maria fainted. The housekeeper told the lady of the house and asked if she should call a doctor. The woman said no, it was just hysterics but later that evening, when her guests had gone, she confronted Maria in her room. That's when she told her she'd been raped."

"In the surgery?"

Judy nodded. "She said Chambers gave her an injection and although she remained conscious she couldn't move a muscle. He had presumably given her a triple dose of sedative and, thinking I was already off the premises, jumped her."

"And you believed this story?"

"Maria was a mouse. Convent educated and very pious. She wouldn't lie to a priest. Why should she? And we assume she confessed the whole thing to him before telling anyone else. Why make it up?"

"To screw money out of the dentist? The priest would be a respectable ally if it came to the crunch."

"She wasn't that bright. Far from it. She didn't even want her employer to know about it at first but when Madame threatened to call a doctor the poor soul admitted what had happened. The priest was bound to secrecy and refused to discuss it with the Arab woman unless Maria agreed."

"How did Mr Chambers explain it?"

"He blamed the drugs for giving the girl wet dreams. Said it was all rubbish, of course, and quite honestly he doesn't look like a rapist, does he? Who would believe the girl? She could easily have had a boyfriend on the quiet, met him after the appointment at the surgery and got rolled."

"And decided to blame the dentist?"

"Sounds feasable. This employer person didn't let her staff have much time off and certainly would not have allowed any fancy man near the house. London's a trap for simple girls like Maria."

"But you believed her right away. Had you any suspicions about Mr Chambers before? Had he groped other patients?"

"Not as far as I know but picking on a girl like Maria was a cunning move. She was too naive to see it coming and too vulnerable to complain afterwards. Chambers and the employer agreed to ship her back to Manila without any fuss. Neither of them wished for any official enquiry and Maria just wanted to go home. He paid handsomely for that little romp – I handled all the negotiations and in the course of several visits I became friendly with the girl. She even introduced me to her priest and naturally he tried to persuade her to report it. But she was desperately anxious no one at home should find out, silly girl, and really it was kinder to let her have it her own way."

"Didn't you confront Mr Chambers yourself?"

"You bet I did. I said I would *never* get involved in another trick like that again and he had better watch out because, for my money, his talk about the girl getting the wrong idea while under sedation was bullshit. I saw her straight after it happened. The poor kid could hardly move. If she was scared of the needle, she needn't have had an injection at all for a temporary filling let alone a blockbuster which left her practically legless."

"He kept you on as his nurse."

"Gave me a rise. You bet he did. And I saw to it he didn't put a foot wrong again. Trouble was, I wasn't in a very good position myself. I *had* been there when it happened. Any scandal supporting the claim that I had been an accessory would have killed my future job prospects stone dead. I can't do anything else, Mimsie. I can't even type."

Mimsie sat rigid, rocked to the core by these accusations. Mr Chambers a rapist? Even the roughest bloke on Steve's Chain Gang wouldn't play that card. After a moment she ventured another question.

"And Khan. How does he fit in?"

Lynne pursed her lips, turning her back to replace Maria's photograph with the other letters behind the clock. The music overhead burst into Wagner with renewed frenzy. "Oh, bugger it," she muttered, going out of the room and bolting upstairs to remonstrate with her aurally challenged lodger. She returned, her face set as if those few minutes respite had been enough to make up her mind.

"Listen, from what you tell me, it seems poor old Phoebe's got the mucky end of the stick in this. She was told, or guessed, about Maria but probably prefers to believe her brother's story, that the girl was making it all up or just got hysterical. This Khan and his brother who destroyed the surgery and tied up Chambers are in a different category altogether, especially if thousands of pounds were levered out of the old pervert before he decided to top himself. I think I can put the finger on this guy. Phoebe has all the books from the surgery with her, doesn't she?"

"I'm sure she took them to the bungalow with all the other stuff. She was left to tie up all the loose ends of the business. But Khan told me himself – he's never been a patient. You won't find his address that way."

"Well, if I can go over Phoebe's files I think I might be able to trace him. Why don't we drive down there together tomorrow? I can borrow my boyfriend's car and Phoebe seems to trust you. Then, between us, we can build up a decent case against Khan and get him off your back. Let the police deal with it. He's been harassing you and may still be looking for me, not to mention Phoebe. How about it?"

"Yes, sure. But tomorrow's out. I'm staying with an elderly relative and he's alone on Sundays. I can't leave him unless someone's there. He's got a serious heart condition."

"I'm working all week. Doesn't matter, I'll go alone. Give

me her phone number and I'll warn her I'm on my way. Phoebe Watson can't push *me* around any longer."

"She's changed, Lynne. Really broken up since he disappeared."

Mimsie scribbled down the phone number in Sussex and drew a map with directions to the house. Glancing at her watch, she scrambled up. "I must get back. The old boy has the gardener on hand all day Saturday but I like to be about. He's got a terrible niece who stamps about at weekends and gives him the shakes. She's a bus driver in Brighton – a real handful and that's without Cassie, her better half."

Nineteen

W hen she re-entered The Willows that afternoon it was
like the aftermath of an earth tremor: the table heaped
with what looked like old clothes, the gardener leaning against
the Aga in a state of shock and Sally Bowker-Smith, looking
like an old bag lady instead of her usual neat self, in tears.

"What's up? Has Toby been taken ill?"

The woman struggled from her seat, clutching Mimsie's
arm like a drowning person, her normally neatly coiffed hair
on end.

"Worse! Mimsie, Toby's being questioned at the police
station!"

"An accident?"

"No. He went into Kingston before lunch, took a taxi Frank
here tells me. To do some shopping he said."

"He didn't mention it to me at breakfast. I had to meet
a friend in town. When did you get here, Mrs Bowker-
Smith?"

"About twelve. He knew I was coming but he had already
left. I was quite pleased really. I've been helping to clear out
Nina's wardrobe and," she indicated the pile on the table,
"these were the last. I thought he probably chose not to
see them go – you know how distressed he gets about such
things."

She dabbed at her eyes, her hands trembling.

"Here, sit down. I'll make you some tea. I'm sure there's
nothing to worry about." Mimsie pushed Frank ahead of her
into the scullery and, in urgent whispers, got his version.

"The Captain rang up from the police station about half an
hour ago and spoke to the lady. He wanted his solicitor but
when Mrs Smith tried to get through the office was closed.
She left a message with a girl there who was doing some

overtime and she said she thought she knew where she could find Mr Blair. He's usually down the rugby club on Saturdays, she said. She said she'd try to find him for her but we've heard nothing since."

"What's Toby doing at the nick, Frank? Was he robbed?" The man miserably shook his head, as clueless as Mimsie herself.

"Here, make some tea for Mrs Bowker-Smith, there's a good chap. Try and calm her down. I'm sure it's nothing serious. I'll drive over to Kingston – it was Kingston police station, wasn't it? – and sort things out. I'll ring here as soon as there's any news and then Mrs Bowker-Smith should be fit enough to drive herself home. No point in hanging about here till I get back. I may have to take Toby to the doctor's afterwards if he's got himself in a state."

She squeezed Sally's shoulder as she hurried through, assuring her she would telephone just as soon as she discovered what was going on.

Mimsie worked herself into a frenzy with the weekend traffic jams, wondering what on earth had got into the old guy, making secret forays into Kingston like that. Perhaps, as Aileen suspected, he *did* have a little romance on the side or why hadn't he asked *her* to chauffeur him about when, as he well knew, she was more than anxious to justify her pay. Alternatives to this charming idea were much darker. Could he have forgotten to pay for his lunch and been apprehended as he walked out or, worse, been caught inadvertently shoplifting as witless elderly people sometimes did?

The police sergeant looked severely at her tousled hair and flushed cheeks as she burst in, the skimpy skirt and knee-boots adding no gravitas. She insisted on seeing Toby straight away.

"Mr Quinn's solicitor's already here," he said, unimpressed by her irritable stance. He would give nothing away, insisting Mimsie wait in the lobby.

"You're not next-of-kin, are you?"

"Christ! Is he dead?"

"No, miss. Of course he's not dead. Just sit down outside, there's a good lass."

At that moment a plain clothes man appeared from the

rear office and pulled the sergeant aside, both men glancing furtively at the girl drumming her fingers on the counter. She was clearly in no mood to back off. The senior officer faced her, his expression as obstinate as her own.

"My name's Ferguson. Inspector Ferguson. Miss Quinn, is it? Miss Rita Quinn?"

"No, of course I'm bloody well not. Do I look like a bus driver? Just tell me why you are holding Captain Quinn here. Is he a witness to some sort of crime? You *do* realise he's a very sick man. He's certainly not fit enough to hang about here while you play Sherlock Holmes."

"Then *who* are you?"

"My name's Crane, Mimsie Crane, and I'm the nearest Toby Quinn's likely to get to next-of-kin on a Saturday afternoon. I'm his fiancée and I have every right to take him home right away. His doctor will take a dim view of any police harassment."

At that moment Alex Blair emerged from an interview room, Toby, grey-faced, in tow. Mimsie's explosive announcement of her relationship with his client patently caught them all off balance and Toby, thoroughly confused, let her claim go uncontested. Alex Blair looked far from equipped for his emergency appearance, a pair of jogging pants hastily pulled over shorts, bare feet shoved into tasselled moccasins and his striped rugby shirt caked with mud. He looked angry, his irritation directed, oddly enough, at the girl, his demeanor towards the police conciliatory.

"It's okay Mimsie. We've already sorted it out. Let's go."

This was the final straw. "What the hell's going on here? I'm the one responsible for Toby's welfare, not *you*." She turned on the detective, demanding an explanation.

"Your fiancé," he said with heavy emphasis, "has been acting suspiciously. Also, he has admitted making notes of the movement of security vans delivering to the building society premises over a number of days. It's all in his notebook here. And this is not the first time his surveillance has been remarked upon by the staff. Mr Quinn has also been recorded handling an offensive weapon inside the building society office. It's all on video tape."

114

He slammed a revolver onto the counter, the menace of it temporarily taking Mimsie's breath away. Light dawned. She laughed.

"You must be joking. It's just a toy. *Look* at it, man. It's a replica. The only offence you could commit with that is sticking it through your flies."

The sergeant sniggered but quickly recovered himself as the inspector jabbed back at her.

"Replica or not it looks real enough to cause a panic. A man recently held up a post office with a toilet duck, may I tell you. And he went to prison for it."

He elaborated on the full extent of Toby's watch on the building society office both from the pedestrian precinct and, merging with the customers, inside the building.

"But it was a gag. A dare set up by his bridge partners. Really, Inspector, if you have nothing better to do than bring a gentleman in here for questioning on the say-so of a stupid bank clerk you must be really scraping about to clear up your crime sheets. I'm surprised you didn't find it necessary to put out a warning on television about these geriatric terrorists in the neighbourhood."

Alex Blair swiftly intervened, taking Mimsie's arm. "Drop it," he muttered. "Just let's get out of here before the old boy's *really* in trouble."

Mimsie shut up, nodding encouragement to Toby who stood like a man caught in a traffic accident, not knowing what he should do next. His shaded spectacles made his white face appear a mask as if the eyes behind the dark lenses were already dead.

"Let's get home, darling," she croaked, near to tears herself, feeling guilty as hell that she had wasted most of the day buzzing up to Fulham to see Lynne Peters when she could easily have stayed put and done her job properly. Aileen had warned her. *She* had guessed Toby was up to something. It was all Sally Bowker-Smith's fault, setting him up like that. These old people were like children playing with fire, trying to enliven their dull routine with silly escapades. While Alex dealt with the paperwork, she phoned Sally at The Willows and assured her that everything was all right.

Her anger, fuelled as it was by fear, melted as they bundled the old man into the car. Toby *was* her responsibility and she had let him down. Looking at him now sitting beside her on the back seat of the Rover, gripping her hands in both his own, she burst into tears. It was just too sad. He seemed to have lost the power of speech, not a word of recrimination passing his lips. She tried to explain.

"Oh, shut up, Mimsie," Alex muttered, out of his depth with what had at first seemed some sort of practical joke. "Let's get the old chap home, then you'd better tell me how this all started."

Mimsie insisted Toby took to his bed while she phoned the doctor. Dr King was away for the weekend and the senior partner turned up within the hour, a patient man whose quiet ministrations were just what was needed. He assured Alex Blair that no real harm had been done though his patient should rest quietly for a couple of days.

The gardener had eagerly resumed his leaf sweeping as soon as Sally Bowker-Smith had departed, and Mimsie and the solicitor stood at the window watching the rhythmic swing of the man's rake, both somewhat stunned by this emergency turn-out. Alex fervently hoped the ghastly business wouldn't reach the local press; it was just the sort of story to appeal to that stupid editor, Fred Colley. Mimsie described the scenario the bridge four had concocted in response to Sally's crazy notions of a means of safeguarding their financial comforts in old age.

"It was a *joke*, Alex. Really it was. Toby obviously wasn't seriously interested – he was just intrigued by the idea. I expect he kept a note of all the comings and goings of the security vans just to amuse Sally at their bridge evening tonight. It was a gag, don't you see?"

"Writing it all down in a notebook for the police to find was bad enough, but a gun. Was *that* supposed to be a gag?"

Mimsie frowned, deeply disappointed that the most attractive man she had met in *yonks* had absolutely no sense of humour.

"I knew it was a replica and so did the police. He got it in Florida years ago, kept it in his bedside cabinet out of sheer bravado, I imagine. It wasn't any sort of weapon. If he'd wanted to injure someone he could do more damage with

116

his umbrella. Anyway, he wasn't threatening anyone, just moving the gun to his raincoat pocket before he sat down, he said."

"But that's not the point, is it? It frightened the bank clerk out of her wits and, as the manager had already noticed this bloke in dark glasses surveying the place and making notes, no wonder the police were alerted."

Mimsie turned away, her irritation rising, the only bright spot on the horizon being a clear Sunday ahead, Rita having already excused herself as she was working the weekend shift.

"Where were you, anyway? I thought Mondays and Tuesdays were your days off."

"I'm a night nurse."

"Sure! And I'm the Pope."

Mimsie sighed, wishing Steve Epps had been the one to save the day instead of this po-faced solicitor. On second thoughts, chances were Steve would never have sprung Toby from police questioning. Probably ended up in a cell himself for causing obstruction to official enquiries.

"Look, let's start again, shall we? We both have Toby's interests at heart, Alex. Let's not squabble about where *I* was and where *you* were." She smiled, pinching a fold of his muddy rugger shirt. "You didn't exactly look the part yourself this afternoon, you know. Sally was lucky to track you down, poor old girl. I've cancelled Toby's bridge night – they'll have to make do with tiddly-winks instead. Serves them right."

Alex Blair's mood remained sombre, gloomily aware that settling up Quinn's final will and testament may have been ominous after all. It also disturbed him that this miniskirted so-called nurse was claiming to be the old man's 'intended'. If she pulled *that* off, the will would be invalid in any case.

"May I use the phone? I need to get back to Kingston. I left my car at the station."

"I'll drive you."

"Better not. What about Rita Quinn? Will you let her know?"

Mimsie bit her lip. "I'd rather not. The doctor did say 'a

117

quiet weekend', didn't he? Rita will make a real dog's dinner out of all this. Give the poor man a stroke."

"Well, it's your responsibility," he said as he dialled for a taxi. "As his fiancé, that is."

She let it go and offered him a beer while he waited for his cab. He declined.

"If you're so worried about him, why don't you come back for supper? Toby will be feeling better by then, we can lay a table in his study and light the fire. Just the three of us. I shall be tied up here all week – I can't take any time off till I know he's recovered – and I've got something to ask you. I need some advice. It's about my former employer."

The doorbell chimed and Alex followed her into the hall, his mind in turmoil.

"Okay. I'd like to reassure him about that nonsense in Kingston. But don't go to any trouble. Egg and chips'll do."

"No it won't. I have to watch my patient's diet," she said with a grin. "Aileen leaves a casserole at weekends. Toby's not allowed fatty food."

They stood on the doorstep, tense as two cats watching the milk bottles. He signalled for the cab driver to wait.

"What's all this about a former employer of yours?"

"It's about a claim on his life insurance. He died a few weeks ago."

Twenty

Their little supper party was useful in that it put Mimsie on a more amicable footing with Toby's solicitor but the old man was distinctly out of sorts and hardly spoke. No one alluded to the traumatic events in Kingston but the bitter aftertaste lingered, blighting Mimsie's efforts to make an evening of it.

Alex Blair's appearance at the police station in his football gear had robbed him of any pretence of formality with Mimsie whose own explosive emergence as a veritable virago had been an eye-opener all round. But, on balance, it had worked out well: Toby had been discharged with a warning, his dicky heart had not flipped despite the strain of it all, and, to Alex's own private satisfaction, the girl seemed to have warmed to him. His own first impression had also shifted. Mimsie was the sort of girl who grew on you – loony but all heart. She seemed genuinely *fond* of the old guy but was she actually intent on *marrying* him? Surely not . . .

As soon as the plates were cleared away, Toby rose from the table and made his excuses, insisting there was no need for Alex to rush away.

"The evening's young, my boy. Stay and keep Mimsie company." He pressed his hand to his chest. "I think Aileen's pork and prunes have given me indigestion. Don't disturb yourself, Mimsie. But if you wouldn't mind setting the alarm when you lock up."

Alex stood awkwardly by the door, still clutching his napkin, his knuckles skinned from a boot strategically stamped on his hand in one of the rugger scrums that afternoon. When Toby had gone, they resettled on the sofa, and he found himself mesmerised by the curve of her cheek against the firelight.

Mimsie poured more coffee and talked about her medley of jobs before being buffeted into the current one.

"It's all Steve's doing. Steve Epps is Toby's builder, not a bad bloke at heart but needs watching. He's got his eye on the development potential of this house and has some sort of understanding with Rita Quinn when she inherits."

"*If* she inherits," he remarked, hoping to get a first-hand admission from the girl about her supposed 'engagement' to her boss.

Mimsie missed the point and rattled on about Steve and the Chain Gang.

"He knows Rita quite well then?"

"Apparently. They're long-established sparring partners. But things have got vicious since I moved in. She thinks I am some sort of spy, I suspect. Someone out to influence Toby against her. All rot, of course. My only concern is to keep her as far away from here as possible. Her friend Cassie works at a hospital near Leatherhead, which is too close for comfort – she has a habit of popping in on the sly and questioning Aileen, I gather – but Rita's the only one who makes him hop. She never got over Nina, of course. Toby marrying late in life like that gave Rita a nasty turn. Luckily for Rita, she died young."

Alex tried another tack. "You said your previous employer died recently. There was some problem with his insurance."

She laughed, sensing his disquiet. "Don't look so worried. I didn't bump him off for his money. In fact, it's not altogether certain he's actually dead. I'm worried about his sister. She's living a wretched existence in a sort of limbo, waiting for news, and until the insurance people are satisfied she has nothing to live on."

"No savings?"

"Mr Chambers was being blackmailed. Enormous sums which probably mopped up any spare cash which hadn't already gone to his psychiatrist."

Alex's square manly jaw dropped as if she had delivered a straight left.

"Blackmail! What about?"

Mimsie shrugged. "Search me."

She delved in her bag and produced the scrappy demand

note in its envelope. "I hid this when I visited Phoebe – the insurance investigator suddenly arrived and she was horrified he might find out about it and tell the police."

"Why? Was she involved?"

"It's complicated." Mimsie mentally balanced the pros and cons of letting this straight-up guy know the details – he wasn't the sort of man she was used to. With Steve she knew exactly where she stood but a suburban solicitor was as unknown to her as Mr Wolf, her childhood nightmare – partly fearsome, partly fun. "In a nutshell, my boss – a dentist by the way – had a couple of things he didn't want anyone to know about. Firstly, he was diddling the taxman but, worse, there was some trouble with a patient who had been paid to disappear. Then his surgery was vandalised and all this naturally put the fear of God into the man and he had a breakdown."

"Hence the psychiatrist's bills?"

"Oh, Mr Chambers didn't do things by halves! He booked himself into a very expensive clinic near Eastbourne and having closed his practice which was his only source of income, proceeded to run up horrendous medical bills. That's why I feel sorry for poor old Phoebe. She's not one of nature's charmers but she didn't deserve to be left in the lurch like this."

"You can't blame the poor dentist for *dying!*"

"But it was his fault! He left his clothes on the beach and jumped into the sea."

"When was this?"

"Four months ago. The insurance people are dragging their feet and to complicate things even further a man to all intents and purposes *identified* as Mr Chambers was killed in a car accident a couple of weeks ago."

"You're saying he staged a fake suicide to claim the insurance?"

"It has been known. The fly in the ointment is the beneficiary. Phoebe won't believe he drowned and denies the body in the mortuary is her brother."

"So she knew nothing of any plan to defraud the insurance company?"

"I'm certain of it. If she were in on it with him she would

be busting a gut to agree with the police scenario. They've shut the files on the case. They think Phoebe's as potty as Mr Chambers was and is just refusing to face facts."

"And the insurance inspector?"

"Oh, he agrees with her. Well, he would, wouldn't he?"

"But he wasn't told the dentist was being blackmailed?"

"No. I thought I would try and persuade Phoebe to come clean over all this. Her brother's *not* coming back, is he? Someone else is helping me to talk her round. I was visiting this woman only this morning – that's why I was off out when Toby went into Kingston. Lynne is going down to see Phoebe tomorrow to try and sort her out. She's known the Chambers for much longer than I and they've got this other secret in common – the person who freaked out in the surgery. Now Mr Chambers is off the scene we thought, Lynne and I, it was about time Phoebe ditched him and made a life for herself with the insurance money."

"Got it all worked out, haven't you? Even with all these accusations levelled at her brother – unproven, I might add – I can't see the poor woman suddenly ditching the man as you put it."

"She wants to protect his reputation. Even if he *is* dead. What's the sense in that?"

He stiffened, stung by her scatty argument, recognising the logic of it but unhappy with the principle. Family feeling was deeply engrained in Alex Blair and the slick disposal of it by this pretty girl was a hard pill to swallow. Perhaps her loyalties lay only with her friends. Perhaps Mimsie Crane *had* no family.

"Would you like me to help?"

She flung her arms around his neck and plonked a kiss on each cheek. "I thought you'd never ask!"

He sighed. "What do you suggest?"

"Well, for a start it would be nice if we could get the Greenwood Clinic off her back. There's no point in them banging on at poor old Phoebe about Chambers's unpaid bills just yet and she *is* fretting about his few personal possessions they're keeping until they're paid. They can't do that, can they?"

"Hardly worth it if it's just socks and ties. It depends. If you like, we could run down there together and see what's what. I've got a few days' holiday still due. Has your friend Phoebe got a solicitor?"

"I don't think she can afford it. I thought I would just speak to Doctor Wellington as a family friend, explain how upsetting it is for Phoebe while she's trying to bridge the gap till the money comes through. I'm sure I could persuade him. After all, it's not exactly good PR for the Greenwood is it, a patient drowning himself when the psychiatrist was about to sign him off?"

Alex grinned, quite certain Dr Wellington didn't stand a chance against this girl.

"Okay. I'll just come along as an advisor. But it's unofficial, mind. I'm curious to meet this Phoebe Chambers myself."

"It's Mrs Watson actually. She's just your sort of lady," she added with a lift of her scarred eyebrow.

"Do we admit I know about the blackmail note?"

"Oh yes. All this pussyfooting has gone on too long. Once Lynne has had a sensible word with her Phoebe may be glad to talk about it. Also, I'd like to ask how it was Mr Chambers got leave from the clinic to go home and borrow her car before he drove to the beach on his suicide mission. She said he was strictly supervised."

"If it *was* her car. He could have hired one or borrowed it from another patient."

"Or one of the nurses? I'd assumed it was her car but the question never came up." She told him about the suicide note in the glove compartment and the credit cards and engraved watch which the unidentified corpse in Birmingham had on it.

"Sounds as if he dumped the car and just walked away."

"With no clothes on?"

"Just because he'd left his coat and trousers behind doesn't mean he didn't have anything else to wear. What about shoes? Didn't anyone *see* him leave the car?"

"It was dark apparently. Phoebe thought he was tucked up at the clinic and Dr Wellington thought he was on home leave. It was well planned but then Mr Chambers was always very meticulous. Dentists usually are."

The logs in the fire shifted, sending sparks up the chimney.

Alex slid his arm around her and playfully tapped her nose. "Solicitors are nit-pickers, too, you know."

Mimsie relaxed, snuggling into his woolly embrace, hoping this whisper of self-parody hinted at a humourous vein yet unmined. She regarded him closely for the first time. He wasn't the sort of man she was familiar with. For a start he had none of the smart backchat of the futures dealer she had briefly moved in with. She choked back a giggle. One thing was certain. If this solicitor guy ever got himself a fiancée, she wouldn't be able to steer him away from the engagement rings to the Rolex counter.

They were just getting acquainted when the phone shrilled. Mimsie leapt up, anxious Toby should not be aroused, and ran into the hall to answer it.

"It's Rita Quinn here."

"Toby's asleep. He's had a tiring day."

"It's not my uncle I want to talk to." She sounded a bit sozzled. The voice was harsh and Mimsie tensed, waiting for the explosion. How on earth had she heard about Toby's Kingston escapade so soon?

"Well?"

"I don't know what your game is but you can tell your friend Steve Epps he's *had* it."

"Why's that?"

"Isn't it obvious? He's already conned my stupid uncle into building that gold-plated gazebo in the garden and thinks he's on to a good thing. Now he's got you squatting in the house selling off Nina's clothes. And *you* think I'm going to sit back and let you all get away with it?"

"What makes you think I'm in the old clothes business?"

"Cassie saw the gardener playing bowls with his away team in Leatherhead last week. He said Toby was having a turnout and if Cassie fancied some good stuff it was going cheap at that dress agency in the village. She called in and checked with the manageress where it all came from. Designer rags – cost a bomb."

"Nothing to do with me, Rita. Anyway, it's a charity shop."

"Toby would never let *me* touch her stuff and the clothes are just the thin end of the wedge. You think you've got him on a string, don't you? What about all that jewellery of hers I'd like to know. Or are you already wearing it?"

"If you have nothing more to say, I have things to do."

"I'll see you out on your ear over this, my girl. Don't think I haven't heard about that new will he's planning either."

"Who told you about that?"

"He admitted as much to me himself. 'Up-date it,' he said. Up-date, my arse. You're trying to weedle him into writing in a chunk for yourself, aren't you, you sly bitch. I'll be over on Thursday. It's my only day off this week so *be there!*"

"Actually, Rita, the will's already been redrafted and signed. Perhaps you should watch your behaviour in front of Toby. His heart isn't fireproof against your horrible tantrums and if I have to *marry* the poor man to ease him from your clutches, don't think I haven't thought of it."

She slammed down the phone, hoping Alex Blair had been too much of a gentleman to eavesdrop. What had she said? Twice in one day too. Did she subconsciously imagine herself the second Mrs Toby Quinn?

Twenty-One

S unday passed without incident, Toby making brave attempts at seeming his normal self but Mimsie was seriously worried. He refused her offer of bacon and eggs for breakfast, one of their little 'naughties' in which she often indulged him before Aileen arrived to enforce Doctor King's healthy diet.

After coffee he shut himself in the study with the newspapers, leaving Mimsie's anxieties to bubble like scum in a witch's cauldron. When Sally Bowker-Smith appeared on the doorstep after church, she fell upon her with enthusiasm. Sally was what Toby called 'a card' and if anyone could lift his depression, she could.

On Monday he took to his bed, having no real symptoms but seeming unwilling to socialise, preferring the radio and his own company. Aileen banged about the house tight-lipped, anxious that the story of Toby's little jaunt did not get about, doubly anxious that the niece never got to hear of it.

On Tuesday Mimsie phoned Steve to tell him that Rita was on the warpath and was calling in for a showdown with her in two days' time. Steve was unperturbed and told her to ignore it.

"Go out for the day, Mims. Let the silly tart stew. She can't cause any trouble if she's got no one to bundle with – even Rita don't want to antagonise the old bloke over a pile of second-hand clothes."

"Do you really think I should?"

"Sure! Get yourself up to the smoke for a breather. The suburbs choke the life out of you if you let 'em. Incidentally, babe, I had a drink with my police pal last night. Norry. You remember Norry, don't you?"

"So?"

"That John Doe they've been keeping in the ice tray in Birmingham's been tagged."

"The man they dragged from the burning car?"

"Yeah. Old Phoebe was right. It wasn't Chambers after all. The cops got a tip-off about a bloke in out-patients with a broken wrist and burns, a known villain with form for nicking cars to order. They tracked him down to this breakers' yard in Walsall to check him out in connection with a trading ring and he got himself a deal."

"He *knew* the man who died?"

"It was his aunt's ex apparently. A layabout called Micky Sullivan who took to the open road when Auntie kicked him out three years ago."

"Does anyone know how he had Mr Chambers's watch and everything?"

"The story goes, Sullivan was doing a circuit of the south coast at the start of the summer season like he does and comes across this unlocked car parked overnight. He climbs in, dosses down and it's early next morning before he falls over the clothes laid out on the sand nearby, including a wallet and a nice gold watch. He hops it with the valuables and gets back on the gypsy trail, ending up three weeks ago knocking on his ex-wife's door asking for a handout. Auntie gets her favourite nephew to drive him out of town and, as bad luck would have it, they had a tyre blow-out and the motor goes out of control and flips into a concrete wall."

"And burst into flames, trapping Sullivan."

"Simple when you think about it. How could Chambers stage a suicide? A dentist is like a babe in the jungle out there, wouldn't last a week. The local fuzz are none too proud of themselves fitting Chambers into the empty slot and if they hadn't got lucky with the car thieving ring which led to Sullivan, nobody would have been the wiser. Too many unsolved crimes, that's the trouble. They shuffle all the offcuts of information together and try to patch over a few missing persons while they're about it. Listen, Mimsie, I've got to go. Come in the office next time you're up. I've got Eva off the desk so no need to lurk about in the hut."

"Is Austen back?"

"Yeah. They've put his Olivier award on ice. Still, it does

the silly old trouper a power of good to air his lungs now and again. Comes back a new man."

By Tuesday Toby had regained a bit of his old style and, with Sally Bowker-Smith's encouragement, was persuaded to make up a bridge four at her house the following evening. Mimsie tried to phone Lynne Peters a couple of times but got no reply. Since the weekend, Alex Blair had taken to ringing Mimsie after Toby had turned in, and their tentative love affair seemed to gather momentum if only at a distance. Aileen encouraged her to take a day off and Toby's depression certainly seemed to have lifted, helped, no doubt, by the absence of 'Butch & Cassidy' as Steve labelled them. It was eventually agreed that Mimsie would take Wednesday off and Alex jumped at the chance to have her to himself for a whole day.

"Lunch in Brighton?"

"First the Greenwood Clinic, then Phoebe's if you can bear it. I hope the police have put her mind at rest about that unidentified body in the mortuary. I wonder if they've returned Mr Chambers's watch? If we could prize his other personal things from Doctor Wellington, I'm sure she would feel able to face the fact that the man really *is* dead."

"I'd like to hear what the insurance inspector's angle is. The claim could drag on for months if not years, you realise."

"Don't be so pessimistic!"

"Well, he's only doing his job."

"What a way to earn a living."

Toby's friend George Sutton had suggested they retired to his club at midday, making up a four at Sally's later that evening, Boy Levinson's wife having cried off with a bad cold. Aileen packed the girl off, glad to have the house to herself for a change.

They arrived at the clinic about eleven, impressed by the discreet entrance and smooth lawns. It looked like a large vicarage, the only clue to its true status being a modern annexe tucked away at the rear which had its own exit onto a side road.

"Staff quarters, I imagine."

They parked the car at the end of a line of disparate

vehicles ranging from a few old bangers to models strictly in the executive range.

"What sort of car did Chambers run?"

"A BMW, but it's not here. Phoebe has her own little Renault but I didn't spot it when I called at the bungalow. There's no garage so I expect she has to leave it on the road."

The receptionist seemed upset by their unscheduled arrival, Mimsie's polite request to see Dr Wellington swiftly denied.

"He's not here on Wednesdays, I'm afraid. He has consulting rooms in London you see. Are you related to one of the patients?"

Mimsie explained her purpose in calling, citing her approval as Mrs Watson's agent.

"Regrettably there's nothing I can do for you. I couldn't possibly hand over a patient's possessions without the doctor's permission."

"But you do have them ready for collection, don't you? Mrs Watson was assured we could call in at *any* time."

"As a matter of fact, Mr Chambers's bag is locked in the luggage room. In the annexe. If you had spoken to Dr Wellington before coming, I feel sure there would have been no difficulty. I've typed letters to Mrs Watson on the subject several times myself."

Alex butted in, presenting his card. "I have no wish to make an issue of this but we have travelled here specially, and as no valuables are in question and Mrs Watson has expressly been asked to arrange collection, I feel sure Dr Wellington would wish you to cooperate. You *do* know the sad circumstances of my late client's disappearance from here?"

The woman blushed, disconcerted by this double assault.

"If you'll excuse me, I'll telephone Dr Wellington and see what can be done."

"I would appreciate that. Would you mention that Mr Miller, the insurance inspector, is particularly anxious to close this enquiry and the sooner the details are out of the way, the sooner Mrs Watson's affairs may be concluded to everyone's satisfaction."

The woman scuttled off into a back room and Mimsie squeezed his arm, mouthing words of silent approval which he chose to ignore, his professional demeanour wobbling dangerously whenever he was within range of her awfully beguiling scent.

The receptionist returned within a few minutes, Dr Wellington being one of those who wasted no time on minor irritations. Having a legal go-between such as Blair, especially a man claiming to be acting in a purely informal capacity, could only speed up the end of a messy affair which, since the appearance on the scene of Miller, was taking on dark undertones. Chambers had been an unprofitable patient in more ways than one and the sooner the case was closed the better.

The receptionist called up a porter to fetch the flight bag from the luggage room and typed out a receipt which Alex initialled, afterwards steering Mimsie outside to wait in the privacy of the car park.

The porter proved to be little more than a teenager, his acne flaring painfully under a thatch of red hair. Alex palmed a fiver into his hand as he passed over the bag and offered the boy a cigarette. Mimsie fidgeted, impatient with all this unnecessary diplomacy.

"Have you worked here long?"

"Since Christmas. Pay's rotten but I get to live in which saves on rent and there's perks on top."

"The patients are generous?"

"Some is. They get me to do little errands, like. They're not allowed out at first."

"But Mr Chambers was? You *did* know him, didn't you?"

"'Course I did. There's only the two porters so we get to know them all one way an' anuvver. He was okay, old Chambers. Bit of a misery but then most of them are. He didn't get leave till the last week. Before that his sister used to bring anythink he wanted, stamps and postal orders and that."

"He wrote a lot of letters then?"

"Well, no, not a lot. Mostly mail orders and competitions. But now and then I used to get things from the Post Office in the village, stuff he didn't want his sister to see."

"What sort of stuff?"

"He used to send off for these dirty books from some place in Liverpool."

"Magazines?"

"Yeah. Mr Chambers put the money in the envelope and I posted it when I went home at weekends."

"And where's that?"

"My mum got a new flat off the council. In Victoria."

"In London? That's handy for the coach station for you. More lively for a chap like you than being stuck here out in the country."

"When I've got a bit of cash saved up, I'll try for a job in London. But you know how it is. 'Jobs don't fall off trees these days, Dave,' Mum says."

Mimsie wound down the window and made impatient signals, anxious not to waste the *entire* day walzing round a spotty baggage handler. Alex tossed the bag in the back and they accelerated away from the Greenwood in a swirl of gravel, his driving, Mimsie decided, being in direct contrast to the prosaic style he affected at work.

It started to rain, huge drops rattling the leaking soft top of the car as if they were under canvas. Mimsie wished she had borrowed the Rover.

Phoebe's seedy looking bungalow didn't improve on second impression and she wasn't altogether sorry to find Phoebe was out. A polite half-hour listening to her account of Lynne Peter's visit could easily be dragged out to lunchtime if Alex's exchange with the Greenwood's porter was anything to go by.

When they got back it was well after midnight and they were shocked to discover the gates wide open and Aileen's car still on the drive. Mimsie flew up the steps and opened the door, leaving Alex standing by the car.

"What's happened?" she gasped, grabbing her arm before Aileen had got halfway up the hall.

"It's that Rita. She came busting in here with her so-called friend just after you left. Both of 'em. A right couple of fishwives."

"But Rita said *Thursday*! She told me she couldn't get time off till tomorrow. I'd never have gone otherwise."

"Well, fat's in the fire good and proper."

"How is he?"

"Poorly. His friend, Mr Sutton, came to fetch him for lunch which gave the poor man an excuse to escape but not before they'd breezed upstairs to check the spare rooms and given Toby a right dusting over."

"She'd heard about Nina's clothes going to the charity shop. Sorry. I should have warned you, Aileen."

"It wasn't just that. Some busybody telephoned the local radio station and told them about the Captain's little do in Kingston."

"It wasn't on the *air*!"

"No names mentioned, just said a retired sea captain, but that disc jockey Wayne Boyton made it sound really daft. 'Old man threatens customers in a mock bank raid with a toy pistol.' You know the sort of thing. Cassie heard it when she was driving back to Brighton and wondered if it could be Toby – just the sort of thing he *would* think funny as Rita said. Cassie rang the building society to check it out and put two and two together."

"But nobody Toby knows ever listens to that sort of programme, Aileen."

"I *told* him that. But by the time Rita had finished shouting the odds, he was trembling like a leaf."

"But he went to his bridge party later, didn't he? She didn't upset him that much, surely?"

Aileen beckoned Alex inside, closing the door behind them. They moved into the kitchen, talking in whispers, Mimsie pale as a ghost at the havoc Rita's unscheduled pit stop had caused.

"He stayed out *all* day, till well after ten. Too fussed to come home if you ask me. I wouldn't leave till you got home, Mimsie."

"Why should Toby be afraid of that stupid pair? He's not a wimp."

"Cassie told him he wasn't fit to be out on his own. She's getting a second opinion about his mental state. She even hinted at 'Alzheimer's' which hit him right between the eyes. He went up to bed with the whisky bottle."

"Oh, God." Mimsie sank down at the table, her head in her hands.

"I'd better go," Alex murmured. "I'll call you in the morning."

"I'll be off then." Aileen put on her coat and squeezed the girl's arm. "I'm ever so glad you're home, dear."

An hour later when Mimsie was still tossing about trying to sleep, the phone rang by her bed. It was Alex.

"I didn't wake you, did I?"

"How can I *sleep*, idiot! Doctor King will *kill* me if he's worse. She'll say I should have been here."

"Cut it out, Mimsie, you're not his babysitter. No, this is something else. I've been nosing through that flight bag."

"Mr Chambers's? You shouldn't have done that."

"It wasn't locked. Do you know how to get in touch with this investigator? Miller, wasn't it?"

"I could ask Phoebe. Why?"

"I'll talk to you later. You've still got the blackmail note, I hope."

"Of course I have. I intended to give it back to Phoebe yesterday with her brother's bag."

"Just hang onto it, Mimsie. I'll call in tomorrow. I'm off till the weekend. How about lunch in Richmond?"

"I can't possibly. I'll have to call Doctor King in the morning. I'm worried, Alex."

"I'll drop in anyway. Don't fret, I think I'm on to something."

Twenty-Two

She awoke with a start to the sound of breaking glass. A break-in? But no burglar alarm shrieked and the house lay silent. She tensed, listening, horrified at the prospect of a rerun of her ordeal at Pollard Place. A faint moan percolated the connecting door which had, since her arrival, remained locked, and she sprang out of bed. The noise was coming from Toby's room. Dragging on her kimono, she sped along the landing.

She listened at his door, hearing nothing, and, knocking very softly, finally got a response.

Mimsie never entered Toby's room at night and was surprised to discover he slept with a night light burning on the chest of drawers. A window was slightly open and the curtains drawn fully back, allowing shafts of bright moonlight to augment the candle's luminosity. Toby stirred against heaped-up pillows, his body slumped half out of the bed, the shards of a whisky tumbler littering the waxed floorboards. She crept forward, touching his hand, the fuzzy halo of hair silver in the half-light, his pupils dark, vunerable as a blind man's without his spectacles.

"Toby! Are you all right? I heard the glass—"

He gripped her hand, a smile breaking through.

"My darling. You've come. How lovely you are – I'd almost forgotten."

His voice was soft with emotion, tears glinting, the smell of whisky strong on his breath. Mimsie relaxed. The poor old boy was merely sozzled. She picked up the largest bits of broken glass and placed them on a dish on the bedside table, collecting up the magazines strewn across the eiderdown and piling them neatly on a chair. He watched her, couched in his pillows, an atmosphere of longing almost palpable. She stood by the bed, her face pale in the moonlight, her tall spare figure indeterminate within the loose folds of the Japanese gown.

"Can I get anything for you, Toby? A sleeping tablet? A glass of water?"

"My own love. Please don't stand so far away." His breathing shortened to soft feathery gasps, his eyes burning. Mimsie leaned against the bed and he took her hand in both his own, gently, stroking her fingers, his eyes ranging over the smooth column of the kimono on which huge splashes of white flowered like water lilies. He rose, standing straight as an arrow, the navy silk pyjamas formal as a uniform in the gloom.

"Are you okay?" she whispered, reassured by his calm. It was all so tragically clear. It was as if he were sleepwalking. In his drunken dreams he saw only Nina.

"I can't *see* you properly, my darling." He touched her shoulder, his eyes wet with tears. "Let me see you."

Slowly, she untied the sash and shrugged from the silky garment, her body pale against the shadowy background of his room, her face serene, smooth as alabaster.

He ran his fingers through her hair, smelling the indefinable fragrance of her skin, stroking her thin shoulders and the delicately moulded breasts. As his hands closed over her hips, Toby dropped to his knees, resting his head against her belly, closing his eyes. They remained so for several minutes, his breath soft as a child's. For a moment Mimsie thought he had stopped breathing altogether and she drew back, holding his head away. His eyes stayed closed, his expression placid as a lagoon.

Gently Mimsie eased him back onto the bed, placing his feet under the covers, suddenly feeling a shiver ripple across her bare skin as the curtains stirred. She gathered her kimono from the floor and looked at her watch. It was just after three.

She sat in the room for another hour, listening to his regular breathing, then slipped back to her own room, taking the whisky bottle out of harm's way.

Next morning she warned Aileen that Toby had had a bad night.

135

"Probably got a hangover," she said with a smile.

"Hasn't he been down for his breakfast?"

"Not yet. I didn't want to disturb him. I thought I'd let him pull himself together before I called Doctor King. I'd better tell her about yesterday's little upset – she might want to check him over."

"It was all that business with Rita what started it off." Aileen attacked the kitchen floor, wielding her mop like a lance. "I'll take him some tea up directly," she said. "Get him in the shower before that new doctor comes pushing herself in. You'd better ring the surgery – he's not himself, not by a long chalk."

Mimsie drifted into the study and telephoned Alex, saying nothing about her night vigil. He was at home, clearing out the garage, making the most of his few days off as he put it. Mimsie could think of better ways to relax.

"How about another run down to Phoebe's place?" he suggested. "See if this girl Lynne Peters got anywhere with her." It wasn't really what she had in mind.

She was about to make her excuses when Aileen's scream from the landing cut her short. She dropped the phone back in the cradle and flew upstairs. Aileen was leaning against the wall, her hand to her mouth, gabbling incoherently.

"What's up?"

Getting no reply, Mimsie ran into Toby's room, the head on the pillow her first glimpse of death. He looked younger, his face smoothed out, the expression bland as that of a stranger. She drew back, appalled by the sheer unexpectedness of it all. He had seemed so settled when she left him. Peacefully sleeping. Hadn't he?

She phoned Doctor King from her own room and urged Aileen to go downstairs, afterwards making herself go back to Toby, feeling impelled to keep him company in some strange way. While she waited, she glanced round the bedroom, the clear daylight reducing the events of the night before to a dream sequence, the only point of focus the flame of the stubby candle guttering in the downdraught sifting through the two inches of open window. Mimsie determined to say nothing to anyone about Toby's hallucination, not even Alex.

136

She removed the tea tray Aileen had dropped onto the bed, the milk jug overturned, soaking into the eiderdown, and stood looking out over the garden. The doric temple gleamed in the early autumn sunshine like a remembrance of warmer days. She wept, hardly knowing what for.

She was still standing by the window when the doctor hurried in, bustling the girl outside while she examined her patient, frowning at the pieces of broken glass on the bedside table.

The next hour passed like an old newsreel, question and answer dealt with in a matter-of-fact exchange which reduced both Aileen's and Mimsie's distress to a bearable level.

Alex Blair drifted in later, unaware of the tragedy, proving a pillar of strength in the wretched household. He packed off the two women into the kitchen, closeting himself with Doctor King in Toby's study and making initial arrangements. It was Alex who broke the news to Rita Quinn, his official stance disseminating the shock. He dealt with all the arrangements and telephone calls, messages seeming to multiply by the hour, bad news travelling at the speed of light it seemed.

When the police rang, he assumed it to be a routine call, possibly an overspill from the Kingston debacle. In fact, they wanted to check on Mimsie's whereabouts and, being assured she was on the premises, the sergeant passed the receiver to a senior officer who introduced himself as Detective Inspector Blakeney. Alex feared some sort of fall-out from Rita, an hysterical accusation about Toby's sudden death.

"My name's Blair, Miss Crane's solicitor. She is naturally in a state of shock. Perhaps you could postpone your enquiry for a day or two."

"Is she, by God!" The reaction was explosive. The voice took on an official tone. "This is a murder investigation, Mr Blair. I shall be there directly."

"Hang on! You've been conned, Inspector. Toby Quinn's death was from natural causes. A massive heart attack. He had been in poor health for a considerable time – you can check all this with Doctor King. There's no call to distress my client by pernicious accusations."

"Quinn? I'm not talking about anyone called Quinn. My case concerns the death of a woman, a friend of Miss Crane's, and, if I may say so, your client's anxiety to field a solicitor at this stage of the game would seem suspiciously premature – the news only appeared in the papers this morning!"

Alex gripped the phone, lost for words.

"We shall be with you in half an hour, sir."

"Er, that won't be at all convenient, I'm afraid. We have a situation here. Miss Crane is just leaving."

"Really? I must insist, nevertheless. Tell her to wait."

Alex drew a deep breath and, in an attempt to hold the initiative, threw in a compromise.

"Well, if it's that urgent I can arrange for her to meet you at my office in an hour." He gave the address and Blakeney agreed, surprised by the solicitor's determined response – one might almost imagine, he thought, they had been waiting for the call.

"Please don't try any legal acrobatics with me, Mr Blair. A letter from your client was found at the scene and the same witness who saw her deliver it recognised her when she came to the house again at the weekend. Miss Crane was the last person to be seen on the premises."

"You mean Phoebe Watson's *dead*?"

The detective let out an involuntary expletive, confounded by the miles of red tape in which these lawyers tried to tangle even the simplest procedure.

"The dead woman's name is Peters. Lynne Angela Peters, so let's stop all this messing about, shall we, sir?"

Twenty-Three

At Alex's appearance at the kitchen door, four pairs of eyes swivelled to his oil-spattered denims and frayed sweater. He touched his chest.

"Sorry. I was working on my car—" he muttered.

Sally Bowker-Smith sat at the table with Aileen, her eyes red-rimmed, her escort, a military-looking cove who introduced himself as George Sutton, standing by Mimsie sipping coffee.

"I had better warn you," Alex continued, "Rita Quinn's on her way over. She's threatening to bring in a second medical opinion. Possibly ask for a post mortem."

Mimsie sprang towards the door, spilling Sutton's coffee as she went.

"That's it! I'm away from here," she said, trying to push past. Alex spun round, holding her back.

"Come into the study for a minute, Mimsie. There's something else—" But before he could finish she had shoved him off and was making for the stairs.

He followed her up to her room and watched her flinging clothes into a bag she fetched from the dressing room, upending drawers into the suitcase like a professional burglar.

"Where are you going?"

"Back to London. Why should I hang about round here to be the object of Rita's rantings?"

"The police want to interview you," he said.

"Tough!"

"It's nothing to do with Rita. A CID man's on his way. He wants to ask you about Lynne Peters."

She paused. "Why? Has something happened to her?"

He took her hand, anticipating a fresh outburst. "She died. I haven't any details. The police want to ask about your visits

139

– you pushed a note through the door apparently and at the weekend you were seen leaving."

"That was days ago."

"But you were seen twice by the same witness. This Peters woman didn't have many callers it seems. You know how curious people can be. What's all this about, Mimsie?"

"You tell me! She 'died' you say. A hit and run? An overdose, or what? You can't just baldly say 'she died' like that, as if her library books were overdue or something."

"She may have been murdered. The police didn't say when exactly."

She slumped onto the bed, her face ashen, all the fight gone out of her.

"It's Khan," she croaked. "He finally got to her. First Chambers, then Lynne. Me next?"

"Khan? Who's he? For God's sake, Mimsie, tell me what's going on."

She resumed her packing, more methodically this time, but her hands shook. "Well, that's *it*. I can't go back to my flat now. I'll have to go to Steve's."

He pulled her to him, his grip painful.

"Stop it! Stop it, Mimsie, do you hear me? You can't go *anywhere* – not until you've spoken to the police about this girl. Tell me. What are you hiding? Anyway, who's Khan?"

She faced him squarely, her mouth set.

"Khan was the reason I came here in the first place, Alex. He's been hounding me for weeks. It was Khan and his brother who vandalised Mr Chambers's surgery. I ran away."

"Who told you this about Khan?"

"Mr Chambers told Phoebe. Four months afterwards, I started being followed. I got notes from this Khan guy, messages left on Steve's answerphone, veiled threats."

"Why you?"

"He thought I was involved with Chambers in some sort of scam and that I knew where the bloody man was hiding out – presumably didn't believe the drowning scenario. He wanted the dentist, then the nurse and probably Phoebe as well. Trouble was I *wasn't* the nurse, it was Lynne who knew what was going on. I knew *nothing*. I *still*

140

know nothing, believe me. They should be grilling Phoebe, not *me*."

"Well, why don't you phone her?"

"I've tried. She never answers. I thought I'd pop down to see her again this week, give her back the flight bag and ask her about Lynne's visit. But there's never any reply." Her mouth dropped. "Hey! Do you think *Phoebe's* dead too, Alex?"

He attempted a laugh but it came out like a strangulated gurgle. "Of course she's not. This isn't some gothic horror movie. I don't even know what happened to Lynne Peters in any detail. This Detective Inspector Blakeney may just be winding us up. He said the news broke this morning."

"I *told* Steve that Khan was violent. Nobody believed me. All Phoebe was concerned about was her horrible brother."

He took her firmly by the shoulders, forcing her to give him her full attention.

"Just tell Blakeney what you know, darling. *Don't* try to fob him off with half the picture, you'll only make it worse for yourself. He already thinks you're on the defensive having a tame solicitor on tap. We're meeting at my office in an hour." He smiled weakly but Mimsie remained unresponsive, her head throbbing with the heap of misery which had fallen on her since she woke up that morning.

"What shall we do, Alex? I can't stay here."

"Finish packing. I'll put your stuff in my car. As soon as you're through with Blakeney you're moving in with me, but don't give my address to anyone else, especially not Steve Epps. You can't go back to your flat and if this stalker of yours knows all about Pollard Place he may be waiting for you to surface. Cheer up, darling. It's not all bad. I get to lure you into my bed at least."

She pulled a wry face. "Neat."

She turned away, disappearing into the dressing room for her other suitcase. He followed, his eyes tracking every lithe movement as she fetched and carried. Mimsie was still an enigma. But he was past caring.

"Do you *really* think this man Khan's still after you?" he ventured.

"Lynne *knew* something but she wasn't saying. She wanted

to see Mr Chambers's books – one reason she went down to Phoebe's bungalow, if she ever got there, that is. When was she killed?"

He shrugged. "It must have been several days ago if they think *you* were the last visitor she had." He helped her close the locks and carried the bags out to the car, glancing at his scruffy reflection as he passed the hall mirror. He hurried back inside, hugging her closely as she hovered on the doorstep.

"Look, wait here while I take your stuff home. I'll only be twenty minutes or so. I want to change before I confront this high-powered CID bod."

She watched his nasty little car rattle off down the drive, the sheer enormity of the hole she was in growing deeper by the minute. Despite the warning bells she got a spade and started digging: Mimsie phoned Steve Epps.

As it happened, Alex made it back a good fifteen minutes before Inspector Blakeney and his sergeant were due to put in an appearance, by which time Sally Bowker-Smith and her pal George had departed to spread the bad news. Aileen soldiered on in the kitchen, occasionally wiping her eye as she struggled to come to grips with the prospect of losing Mimsie just when she felt she needed some support.

Mimsie insisted she would be leaving straight away, warning Aileen not to let *anyone* know she was moving in with Alex until things were settled. So much for taking professional advice. She left the reason which precipitated her departure vague and with all the formalities connected with Toby's sudden death to be dealt with, plus the imminent arrival of Rita, it passed without so much as a quibble.

Alex and his partners shared a set of offices overlooking the river in a quiet part of town. The Victorian building looked staid, a million miles from law-breaking in any form and Mimsie guessed the bulk of the business had, before the recession, been concerned with conveyancing, wills and neighbourhood wrangling about boundary fences. Murder would be something quite new.

Alex's room was boxlike, the outer office occupied by a middle-aged secretary called Mrs Devon inherited from a retired senior partner. She greeted Mimsie warmly and it was all too evident the old trout had a soft spot for her new boss.

When the two policemen were shown into the room, the space seemed suddenly to shrink intolerably. Alex rose to introduce himself and the four of them sat facing each other, Mimsie's precise job description couched in vague terms such as 'clerical assistant' and 'companion' to the late Captain Quinn. Once the initial details were out of the way, the Inspector launched into his enquiry.

"Tell me, in your own words, Miss Crane – what was your relationship with Lynne Peters?"

"We met at work but we were hardly friends. I took over as receptionist in Mr Chambers's dental surgery a few days before Lynne left. She was his nurse and—"

"One moment. The address was?" Mimsie filled in the particulars, omiting to enlarge on the sudden collapse of the Chambers set-up.

"And this brief association with the dead woman was when?"

"I started work on March the first this year and Lynne left on the Thursday of that week, the fourth. I left on the twenty-second of April."

The man smiled. A nice smile, uncomplicated. He vaguely reminded her of Toby's friend George. "That wasn't very long, was it? Was this dentist a difficult man to work for?"

"The surgery was damaged. A break-in. Listen, what about his sister, Phoebe Watson? Shouldn't you be asking her about all this?"

"All in good time, Miss Crane."

"Is she all right?" Mimsie blurted out. "Phoebe Watson, I mean?"

The Inspector ignored this last remark and stared around the room, choosing his next line of questioning. He was a stocky man, grey-haired and with a bluff way of speaking, not curt but having a manner which invited no wandering off the point. Mimsie had never been questioned by the police before, apart from abrasive run-ins with speed cops, and she suddenly felt very unsure, as if the ground under her feet was subject to a geological schism.

143

"Let's get back to Lynne Peters, Miss Crane. Did you get on well?"

"As I keep telling you, I hardly knew her! At work I was mostly out in the waiting room and she kept to the surgery and to Mr Chambers's stockroom upstairs where he stored the drugs and supplies. Also she seemed to pretty much please herself about her hours of work and regarded me as a temp, hardly worth bothering with. I assumed she had worked for Mr Chambers and his sister for ages but later I found out from Mrs Garland that Lynne hadn't been there more than two years or so, as it turned out."

"Mrs Garland?"

"The cleaning woman."

"But this informative cleaning woman filled you in with the gossip. She agreed that the nurse seemed on a better wicket than the rest of you?"

"Better paid for a start. Qualified, of course. But cocky, if you know what I mean, and Mr Chambers wasn't a pushover."

"Was Lynne having an affair with the dentist?"

"I thought there might have been something like that when I first arrived but it wasn't that sort of relationship. She was contemptuous if anything."

"And he took it?"

"Yes, he did. Mrs Watson, Phoebe, had to stand in for her often when Lynne didn't turn up for work. She led them both by the nose if you ask me."

"But then she left?"

"Yes. Just walked out in the middle of a morning session. Flounced out, you could say."

"There was a showdown?"

"Nothing I heard about. Mrs Garland was trying to find out why she went but it was lost on me, especially with the nice terms of employment she had worked in for herself."

"But you kept in touch."

"No. I didn't like her very much when she was working at the surgery, if you want to know. But I dug her out recently because I was having trouble with a stalker and I thought the man was only pestering me because he was trying to

144

track down Mr Chambers through Lynne. He assumed *I* was the nurse."

"Who was this stalker?"

"A man called Khan. Later I found out he was the one who broke up Mr Chambers's surgery. Khan was a stranger to me and at first Lynne didn't remember him either but she said she would go down and see Phoebe and find out more about it. The funny thing was both of them had changed since leaving the surgery. Phoebe was awfully bossy when she was running the show yet I became quite fond of her when I got to know her better. And Lynne was very nice on closer acquaintance, too. Perhaps I'm just a rotten judge of character or they both gave a prickly impression at work."

"Perhaps Chambers was the bone of contention. Once he was off stage, they had nothing to be crabby about with a pretty girl like you. Jealousy takes funny guises I've found."

"Why don't you get Phoebe Watson to talk to you about all this? She could tell you why Lynne got the push. When Phoebe told me that it was Khan and his brother who had wrecked the surgery it occurred to me that perhaps Lynne had put them up to it after losing her job, but I may have got it wrong. She was quick tempered but didn't seem the sort to harbour grudges."

Blakeney nodded.

"There is a problem with that. You see we only have your word for it that this man Khan actually exists. We don't have his address and there's no obvious link with the surgery. By your own submission, Phoebe Watson only knows of him from hearsay, from what Mr Chambers said. And if, as you say, this mystery man consistently confused you with the dead woman, Lynne Peters never met him either. Why would a *phantom* stalk you, Miss Crane? Come now, there's more to it, I'm sure."

Mimsie recoiled, unprepared for this assault from such an unexpected angle.

"Well, my landlord saw him! Mr Phidias. He knows the man was pestering me. You can reach him at my flat in Frayne Gardens."

"But an anonymous man trying to chat up a pretty girl could be anyone."

Mimsie's voice began to rise. "And Mrs Garland saw him at the *surgery*. It was Mrs Garland who told him where I live – she knows Mrs Phidias from a bingo club they both belong to in Notting Hill. They got talking and my name cropped up."

"And Mrs Garland's address?"

"I don't know it! You'll have to ask Phoebe Watson about that. Look here, why pursue me? Lynne had a boyfriend, didn't she? She said she was going to borrow his car to run down to Pevensey on Sunday to see Phoebe. I wasn't the last person to see Lynne last weekend."

"We're not sure about her exact movements. We'll check it out. Give the sergeant this address in Pevensey and I'll send him down to see this lady in due course."

"What about the lodger? He would know where she went."

"It was Mr Franklin who put us onto *you*, Miss Crane. He saw you on Saturday and recognised you as the woman who left the note through the door before. We found your note in her handbag. He never saw the victim at all after the weekend. We may find it necessary to ask Mr Franklin to formally identify you, of course."

"He's not exactly an expert witness though, is he? Lynne told me he was old *and* deaf."

Blakeney sighed. "His eyesight's perfect." He jotted down some notes for his own information, finally agreeing that yes, he would check up on Phoebe Watson and yes, they would make more enquiries about a possible boyfriend."

"How was she killed?" Mimsie whispered.

"It's no secret. She was strangled with a pair of tights which were probably taken from the pile of washing on the table where she was found. Taken by surprise we assume. Someone she trusted."

Mimsie felt she had been forced into a corner by a deaf old man she had never set eyes on, backed up by a note she had thoughtlessly shoved through Lynne's letterbox. She decided to toss a grenade into this copper's self-satisfied approach.

"And when you finally get around to questioning Phoebe Watson, ask her why they never reported the vandalism of the surgery or the fact that I found him stripped naked and tied to his dentist's chair? Ask her *why* Mr Chambers was being blackmailed. And Khan – this man you think I've invented – might have been the blackmailer." She produced the scrappy note from her bag which the sergeant pounced on and passed to his superior. The two men tried to disguise their shock and the silence built up like a snowdrift while Blakeney read it.

Alex intervened. "Before we get too deeply into all this, I have something to add, Inspector."

He described their visit to the Greenwood and placed a cheap notepad wrapped in clingfilm on the desk in front of him.

"This is one of the items listed on the receipt I signed at the clinic. I'm sure it's of enormous significance. It came from Chambers's flight bag. If your forensic people examine the top sheet they'll find it exactly matches the paper on which the blackmail demand is written and even with the naked eye it's not difficult to see indentations which match the message in the letter you have in your hand. There's some sort of test, isn't there? With dust sifted across an apparently blank piece of paper?"

The two policemen regarded the potential evidence as if it was likely to explode.

"You're saying Mr Chambers wrote his *own* blackmail letter?" Mimsie stuttered.

Alex butted in, his enthusiasm stripping any remnants of professional discretion. "Khan may have killed Lynne Peters but the blackmail's an entirely different matter. That crafty bloody dentist found a way to disappear, financed by his own money, and got his wretched sister to deliver it for him. Chambers vanished with a means of surviving for some time – until the insurance people paid up."

Twenty-Four

Once the police had gone Alex sent out for some sandwiches and they picnicked in his office while he made several phone calls. Mrs Devon came in with flowered coffee cups and a cafetiere on a tray, and said she had the Captain's housekeeper on the other line.

Mimsie brightened. "For me?"

"She sounds rather anxious. She asked for Mr Blair."

"Thank you, Mrs Devon. I'll take it in your office."

He scuttled out leaving Mimsie feeling distinctly 'de trop'. As suddenly as she had been accepted in the Quinn set-up she now seemed subtly excluded. Perhaps that was the price for being such a bolter, always running out as soon as things got sticky.

Alex returned after a few minutes, swallowed his coffee and made his excuses.

"Rita's turned up at the house. With Cassie. Causing one hell of a dust-up, Aileen says. I'll have to go. Sorry—"

"Rita will calm down once you tell her I'm permanently off the nest."

"The gist of the will is unchanged so there's no earthly reason for Rita to stamp about. Once she realises you haven't snatched the loot she's banked on all these years, she'll drop any complaints. You gave her a nasty fright. They want to sell up and finance some sort of women's aid place in Brighton. Rita won't be looking for trouble."

"Whew!"

Alex grinned, shrugging into a raincoat he unhooked from the back of the door. "I won't be long. Wait here till I get back and we can go to my place when I've tied up the loose ends." He called through to Mrs Devon to get the Quinn file ready and then closed the communicating door to take Mimsie

148

in his arms. She drew back, uneasy with the surroundings, the banks of legal tomes, not to mention the smell of the musty documents which clogged the boxy little office. Alex seemed not to notice, his mood breezy, the light at the end of the Quinn debacle gleaming in his mind like a prize all but within his grasp. He hurried off.

Mimsie poured herself more coffee and picked at the bits of lettuce strewn amid the debris of their picnic. After ten minutes restlessly pacing the square of carpet listening to the soft rattle and ping of Mrs Devon's word processor, she stood at the window, weighing her options. Getting only an increasing sinking feeling, she reached out for the only lifeline she could think of and, picking up the phone, called Steve Epps.

She got him on the mobile and swiftly gave him a rundown on her police interview.

"They say I was the last to be seen leaving Lynne's house last weekend, Steve. They think *I* killed her."

"Why?"

"Presumably because Lynne knew about this scam Mr Chambers was operating and was going to blow the whistle."

"Why would he chose you? You said this Peters woman worked for Chambers for years before you turned up. Surely, if anyone was in it, it would have been her."

"But she was so absolutely broke, Steve. You should see that house! It *must* be Khan. I *told* you he was a killer."

"You *told* me Khan had thrown you down the fire escape! Trouble with you, Mimsie, is too much imagination. Forget Khan. He's just a sad bastard who likes to follow pretty girls. Tell me more about the poor old Captain. He died in the night you say?"

"Yes. Rita's there now. I'm at the solicitor's office."

"Got another job lined up already? Blimey, I always knew you was a fast worker but you could have given me first shout."

"Shut up and listen. I've got to get back to Lynne's place and find those account books she went to Phoebe's for on Sunday. She hinted that was the only way to prove anything against Khan."

"Hold on! How do you know she wasn't already dead before Sunday? If you was the last one seen there—"

"Well, what do *you* suggest?"

"When in doubt, do nothing. Trust me, babe. You'll be putting your head in a noose if you start nosing about. Anyway, the fuzz will still be there. Do you think they'll let you waltz in, search the bloody house and take off with anything what takes your fancy?"

"Well, I can't stay here. I'll suffocate."

Steve sighed. "All right. Meet me at the de Quincy Winery at four o'clock and I'll see what I can do."

Mimsie grabbed her things and bolted, assuring Mrs Devon she would ring Alex later. The woman watched the figure disappearing downstairs with a knowing eye, recognising in Alex Blair's choice a path of pain and delight which the silly young man would never see in a million years. She shook her head and went into his office to stack up the tray.

When Mimsie got to the station, the London train had just left. She bought a newspaper and sat in the waiting room reading about Lynne Peters. The photograph was appealing, obviously taken on holiday, more like the girl Mimsie remembered working at the dental surgery before she got saddled with the millstone of her aunt's house and had her hair cut short. The police were not revealing much information and the story lacked any sort of build-up, merely stating that the victim had no immediate family, no regular boyfriend and before her death worked for a dentist in West Kensington. She had, it appeared, died by strangulation two days before the body was discovered by her lodger, Mr Reginald Franklin, aged eighty-one. It occurred to Mimsie that Lynne had not lost the habit of taking days off from work if they had not questioned her non-appearance. There must be a knack of establishing that sort of arrangement which Mimsie had not yet perfected.

Mimsie at a loose end was naturally drawn to the nearest telephone and, for something to do, tried Phoebe's number again. When a quavery voice answered she was almost taken aback.

"Oh, Phoebe, you *are* still there. I've been trying to ring you. Are you all right?"

150

"No, I'm quite wretched if you must know. I've been in bed for four days with flu. At this time of year too! I'm only answering the phone now because I was on my way to the kitchen to refill my hot-water bottle."

"You're run down, Phoebe. And that place is damp. Why don't you pack up and go home?"

"Not yet."

"Look, I'll pop down. There's something I must ask you. Did Lynne Peters call in to see you on Sunday?"

"Briefly. I was already feeling groggy so she didn't stay. She only came to look at the appointment books and the surgery accounts; said she was trying to trace a former patient. I didn't believe her but it was the only way to get her off the doorstep. She borrowed them. A shifty sort of girl I always thought. Untrustworthy."

"You haven't heard then?"

"Heard? Heard what?"

"She was seriously attacked in her home a few days ago."

"Not dead?"

"I'm afraid so."

The line went very quiet and Mimsie thought they may have been cut off.

"Are you still there, Phoebe?"

"I have to get back to bed."

"The police will want to ask you about Lynne."

"It's no use them coming here. I don't know anything."

"Shall *I* come down? I could bring some shopping for you."

"No! I'll manage. Don't ring again, Mimsie, I don't want to have to crawl out of bed just to answer the telephone."

Mimsie toyed with the idea of warning Phoebe that her brother had double-crossed her over the blackmail demand but it would be a cruel blow and doubly cruel coming over the phone. Anyway, she thought the police would want to question her about it themselves though it surely wasn't a criminal offence to pay off a blackmailer, was it? Perhaps coming from an official source, Phoebe Watson would recognise the sad truth at last: the brother she idolised was a complete shit. But, at least, knowing he had deliberately

151

abandoned her to make a new life for himself, Phoebe could finally relinquish this stupid waiting game.

Mimsie took the charitable view. She could never believe Mr Chambers was ultimately coming back to claim the insurance payout, he wasn't as savage as that. However devious the man was, he had at least *tried* to cushion his sister's old age with the insurance money. She wished now Alex Blair had kept his nose out of it. If he had not so cleverly tied up the blackmail demand with the pad of notepaper recovered from the Greenwood Clinic, no one would be the wiser. Phoebe would have never found out about her brother's deception and eventually even she would have accepted his suicide and taken the money.

Bugger you, Alex Blair, she murmured, drifting along the station platform. That was the trouble with getting mixed up with a solicitor. He *had* warned her: nitpickers all. She shied away from her own part in all this, the niggling reminder that it was Mimsie Crane who had got Alex involved in the first place.

The de Quincy Winery was one of Steve's regular haunts, an informal bar-cum-bistro, open all hours. The place was candlelit even on the brightest summer day, its wooden booths ideal for romantic assignations, not to mention the unromantic kind Steve Epps specialised in. Mimsie arrived first and was greeted by the barman like a long-lost traveller stumbling across the threshold after a desert storm.

"You've been living in the sticks, Steve tells me."

"Well, not exactly, Barney. Esher isn't quite Nowheresville, not in mileage terms anyway."

He looked disbelieving. "White wine?"

Steve strolled in two minutes later, unexpectedly punctual, whipping off his Ray Bans to scan the dimly-lit interior. He greeted a trio of drinking cronies closeted in a corner booth then made his way across to Mimsie perched at the bar. He ordered a beer and drew her to a quiet table.

They picked up their conversation from where he had broken it off, repeating his insistence that she lie low and keep her fingers out of the pie.

"I've at least established I wasn't the last to see Lynne

Peters. She went down to Phoebe's on the Sunday. Phoebe sent her packing – she's got flu or something – won't let me see her either."

"Why do that? Mimsie," he patiently repeated, "stay out of it. What did I tell you?"

"Those account books Lynne wanted. She managed to get them. Phoebe felt too rotten to argue so she let her borrow the stuff to take home. It's probably still there. Nobody else would think there was anything special about a dentist's bookkeeping records."

Steve shook his head. "Perhaps *she* had something to hide. Wanted to destroy the books before the sister started asking awkward questions."

"No! Lynne was after Khan. She was sure that if he had been getting regular cheques from Mr Chambers it would show up in the books in one form or another – Mr Chambers would try to pass it off as some sort of business expense, wouldn't he? Lynne would have spotted what was kosher and what wasn't."

Steve shrugged. "I'll have to think about that one, doll. Seems you've got a whole nest of funny people with their hands in the till. Give it a rest. Why don't you come on this job with me? I've got an emergency over at Queen's Road. A roofing problem. A maisonette on the top two floors of that new block on the corner of Chilcott Square."

They drove west, parking in the car park under the building and taking the lift to the top, Steve producing the keys and entering the empty apartment with little of his usual jauntiness.

The accommodation on the lower floor comprised a hallway, two bedrooms and a bathroom, the living rooms above commanding a panoramic view of Kensington Gardens. Trouble was the place was a shambles, two walls streaked with rain damage, the water flooding through to the bedroom below.

"We got going on this little repair job on the flat roof," he said. "Stupid bugger had been using it to sun himself which wouldn't have been so bad if he'd left it at a deckchair and a few bottles of bubbly but, oh no, he had to start tricking it out with plant pots and stuff, didn't he? Even laid some Astroturf. Kidding himself he'd got a roof garden, see. When

he damaged the roof he called us in to resurface it but, Sod's
Law, over the weekend the tarpaulin Charlie and Kev laid
down blew off and the rain soaked clear through two floors
to the bedroom downstairs."

"Not a happy man."

Steve's gloom suddenly evaporated. "Wrong again! You
should have seen him, Mims. Talk about chuffed. Like a
bleedin' Cheshire cat. Insurance'll pay up. No sweat. And
for afters, he gets his flat redecorated all in."

"And he's giving *you* the job? After wrecking the rooms
in the first place?"

"Course he does. The insurance want three estimates but
we've fixed that. One good turn deserves another. Carter's and
that new outfit, P & Q Properties, are helping me out."

"High estimates?"

"Better than that. Let me have a couple of headed sheets
each. Type me own. Eva's already done one. You can type
the other on Chummy's little laptop in the study there and
then we'll be all square, won't we, Mimsie?"

She gasped. "Steve, you'll end up inside the way you're
going."

"Now, that's where you go wrong, my girl. The way I see
it everyone's happy."

She gave up. "Where's the client?"

"Celebrating in Majorca for a month while I fix up his
pad. Maude Flegge's chosing the new decor and fixing up
some fancy bed drapes an'all while she's measuring up. Why
don't you doss down here till this murder lark's cleared up?
No sense in putting yourself on a plate if this Khan guy
is still stalking you. The spare bedroom's undamaged and
Charlie won't cause you any grief – they'll be a week on
the roof before they move down here. I'll tell the caretaker
you're security while the workmen are here. Say you're Mr
McTann's sister if he asks."

Steve went off downstairs whistling 'Singing in the Rain'.
Mimsie's state of lingering apprehension dissolved like lifting
fog. Suddenly, life seemed safe again. Back to normal.
Steve's brand of 'normal', the sort she could understand.
He reappeared in a pair of stained overalls, a bag of tools
in his hand.

"Where are you going?"

"Make yourself comfortable and stop fussing. Don't answer the intercom and don't touch the telephone but no reason why you can't pop out for a takeaway. I'll leave you the keys. Do you hear me? I'm serious, Mimsie. If you want to know I'm going to Lynne Peters's place to see what I can suss out. Don't you ever say I'm all mouth, Mimsie Crane. In a mess like the crap you've got yourself into, I'm the best mate you're likely to have and don't you forget it."

Twenty-Five

S teve left the van around the corner from Ruskin Street and strolled towards the Peters house casting a professional eye over the properties. Lynne's was an 'end of terrace', separated from its neighbour by an alley leading to a path giving access to the gardens of both Ruskin Street and the houses backing onto it. A policeman stood at the front gate looking bored.

Steve wandered down the alley, the gardens either side partly screened by high fences, most of the backyards clearly viewable. Each strip of back garden had its own exit and most boasted some sort of shed for tools, bicycles and junk. Steve viewed the back elevations, making a mental note to have a word with Jerry Logan about the development potential of this rump end of Fulham. Retracing his steps, he noticed an old man pulling down bean poles in the Peters backyard, presumably the lodger, Reg Franklin. Steve grinned and shouted a greeting but the man continued slashing at the string attached to the poles, entirely unresponsive. Steve unlatched the gate and stepped inside, this time positioning himself in full view.

"Mr Franklin?"

The old man straightened, glaring at the interloper, cupping his right ear.

"What d'you want?" he said, waving his knife about with what Steve considered a wanton lack of hospitality. He produced a business card and passed it over, mouthing his words distinctly, the man clearly a lip-reader.

"Miss Peters booked me in today. To service the boiler. Sorry I'm late, I've had a lot of calls. I tried the doorbell but—"

"Can't hear the doorbell out here, can I? You'd better

come in then. I expect you heard ... We're at sixes and sevens here."

Steve followed him into the house, the kitchen not much more than a narrow galley beyond which a dark passage led towards the stairs. He started to speak but the man shut him up, insisting on going upstairs to fetch his hearing aid. After that, talk between them fairly sparkled, Steve eyeing the ancient coke boiler with disbelief. Luckily, it was unlit.

"What about your bill? I'm only the lodger, you know."

"All paid for, don't you worry, mate. Miss Peters got an account."

"She's gone, you know."

Steve spread his tools on the floor and looked up, all surprised.

"Moved away?"

"Murdered. In this very house. I was the one who found the body. Don't you read the papers?"

"No time. Page Three's all I need to see."

Reg Franklin looked confused but rattled on about the killing, obviously relieved to have someone to share it with.

"Lucky you having the bobby on your doorstep to keep an eye on you then. Vicious devils, these house breakers. Kids these days! Enough to make your hair stand on end."

Steve emptied the ash container and took the front off the contraption, riddling the clinker which had built up at the back.

"You were out when this terrible thing happened, Mr Franklin?"

"Didn't hear a sound. Mind you, we don't pass the time of day the way I used to when Maggie lived here; I didn't even know she'd been killed till I went down to tell her the hot water had run out."

"Got any old newspapers, Dad? To wrap up all this muck?"

"Upstairs. I'll get some."

He shambled off and, quick as a flash, Steve did a swift recce of the downstairs rooms, listening for the old man's footsteps as he shuffled about above. The living room was shambolic, every drawer and cupboard gaping, the contents strewn about. A plastic laundry basket lay on its side on

157

the floor, an ironing board propped up in the corner, the iron with its flex neatly rewound, taking centre spot on the cleared dining table. If the killer had done this he must have really turned the place over or maybe the s.o.c. officers were messy operatives. The bedroom was too small for any sort of concealment and Steve quickly retreated, hearing the lodger's foot on the landing.

He shot back to the kitchen and was kneeling in front of the boiler when Franklin reappeared with a pile of newsprint.

"Have you got any other way of heating the water, Mr—"

"Call me Reg, everyone does. There's an immersion heater in the airing cupboard upstairs."

"Well, if I was you I'd forget about this old furnace. The flue needs sweeping and I'll have to order a new riddler. Shall I have a dekko at the immersion switch and set it up for you, Reg? Just enough to keep you ticking over?"

He parcelled up all the debris from the boiler and put it outside, sweeping up neatly the way he insisted the Chain Gang left a client's property. Reg Franklin led the way to the bathroom and showed Steve the airing cupboard.

"Cup of tea?" he said.

"Don't mind if I do, Reg. All that dust—" He fiddled with the switch and ran a quick check on the wiring. "This new, this gadget?"

"Yes. Maggie had it put in for emergencies when we ran out of coke. Only three years old."

"It'll be safe enough then. Never know in old houses like these." Steve followed Reg into his sitting room which was impressively neat and very cosy, thick rugs overlaying a mottled carpet and a shaded standard lamp spreading a warm glow over the fireside chair.

The old man appeared with mugs on a tin tray, a plate of biscuits to hand. Steve Epps had a winning way with ordinary people which lay hidden for most of his working life with his glitzy clients, a side of him Mimsie had certainly never witnessed.

"Terrible what you was saying downstairs. About your landlady being done in."

158

"Only a young girl, too. Maggie would have been broken hearted."

"Her mother?"

"No. Aunt. Poor Lynne had no one else. Maggie left her this place and I came with it – like the old coke boiler!" He chuckled, a crackly laugh like a scratched gramophone record.

"And you found the body you say."

"Terrible. Terrible it was. Been dead a couple of days, they reckon. All swelled up, her tongue hanging out."

"Strangled?"

"With her own tights, God bless us! The place was in a terrible mess. She must have been in the middle of her ironing, stuff everywhere, the telly still on. Lucky she turned it off before she let this bloke in or there might have been a fire and me asleep upstairs. Don't bear thinking about."

"You mean the iron?"

"Yes. Must have known him to invite someone in late like that. Cunning blighter."

"P'raps it was a woman."

The old man looked incredulous. "No, never! Mind you there was a young lady who came a couple of times lately and poor Lynne didn't ask people here as a rule – I think she wanted to fix the place up a bit before she started entertaining."

"Well, women these days, Reg. Believe me, my old woman can pack a punch if she's put out." Steve laughed and Lynne's lodger relaxed. "What about a boyfriend?"

Reg looked shifty, conspiratorial almost. "I don't like to talk ill of the dead but there *was* someone. Not a nice man."

"You think *he* did it?"

"No! He's abroad. Works as a location finder for a film company. Goes overseas quite a lot, so he *says*."

"What's wrong with this bloke?" Steve took a shot in the dark. "Black, is he?"

Reg looked startled, his rheumy eyes widening. "Oh no, nothing like that. But he's getting divorced! No good to her. No good at all. I told her over and over again. Me being RC makes a difference, of course, but she agreed with me. I know, Reg, she says. You're quite right. Jimmy's not going

159

to make that mistake again. She would have made a lovely wife, poor Lynne. Really tragic the way she went."

"Does he know about the murder?"

The old man shrugged. "Nothing to do with me. I don't even know where he lives – or who with! I'm not going to drag Lynne into any messy divorce business. I wouldn't give those newspaper people the time of day." He touched his ear, nodding sagely. "Pretended I was too deaf to hear their silly questions, didn't I?"

"This Jimmy never stopped here then?"

"Not likely – but it's true, my hearing's none too good. I don't answer the door and I don't come down in the mornings till she's gone to work. I have to go through the kitchen to get to the garden, see. Sometimes she took a couple of days off against her overtime, weekend surgeries she told me so I'm not sure what she got up to. I watch out of the window most days but I don't like to seem nosy. Things are a bit different since Maggie went."

Steve stirred his tea and tried to manoeuvre the old man's recollections into more profitable channels.

"How do you know he was abroad then, Whats-his-name?"

"Jimmy Cheeseman. Oh, he's definitely in South America somewhere. She had a card from him only this week – I saw it on the mat. Also, when he's off on one of his trips – she told me he was looking for a place for a new Tarzan film this time – he leaves her his car; she keeps a spare lot of keys in the hallstand in the little glove box. I told the police they were an old set of Maggie's – she used to run a little Fiesta, you know. Sometimes we used to run down to the coast in the summer and—"

"That's nice. I bet it's a lovely smart car an' all, him being in films."

Reg sniffed. "Nothing special. A middling sort. Another Fiesta, I think Lynne said. Red. Would be red, wouldn't it, a Flash Harry like Jimmy Cheeseman?"

"But you've got no garage here, Reg."

"He rents a lock-up place round the corner. At the side of the Black Cat Caff. Lynne said she was running down to Bognor or some such place only last weekend but I didn't hear any car so I don't know if she went or not. She didn't ask me," he added tersely.

Steve checked his watch, getting to his feet. "Must be off, I've got another job before I finish. Nice meeting you, Reg. Thanks for the tea. I'll pop back as soon as that spare part comes in. Don't bother to see me out, I'll slip out through the kitchen. Don't forget to lock up when you've finished in the garden. Cheers, mate."

The old man nodded and switched on the radio, anxious to catch the news.

It required no sleight of hand to snaffle the car keys on his way out and he dumped the rubbish in the dustbin before securing the back gate. When he appeared in the street he noticed the police constable had left, the scenes of crime officers apparently satisfied that all the juice had been squeezed from the Peters case.

It was getting dark before he dared try the padlock on the lock-up where he hoped Lynne Peters had stowed the Fiesta. Bit of luck the lodger being such a tightarse about her boyfriend, censoring any chance of the police washing all the poor kid's dirty linen in public. Steve guessed Jimmy Cheeseman would also think it a lucky break to be cut out of the picture by the sanctimonious old devil. Nothing like having a watertight alibi if your girlfriend gets topped, especially if you have more than one on the go which to Steve would seem a rational way for a bloke with access to all the starlets to operate.

Searching the Fiesta took a matter of minutes and where presumably Khan had failed, Steve Epps scored, the weighty dental surgery accounts still tucked up in the boot in a Sainsbury's plastic carrier. If the Peters girl had been snuffed for the information locked up in Chambers's dodgy book-keeping, she hadn't even had the chance to slice it out herself before getting strangled. What a waste!

Twenty-Six

S teve went straight home and spent half the night poring over the dentist's accounts. Even to a putative fraudulent converter, the books looked absolutely spotless and he very much doubted that Mimsie's inexperienced eye would see any flaws. Maybe they needed an accountant.

Next morning he surprised Eva by making a seven o'clock start and caught Mimsie fairly breathless, too, having herself just emerged from the shower. She heard the doorbell and surreptitiously scanned the street, relieved to see Steve's new BMW at the kerbside. She lifted the intercom and he chivvied her to get a move on and open up. Pressing the release button, she hurried to throw on some jeans and a sweater before he started beating the door down. Patience was not one of Steve's virtues.

He looked more his normal self dressed in a navy light-weight suit and striped shirt, the overalls and stack of account books jammed under one arm. He followed her into the kitchen and dumped his bundles on the table, waiting for the kettle to boil.

"Sleep all right?" he said.

"Fine. It's a lovely flat. Perhaps I should marry this guy with the leaky roof and settle down."

"Fat chance!"

She nervously eyed the Sainsbury's carrier from which the books protruded. "Are they what I think they are?"

Steve spread his hands expansively, grinning from ear to ear. "But of course. Would your Uncle Steve let you down?"

Mimsie grimaced, passing him a steaming cup of coffee and a plate of fresh croissants warm from the microwave. They settled at the pine table, Mimsie wondering what had pitched Steve out of bed at dawn.

"Where were they? The books I mean."

"In the boot of the boyfriend's car."

"So Lynne hadn't even started to check them before she was killed."

He shrugged. "Maybe. Maybe not. She might have put them back in the car for safety. Once she found what she was looking for."

"Evidence?"

"Well, I'm no slouch when it comes to fudging the numbers but if Chambers was working something you could fool me."

"You've looked?"

"Spent two hours on it last night and buggered if I could spot a wrong turn. That guy was a fantastic bookkeeper, Mimsie. Did he do it all himself?"

"Absolutely unaided. I think it was his only hobby. He was a terrible fusspot – I would have got the sack anyway even if the place hadn't been trashed. Perhaps Phoebe could help?"

"Leave her out of it. For all we know they were cheek to cheek in all this. You said she helped hush up his little nonsense with the little foreign girl – I reckon she would turn a blind eye to anything that bloke did."

"What shall I do?"

"Charlie and two of the boys will be here at eight. I'll get them started on the roof and tell Charlie you're minding the keys so if you take off, pass them over. I'm going to try and get the caretaker to let me have a set for the service entry – there's a separate staff lift which would save messing the main entrance."

"You're not leaving me to sort out all this bookkeeping *on my own*, are you?"

"I can spare an hour at dinnertime but I've got a load of jobs on the go this week, doll. Why don't you tackle this lot from a different angle? Don't frazzle your brainbox on the figures, just see if anything strikes you as *odd*. Too many orders for drugs for the size of the practice, too few patients for the weekly turnover – that sort of stuff."

Mimsie looked appalled. "I'm not Lynne Peters! I only worked for a dentist once and that was only for a few weeks. How would I know what's normal?" The doorbell rang.

163

Steve scoffed the last mouthful before picking up the intercom to admit his foreman. Charlie was early, wanting to size up the mess the previous gang had left before the others clocked on.

When Steve had gone Mimsie slumped at the table, the books spread before her. If Steve could pick no bones from all this, she felt defeated from the start. But if Lynne thought they were so important, there must be *something*.

Being more familiar with the appointment books, Mimsie made a start on the current book dating from January. The accounts were much more of a headache, going back more than three years and presumably covering the time when the Filipina scandal erupted. Trouble was, Lynne was the only one who could pinpoint this particular incident, Mimsie having no knowledge of either the girl's full name or that of her boss. In addition to the hefty accounts and the appointment book there were two receipt books, one printed on better quality paper, the counterfoils in this meticulously anotated with cash payments and, in the case of cheques, the name and address of each patient printed on the counterfoil, a red tick presumably indicating that the cheque had been honoured. No wonder Mr Chambers was such a good dentist if keeping holes out of the bookkeeping was any indication.

She studied the daily appointments for over an hour, listing any patient called Khan on a separate sheet and cross-referencing with both receipt books, one clearly for NHS patients and the other for the private sector. She wondered if there was a third receipt book in a safe somewhere listing his Bayswater surgery outlet, the undeclared treatments which netted some of the cash paid over in the so-called blackmail.

By the time Steve returned at one, Mimsie had reduced her own detective work to a single sheet of scribbled notes. Steve brought in a jumbo parcel of fish and chips, passing half over to Charlie having satisfied himself that the roofing operation was proceding on schedule. He threw his jacket on a chair and tossed the steaming contents of the remaining paper bags onto plates Mimsie had warmed in the oven.

Between mouthfuls, they also chewed over her conclusions. She reminded him of the big payout to finance the maid's air fare and compensation, and between them they roughly worked out the way these payments had been disguised. No further frills in the accounts were discernible so they decided Chambers's sexual romp had been a one-off and concentrated on the private patients' bills.

Mimsie chewed the end of her pencil, looking thoughtful.

"Lynne Peters's walkout happened on March the fourth, the week I started at the surgery, and though at first she pretended his name meant nothing, I feel sure she knew *of* Khan in some way, Steve, even if they had never come face to face."

"So chances are the Khan guy has only been causing trouble *this* year if we can't find any regular payment disappearing abroad or even to Khan in London."

"Well, let's hope so. Without Lynne we're working in the dark. If Khan frightened her off, forcing her to leave a well-paid job with Chambers without warning, it must have been serious. She clearly didn't improve her career by moving on. Do you think she had been milking payouts meant for Khan through Maria? Lynne admitted she was the sole intermediary in that business; Mr Chambers and his sister made sure *their* hands were clean. Incidentally, what did you think of her house, Steve?"

He made a thumbs down gesture, describing poor Reg Franklin's efforts to cope with the disaster. Mimsie looked pensive, clearing away the empty plates and making a pot of tea. Who else would take a chance like that except Steve Epps? Practically walking through a police cordon and snaffling the wretched account books from under their noses?

He urged her to hurry. "I've got a date with Jerry Logan at three. He wants to arrange an urgent meeting with Rita Quinn before she gets tempted by a better offer."

Mimsie lowered her eyes, the recollection of Toby's last encounter with her in his darkened bedroom still raw, a memory she would never share, not even with Steve, her 'best mate' as he called himself.

She pushed her page of notes across the table.

"For lack of anything else to go on, I've listed all the private patients called Khan and linked them with the receipt book stubs and the accounts."

165

"I thought he said he *wasn't* a patient, Mimsie! Why waste time going down a bloody cul-de-sac? We've got to take his word for it on *something*."

"But there's nowhere else to go, Steve! Khan thought I was the nurse and I think Lynne was involved with him in which case the only common factor is the surgery. Maybe he was a technician or something. Fiddling on the gold fillings. There were plenty of those!"

"Is this what you call 'feminine intuition'?" he said sarcastically.

Mimsie ploughed on, pointing at the list. "If we only go back from the beginning of the year through the months before the surgery was shut on April the twenty-first, Mr Chambers treated four people called Khan on his private list and eight on the NHS. As I only have the addresses of the private patients from the receipt book with the smart headed paper, we'll have to fix on those to start with. Fortunately, they all live within five miles of the surgery so it's unlikely they went to the Bayswater place."

"So?"

"I thought I'd call at all these addresses this afternoon and see if I can identify my man."

Steve leaned back in his chair, totally bemused.

"You do realise that if you're right, this bloke has already killed Lynne Peters to protect his own back and you are the only other witness who can point a finger at him. You think you can just knock on his door, take a dekko at the guy and push off and report him to our CID man, Blakeney? And *that* presupposes your stalker is sitting at home in the afternoons, twiddling his thumbs. Mimsie, your powers of self-preservation are non-existent, babe."

She sprang to her feet, eyes blazing. "I'm fed up with you and every other man I know telling me I'm stupid! Where else can I start looking?"

He rose, putting on his jacket, making soothing noises.

"Trust me, kiddo. People out there have a lot to hide. At best this bloke smashed up Chambers's surgery with at least one other guy helping him, even Phoebe acknowledges that. On the dark side, he may also have choked the life out of the nurse who worked there and who knew more than she was admitting to you. When did you say she left? Early March?"

"Yes."

"Okay, let's cut out those Khans who got their teeth fixed after that and if you like we'll drive round to the others and try to get the men out in the open on some pretext so you can give them the once-over from a safe distance. Any way of knowing if any of these on the list are women? We could eliminate them straight off and save ourselves a trip."

"No, not really. Mostly the husbands or parents paid for the Asians' treatment and sometimes the person who settled up wasn't even related – an employer for instance."

"Right." He looked at his watch, slapping her bottom which was Steve Epps's idea of an affectionate gesture. "Now, don't put a foot outside this door till I come for you at eight o'clock. I'll cancel my snooker. Have we got a deal?"

She nodded, miserably aware that dragging Steve on a fruitless tour and spoiling his night out would have repercussions. Someone's head would roll. She hoped Eva's.

Having cleared up and spent half an hour chatting with Charlie on the sunlit roof, the afternoon stretched ahead interminably. She toyed with the idea of ringing Alex Blair and assuring him of her safety but he wasn't the sort to let it go at that. Before she knew it, Alex would be bouncing into her life, warning her off all these undercover operations with Steve Epps, appalled at her occupation of a total stranger's flat without his permission, disapproving of her apparent inability to stay put for more than one day at a time.

Aching to do *something* she telephoned Phoebe Watson, hardly expecting an answer. In fact, Phoebe must have felt a good deal improved as she picked up the phone immediately, her voice firm.

"Oh, Phoebe! You're better. I wouldn't have rung you but I think I'm really on to something at last. Those account books and things you loaned to Lynne. I've got them."

"How?"

"It's a long story. How about if I run down to see you in the morning? I could bring your brother's flight bag as well, his belongings from the Greenwood. A solicitor friend of mine went down there with me and I think he's convinced

167

them to stop pressing for that overdue account. He said you'd be in touch with Dr Wellington just as soon as the insurance came through."

"How kind." Her response was dry and Mimsie hesitated, wondering if she had put her foot in it.

"I must see you, Phoebe. There's something I think you should know. It's about the blackmail letter."

"I'm sorry but I really don't wish to discuss it."

"But it means you don't have to hang about in that horrible bungalow any longer. You see you were right. Your brother isn't dead. I hate to tell you this over the phone but if you won't let me drive down there's no time to waste. You should know before Inspector Blakeney questions you. They've established that it was *Mr Chambers* who wrote that letter, Phoebe. He needed the money to get away, start afresh somewhere abroad, I suppose. He isn't coming back, Phoebe. You *must* get on with *your* life, you're making yourself ill and really Mr Chambers wouldn't want you to moulder away in that awful hole for ever."

"I don't believe you," she said, the tone weakly defiant but not exactly outraged and it occurred to Mimsie that Phoebe was not alone.

"Is Mr Miller, the insurance inspector, there? You can't talk?"

"That's right."

"Well, listen anyway. There's more news, Phoebe. We've found a possible lead to Khan, the man who vandalised the surgery. If I'm right we can tell the police his address and they'll pick him up. You see, it's dreadfully probable he was the one who killed Lynne Peters."

Phoebe's reply was curt. "It's very nice of you to ring, Hazel, but I'm in the middle of packing. I've got a train to catch. I'm going back to London this afternoon, you see. Goodbye." And the line went dead before Mimsie had a chance to explain. She wondered if it would be possible to catch Phoebe later, when the insurance man had gone, but if she *was* on the way to the station Mimsie could always call in on her at Phoebe's home in London, an address which Blakeney didn't know about yet. Much better to let it go, at least until Khan was under lock and key.

She drifted back to the kitchen feeling deflated. It was like a rerun of the brush-off she sensed on quitting the Quinn household, the drifting lifestyle she had chosen reducing her to surface relationships all too swiftly borne away by events. First Aileen and now Phoebe. One couldn't blame these people but it suddenly occurred to her that living from day to day, killing time, was not a way to live.

Steve picked her up at eight and they tacked across town. He passed her his sunglasses and a gypsyish headscarf of Eva's and told her stay in the car whatever happened. The late summer evening was still and golden, the air balmy as only September days can be.

He drove slowly past the first address on her list, an Edwardian semi in an affluent backwater behind Kensington Town Hall, the resident's parking spaces already closely packed.

"Just watch and whatever you do, don't interfere."

He drove round again and double parked; taking a stubby, retractable umbrella from under the dashboard, he strode up the garden path. A dark-haired child about ten years old opened the door in answer to his ring and Steve conducted a brief conversation with the boy, gesticulating with the brolly. The child disappeared inside and a man, presumably his father, emerged to join Steve who had retreated to the gate, pointing at the roof, turning the man this way and that as he talked. Then, touching his forehead in a gesture of apology, Steve returned to the car and accelerated away.

"And what was all that about?" she said, laughing.

"Wasn't he your stalker?"

"No, of course he wasn't. My man's younger and very thin. What did you say?"

"Said my cat was stranded on his roof."

"Your *cat*?"

"Mimsie," he said irritably, "it was just something to get the guy out in the open. When he looked up, of course there was nothing there. I said the bloody moggy must have moved over to the next house and sorry to have troubled him."

"What was the umbrella for? It's not raining."

"Protection. If your bloke *is* dangerous, a nice bit of lead piping tucked inside a brolly's as good as a cosh."

"Oh!"

They did a run round the one-way system to the second address and Steve went through the pantomime cat routine again, and drew another blank. The third stop was more hopeful, turning out to be a health food shop with accommodation above, the owner still working behind closed doors, stocktaking, the street busy with passers-by. The shop was double fronted and in a good location, handy for the lentil freaks of Notting Hill and clearly a very successful enterprise.

Steve parked on double yellow lines right outside and rapped on the shop window with his umbrella. The man looked up, pointing to the 'Closed' sign hanging inside the door. Steve persisted, his smart city suit and the BMW evidently convincing the man that if it did turn out to be daylight robbery, thugs were getting very upmarket.

Steve coaxed him outside, pointing to a broken gutter hanging by a single bracket right over the shop doorway. They talked for a few moments and Steve passed over a business card, patting the man's shoulder in a gesture of goodwill as he turned to go.

Mimsie crouched in her seat as they drove away, her eyes wide with excitement.

"That's him! That's my stalker. Steve, you're brilliant, absolutely brilliant! Let's call Blakeney right away."

"Not on your nelly! Don't put *my* name in the frame, Mimsie Crane. Leave it with me. I'll phone my police contact, Norry, and give him a tip-off. That way I'm not involved and neither are you. He can deal with Blakeney."

"Will you tell Norry about the link between Lynne's murder and Mr Chambers's fake suicide?"

"I'll tell him the lot. You can talk to him yourself if you like. I'll even dump the account books back in the boyfriend's car if you say so."

"Don't get on your high horse, Steve. But you will get onto your contact tonight, won't you? If he persuades Blakeney to take Khan in straight away I can move back to my own flat."

"Hold on! Wait till I see what Norry's got to say first. They'll need evidence to hang on to him, fingerprints at least. Reg Franklin heard nothing and there was no break-in so they'd have to assume the dead girl knew the guy well enough to invite him inside, wouldn't they? It all takes time, kid. Why don't we go back to my place for a bite to eat and then I'll give him a bell at home?"

"What about Eva? She thinks you're playing snooker, doesn't she?"

"Well, Eva's used to my little U-turns, babe. I got diverted, didn't I? Picked you off the street like the Good Samaritan I am."

Mimsie decided that being the focus of Eva's evil eye would be a small price to pay for getting Khan out of circulation once and for all.

Twenty-Seven

S teve's police contact Norry was none too pleased to be phoned at his house. He was trying to watch television, the second round replay of a World Cup match, and an evening at home was a rare event, the way criminals in the royal borough gave scant regard to office hours.

Steve patiently filled in the background, Mimsie jogging his elbow, mouthing unwanted prompts and generally getting in the way. As an informant, Steve Epps was worth cultivating but putting himself in the middle of a current CID investigation was not worth the candle in Norry's book. Steve replaced the receiver, secretly relieved, putting an arm round Mimsie's shoulder in a gesture of sympathy.

"Sorry, no can do, kid. You'll have to go solo. Norry says best thing is for you to go straight to Blakeney yourself."

"But that'll mean telling him about you stealing the account books and everything."

"Why? Just say you was strolling past the Khan's health food shop and saw the bloke who had been hassling you working behind the counter. Recognised him straight away. Bingo!"

"What about you being at Lynne's house pretending to be a boiler mechanic?"

Steve steered her to the sofa, looking pained, Eva glaring at the two of them through narrowed eyes.

"Look, here's how we play it. You say you came to my place yesterday to ask if you could borrow the van to fetch your stuff from Esher now your job with Quinn's folded. Stayed one night here with me and Eva and when you was walking round the shops you spotted Khan and like a good citizen you've come in to report it. Blakeney already knows about your stalker and here you are putting a murder suspect on a plate for him. Blakeney only has to check the bloke's fingerprints with those at Lynne's place and Khan's in the cells. What could be simpler?"

"But what about the surgery account books?" she persisted.

"Forget the bloody accounts! The books are of no interest whatsoever at this stage. Just give Khan to Blakeney and let him put his own case together. If you start blabbing about *my* part in all this we'll both be locked up. I'll put the books back in the boyfriend's Fiesta and no one's any the wiser. The car keys and the padlock key will have to go missing – I can't risk going back to the old boy's digs. Chances are Cheeseman will assume his spare keys got mopped up in the police search and he'll be the last one to want to draw attention to himself."

Mimsie reluctantly agreed and endured Steve's recapitulation of her 'story'. Actually, borrowing the van to fetch her suitcases from Alex Blair's sounded a good idea. She could reclaim Mr Chambers's flight bag while she was about it.

Mimsie agreed to stay overnight at Steve's place, Eva gracelessly shelling out nightclothes, clean underwear and a new toothbrush.

Early next morning she phoned Alex at home and told him she was moving back to Frayne Gardens and could she pick up her suitcases before eleven. His response was guarded but she cut him short, saying she couldn't talk – she was using her girlfriend's mobile and it was expensive.

They agreed to meet at his office, his arrangements with Rita Quinn about Toby's funeral demanding urgent attention. Steve drove her to Pollard Place and handed over the keys of the van, Mimsie feeling a lump come into her throat seeing Austen and the old gang again, the rough and tumble of working with Epps Building Services suddenly seeming a world away from the wretched morass she was in now.

She drove to Esher with grim determination, hardly taking her foot off the accelerator, dreading her encounter with Alex, his hurt feelings, the unspoken recriminations. She decided to say nothing about tracing her mysterious stalker and her coming interview with Blakeney. Despite her careless treatment of Alex, he was the sort of man to feel duty bound to accompany her, protect her from a police grilling. Mimsie was doubtful enough of her ability to tell it according to Steve's abbreviated scenario without the added anxiety of having legal representation at her elbow, censoring even the half-truths she was prepared to utter in order to put the Khan man inside.

As luck would have it, she got off lightly, Alex being genuinely due at a meeting. He helped stow the bags in the van, giving up Chambers's flight bag without so much as a quibble, his expression as steadfast as the strong, silent types illustrating the covers of supermarket novelettes. She promised to ring, 'have lunch sometime', the usual phrases with which civilised people smoothed out an exit line. Alex's eyes darkened as if she had inflicted actual bruises but he said nothing, her words curdling in his stomach like bile. Why? What had brought this on? What had he *done* for God's sake?

Mimsie drove away, feeling oddly bereft, wondering if she had, from sheer lack of courage, thrown away her last chance of a nice family life. But then, glancing at the time, the Rolex glinted back at her like a wink of encouragement.

"Oh, what the hell," she muttered, grinding gears at the traffic lights.

Detective Inspector Blakeney was surprised when Ms Crane was ushered into his office and rose from his desk in a flurry of politeness. She had written down the address of Khan's shop and passed it over, her fingers shaking. Blakeney called in his sergeant, insisting she stay put at Frayne Gardens until his interrogation of Khan was complete. "I'll ring and give you the all clear."

"But I have to go out," she insisted. "I have things to do. I have to – er – have to find another job."

It was finally agreed that she would telephone in if she intended to stay away overnight. Mimsie signed her statement and left the police station almost at a run, horribly aware that being on a police computer was inevitable. What about her 'cash-in-hand' temping jobs with Steve? Would her entire life be brought out in the open when Khan eventually came to trial? In the *papers* even! Suddenly Gozo beckoned like

174

a golden haven of repose. She had promised herself that as soon as she got back her Rolex she would buy an air ticket and get the hell out. She should have done just that. Waved goodbye to all the misery that little shit Chambers had shoved her into. If she wasn't allowed to leave London she dare not sit about at home waiting for Blakeney to assure her she was out of danger. She would just have to keep her head down.

Mimsie caught a taxi and made like an arrow for Leicester Square, sitting through two full-length movies one after the other, the almost empty auditoria womblike and safe.

When she emerged, the day had faded, the sky streaked with the first gold bars of a summer twilight. She wandered around Covent Garden among the tourists and pickpockets thinking about what she should do, the prospect of a lonely night stretching like a dark tunnel ahead simply appalling.

Perhaps it would be better to get right away. Even Esher with Rita on the rampage was safer that Frayne Gardens, an address with which Khan was all too familiar. Why should she be a sitting duck just to convenience Blakeney? She let herself into the flat and spent the next hour giving the place a bit of a spring clean, the sheer mindlessness of vacuuming and polishing taking the edge off her fears. She took a chance and rang The Willows. No one answered but she left a message and her number on the machine.

"It's Mimsie. Sorry I ran out on you, Aileen. Can I come down and see you tomorrow morning?" As she replaced the receiver she heard her landlord, Mr Phidias, shouting at someone in the street. The abuse got louder, more threatening, and instantly she knew who was on the receiving end. There was only one man who could pitch the Cypriot into such a rage: Khan. Her heart thumped in her chest like a hammer on an anvil. Voices were raised in the quiet cul-de-sac, Mr P's curlicue phrases peppered with backstreet insults. Khan had been let out! Why hadn't the bloody policeman warned her?

Checking the locks on her door and gaining courage from the continuing tirade on the pavement, Mimsie crept to the window and twitched the curtain. The street lights illuminated the street like a stage set, the stocky figure of Phidias, arms flailing, overshadowing his victim as their exchanges grew more heated.

175

Mimsie let out a gasp, bunching the curtain in her fingers, suddenly realising what it was all about. Fumbling with the window lock, she threw up the sash in a rush, leaning over the sill like a nosy neighbour intent on a ringside seat.

"Hey! Mr Phidias. Hang on! It's okay – I'll come down."

She flung herself downstairs, giggling in a witless reaction to the fright the silly old fart had given her. Outside, the two men faced each other at the kerbside, Mimsie's landlord brandishing what looked like an axe handle, the other man squaring up to a full-scale street fight. Three youths excitedly jigged about on the other side of the road, yelling encouragement.

The combatants swung round as Mimsie burst onto the scene, turning on her beligerently as if she were an unwanted umpire in a bout which was just getting into its stride.

"Alex! Stop it. For Christ's sake, what's got *into* you?"

"You *know* this bloke, Miss Crane?" The arm wielding the axe handle hesitated, the man seeming to deflate like a flat tyre. Phidias glared at Alex whose jeans and oil-stained bomber jacket gave off all the signals the Cypriot had learned to distrust. The boys across the street moved in. It didn't help that the suburban solicitor was clearly under the influence, the latent aggression giving Mimsie a brand-new aspect of the man she thought she had placed firmly in his slot.

She touched Phidias's hairy forearm, the odour of stale sweat forming an invisible nimbus of BO which gave instant recall of the Chain Gang in Steve Epps's builders' yard.

"He's a friend of mine, Mr Phidias. It okay. Really! Did you think I'd got another stalker?"

"He's been 'anging round here since six o'clock – I seen him from my basement. That policeman, Sergeant Moss, 'e dropped in on me when I was 'aving my tea break – he was lookin' for you, Miss Crane. Said you was a 'target'. Said I was to keep an eye out – that black bastard was likely to get off and the press would be after you, 'e say. Not in *my* 'ouse! I say to 'im. I keep *all* the filth off my steps. Dogshit they are!" He spat in the gutter to emphasise his point.

"I merely tried to ring your bell," Alex muttered. "And this gorilla *jumped* me! Before I could get a word in he—"

"I thinkin' you was one of them tabloid rubbish chasing *my* tenant."

Mimsie's voice softened, and, drawing Phidias to his area steps, whispered urgently in his ear, patting his arm in small gestures of contrition. He vented the final blasts of his punctured ego on the teenage trio who had now skimmed across the road to lounge against his railings, riveted to the dwindling drama, elbowing each other and grinning, taunting the sweating landlord with the accuracy of picadors.

Alex brushed ineffectively at his scruffy denims, his face grey with either temper or nausea. Mimsie broke away, miming more apologies to Phidias as she steered Alex through the open door and led him unsteadily upstairs.

He slumped on the sofa, staring at her with bloodshot eyes.

"Coffee, I think. Don't move, Alex. By the way, you didn't drive here, I hope?"

"Taxi," he mumbled, the embarrassment of the fracas on Mimsie's doorstep already mercifully receding. He leaned forward, burying his head in his hands, trying to blank out the hours he had spent trying to locate the wretched girl since she walked out on him. So many unanswered questions. Only Mimsie could disappear like that, assuming no explanation was called for. He dragged off his jacket, his office shirt, minus the tie, still neatly buttoned, the striped front liberally spattered with speckles of what was probably whisky. He felt like shit.

The coffee helped but not much. Mimsie glanced at the Rolex, suddenly tired of the whole business. Alex had clearly endured his own torments and was even more frazzled than she but, all the same . . . Wordlessly, she steered him into the bedroom, gently shoving him onto the soft mattress where he subsided without a murmur, starting to snore almost as his head hit the pillow. She pulled off his shoes, draping the inert body with a spare blanket, and stood back, wryly admitting to herself that the poor bloke was indeed all at sea. There was nothing else for it. She would have to keep him off the streets till he sobered up. On the bright side, she wouldn't have to sit up all night waiting for Khan to break in on her solitary state – not that this unconscious hunk occupying *her*

177

bed would prove much of a bodyguard if it came to it. Ah well . . .

She started off on the sofa, a cheap two-seater none too cosy to sit on but impossible as a bed. By 2 a.m. she was still wide awake, irritable as hell, her shoulders stiff with the sheer torment of finding any sort of sleeping position. She gave up and slid in beside Alex. Even boozed to the eyeballs his warm nearness was undeniably sexy. Perhaps being out for the count even added to the man's appeal? She pushed aside this unwelcome shaft of self-insight and relaxed in the bliss of being in her own bed at last.

Alex woke first, calling her in a soft repetitive monotone, lightly tracing her profile with his thumb. She barely stirred. He whispered her name, his voice gradually infiltrating her brain like the insistent burble of morning coffee starting to perc in the kitchen.

"Oh, Alex—"

"Don't talk."

Rough hands smoothed her hair, his body pressing against her, gradually moving into an insistent rhythm, strong as an undertow, impossible to resist. Mimsie tried to speak but his mouth closed over hers, the inevitability of all this seeming, in her dreamy state, hardly to matter after all.

Later they lay in the pale luminescence of a grey dawn, the soft rattle of a rainy day pit-pattering against the windows. Mimsie, curled in his arms, nuzzled his soft chest hairs, drowsily aware of the repetitive coo-coo of a pigeon perched on her windowbox preening its wet feathers.

"Why didn't you want to stay with me, Mimsie?"

"I couldn't."

He shook his head, smiling, impossible to sidetrack.

"Tell me why," he repeated.

"I was frightened."

"Of Khan? But you're a sitting target *here*. I don't believe a word of it. It was me, wasn't it?"

"Not specially *you*. I didn't want to be hassled. I don't sleep around – and anyway I hardly knew you. It just didn't seem a good idea," she finished lamely.

"I want us to be together, Mimsie. What's frightening in that?"

"You don't know me."

"I don't have to. I love you. What else is there to know?" He lifted her chin, insisting on a straight answer. "Look, I know I behaved like an idiot last night. You throwing everything back in my face so coolly yesterday morning hit me hard. I couldn't let it go like *that*. I had to see you again. I'd been hanging about here for hours on and off before that bloody Greek attacked me, wondering if you'd ever surface. What did I do wrong?"

"Nothing." She irritably shook him off, trying to slide out from under the blanket but he held on. Seconds ticked by, the rain rattling the glass like an impatient eavesdropper demanding a response.

With tired resignation she finally said, "Listen, Alex, I'm not your sort of girl, believe me."

"You're not married, for Christ's sake?"

Mimsie laughed, relaxing back against the pillows. "You *were* worried about my designs on poor old Toby, weren't you, Alex? No, I'm not married."

"This fellow in Gozo. He's special?"

"Guy? Honestly, you are *so* old-fashioned! You don't have any conception of a girl having 'friends', do you?"

"Not with you, darling, of course I don't. Who would? I only have to *look* at you, Mimsie, and I'm a dead duck. You saying this man's gay?"

"No! But we don't *do* it. We're mates. Just that. We don't gel in *that* way."

"Who is it then? Surely not Epps, that crappy builder?"

She shook with laughter. "Hell, no! Not that Steve wouldn't go for it given half a chance."

Mimsie turned to face him, stilling his roaming hands in a firm grasp, making up her mind at last.

"Listen. I haven't been with *anyone* for nearly two years. The fact is I've been scared to death. I got tight at a Christmas party, really rat-arsed – someone must have spiked my drink – and ended up in a one-nighter with this American guy. Never even knew his name," she bitterly added. "He gave me a dose and it really freaked me out. I've been having treatment. It's

179

okay. You needn't worry. It's under control. But I just haven't fancied men much lately. Maybe being lulled into *this* was the only way out."

"You could have said. I wasn't born yesterday, you know."

"I hardly knew you, Alex! It's not exactly the sort of thing you gas about on a first date. Scared me shitless, I don't mind telling you."

"Infections are hardly news these days, my chicken-hearted darling – even in 'the Sticks' as you smart cats call it." He sobered, kissing the frown lines creasing her forehead. "It could have been *much* worse."

She reared up, stung by his complacency. "HIV, you mean? Aids even? Don't think I haven't had nightmares about it, Alex Blair!"

"Calm down, sweetheart. Shush. No more fighting . . ." He drew her to him, murmuring soothing meaningless phrases, waiting for the squall to pass. The pigeon on the windowsill added its own version of the same magic and she closed her eyes and just let go, the rain now reduced to a drizzle, misting the windows as if to shut out the demons still hovering just out of sight. She decided to shake out the whole bag of nasties while she was at it and told him about her police interview. Alex tried to play down her fears but in fairness Mimsie had to admit to herself the poor bloke still only knew the half of it. She refused to elaborate and turned over, pleading exhaustion. He relented and, dog-tired, Mimsie finally dozed off, only the shrill telephone reveille shooting her out of bed soon after nine. Alex had gone. She picked up the phone. It was Aileen.

"Mimsie! I got your message. Rita's gone back home till the funeral – why don't you come over and stay for a bit? Your old room's still here for you, love. Toby would have wanted you to feel it's your home while there's still time."

This last bit clearly left a lot unsaid, Rita's in-your-face attitude hard to take at any time, least of all to Aileen in the throes of closing down the house she had cared for for so long.

"I can't stay over but I'd like to be with you for a bit. To say goodbye—"

When she put down the receiver, she made straight for the

kettle. Alex had left a note propped up by the coffee pot. 'I'll call for you tonight. About 8.30. We'll eat out. For God's sake get away from that flat of yours until we find out if Khan's out on the streets again. Ring me at the office to tell me where to pick you up.'

His anxious demands were both irritating and alluring. She wasn't used to being told what to do. Suddenly her terror of Khan and the possibility of his release seemed pathetic. Was Alex the factor which altered the equation? Was Mimsie Crane getting tired of looking after herself all of a sudden?

Mimsie spent the day helping Aileen sort out Toby's things and between them they made good progress. When they parted just before five, her mood remained buoyant, the fears about returning to the empty flat reduced to a rational understanding. Mimsie had just closed the door of the flat behind her when the phone rang. It was Blakeney. He gave her a run-down on his interview with Khan, reassuring her that the man no longer presented any sort of threat.

"You sure?"

"Absolutely. Goodnight, Miss Crane."

She wasn't convinced. Khan wouldn't give up as easily as that. The horrors re-emerged like bats in the twilight. She *must* speak to someone about all this and Alex wasn't the answer. And Steve Epps had had more than enough of sailing too close to murder. On impulse she phoned for a minicab and told the driver to wait while she fetched the flight bag. She would force herself on Phoebe Watson.

Since that last brusque telephone conversation with Phoebe, Mimsie felt certain there was more, much more the woman hadn't told her. And now Lynne, the only other person she could discuss it with, was *dead*. It was Chambers and his sister who had got her into this mess in the first place. She would make Phoebe come clean. They both owed her that much.

She stood on the doorstep of the neat semi in Harefield Avenue comparing its solid affluence with the flimsy seaside bungalow Phoebe had put up with all summer, and waited for someone to answer the bell. The woman who came was the old Phoebe Watson she remembered, fully restored, her erect carriage shown to advantage in a Donegal tweed suit, her ears twinkling with diamond studs.

"Oh, Mimsie, come in, dear. I've been expecting you."

Twenty-Eight

A fter his first interview with the Crane girl, D.I. Blakeney had despatched his sergeant to seek out the cleaning woman from the dental surgery, a Mrs Joyce Garland, an investigator's dream: loose-lipped, vitriolic and very well informed about her employers. Sergeant Moss let her run on.

"Mrs Garland confirmed that about that Khan bloke coming to the surgery, sir. He's not just a fairy story cooked up by the girl. He first surfaced some time after Easter asking where Chambers had gone."

"I thought the surgery was closed by the end of April."

"Well, the cleaner continued to go in twice a week after the builders were in. She was also keeping an eye on the dentist's sister's house round the corner while she was living on the coast all summer."

"Chambers's sister?"

"Mrs Watson. She engaged the staff and paid the wages. Chambers had a flat over the surgery but his sister's got a nice place this Mrs Garland told me. Ran a mop over that too while it was empty – talk about money for old rope."

"How was she paid?"

"Got a cheque by post; didn't know exactly where they'd gone but said the Post Office forwarded mail from the surgery and from Watson's place which kept Mrs Garland's nose out of their affairs quite effectively."

"But none of the other staff enjoyed any sort of retainer?"

"No. The business was definitely closed – up for sale, in fact."

"And this Garland female was the one who gave Crane's address to Khan?"

"Oh, yes. She admitted that – saw nothing wrong in putting

the guy on the right track, she said. He nobbled her when she was cleaning up at the surgery one morning. She thought he was a patient."

"He was asking about the dentist you said?"

Moss nodded. "Wanted to know if he'd moved to another premises. She said, Hadn't he heard? Mr Chambers had gone missing. Told him he'd better phone the NHS people. Then Khan came out with what he *really* wanted – to get in touch with Mr Chambers's nurse, the one he'd spoken to on the phone. And Mrs Garland, being a dirty-minded old bat, assumed he wanted a date with Mimsie Crane who always got a lot of attention from the men in the waiting room. Never one to lose an opportunity to get her own back on the smart-talking totties Chambers employed, she gave Khan the girl's address where, as luck would have it, she knew a Cypriot woman who lets rooms in the house."

"But Crane wasn't the *nurse*."

"I said that. But she insisted he said he'd talked to her on the phone a couple of times and Garland assumed that as Mimsie Crane was the one who *always* answered the phones on reception, she was the one he was looking for. Anyway, she didn't know where the other girls came from – they were agency nurses, different ones each week."

"No mention of Lynne Peters?"

"I put it to her squarely – had Mrs Garland ever given Peters's address to him? She said quite definitely not – she didn't even know it and anyway the girl had gone months before the surgery closed and in Mrs Garland's opinion never had any boyfriends. Her exact words were, 'And even if she did, Lynne was too much of a lady to go out with a Paki'." Moss read this juicy morsel straight off his notebook, his face grave, racial insults looming large in his personal no-go area. Blakeney, on the other hand, supported no such sensitivities and roared with laughter, picturing this prime witness's tête-à-tête with Moss, a thick-set copper in his forties with a broken nose and a useful knack with older women.

Blakeney leaned back, looking thoughtful, mentally juggling the weeks which separated the dramatic events in the Chambers Surgery Saga. "Remind me, Moss. When was the last conversation Mrs Garland had with Khan about Mimsie?"

"In August. She was quite chummy with him by then, reckoned she'd seen the guy hanging about on and off since their original chat. If she was cleaning in the waiting room at the front he would knock on the window and pass the time of day. He had even slipped in to talk to the builder's foreman when they were clearing up after the break-in when the place was vandalised. April, wasn't it?"

"Keeping an eye on the place, you think?"

"I should say so. Mrs G. was always ready to break off for a gossip and she eventually assured Khan Mr Chambers was *never* coming back. She told him it was more than likely the poor man had drowned at sea which I suppose sounded a lot more polite than 'Your dentist got so fed up with looking at his patients' rotten teeth, he killed himself'."

In private Moss enjoyed a certain latitude with the inspector which the younger members of the CID team only suspected. One area of common ground was a mutual distrust of the new computerised methods of investigation, Blakeney and Moss being the rump end of the old school who laid more weight on the slow accumulation of evidence by archaic interviewing procedures, these not accelerated by the nature of their lying clientele.

"What else did this fount of all knowledge give away?"

"She hinted that there had been a scandal a couple of years ago but it had all been hushed up."

"The Filipina?"

"Not specially. She may have been talking about something else – Garland just said, 'an Arab woman made a hullabaloo in the waiting room one morning when I was there.' Mrs Watson told her afterwards a silly girl had had a bad reaction to an injection the previous day and the patient's boss had come in to bawl out the dentist."

"She said this kid was from the Philippines?"

"No, she never saw her, just the girl's boss."

"Do you think it's the same one Crane was going on about?"

"Who knows? Could be."

"And Mrs Garland told Khan about this?"

"No, quite definitely not, she said. I asked her specifically. Got quite fluffed up about such a suggestion! But in my opinion she would have done if it had come up. Mrs Garland's not the sort to waste a juicy bit of gossip but the guy's only interest was focussed on the girl, she said, so being 'a romantic' as she put it, she gave him Crane's address without a thought."

"Has the surgery been sold?"

"Not so far. Until the dentist is declared dead it's tricky but I had a word with the estate agent and there hasn't been much interest. The sister, Mrs Watson's handling all Chambers' affairs."

Blakeney made some notes and queried one or two points with Moss but the cultivation of the cleaner by Khan seemed to have been laid down over a period of weeks and months though the exact purpose of this seemed unclear. A man who could overcome the older woman's prejudice in such a short time hardly seemed to match up with the terrorising stalker described by the streetwise Mimsie Crane. Blakeney decided to give Mimsie's bogeyman some priority treatment. He told Moss to get on to it and leave the Watson interview till later.

In fact, Mimsie's intervention saved Sergeant Moss a lot of trouble and as soon as she had produced Khan's address, Blakeney wasted no time pulling in their suspect for questioning. Moss led him to an interview room, a bleak place guaranteed to overawe a seemingly mild culprit such as the neatly dressed shop keeper sitting before them who, on first impression, was not your regular graffiti artist, let alone vandal. The trouble was, although Arif Khan had been brought to the station as the possible assailant in the Peters case, there was – as Blakeney admitted to his sergeant – no evidence against him, not even fingerprints, the only ones, apart from the victim's, being those of an unidentified person and a few smudges which might or might not be Mimsie Crane's. Even Reg Franklin, the lodger, had submitted to having his prints taken as a means of elimination though, in his case, the old chap seemed quite taken with the procedure, the excitement of the continuing drama bringing a sparkle to his otherwise dull routine. He hadn't seemed too distressed by the girl's death either which was surprising, though they seemed to rub along well enough, Reg Franklin's affections harking back repeatedly to the good old days when the aunt, a Mrs Maggie Peters, had ruled the roost.

After the initial preliminaries, being anxious not to have so much as a whisper of racial bias levelled against him later, Blakeney confirmed with Khan that he required no solicitor present. He offered a cigarette but Khan refused which seemed reasonable in a man who made his living selling health foods and natural remedies. In fact, Arif Khan was more than willing to cooperate, his eyes unclouded by this unexpected request 'to assist with police enquiries'.

Blakeney felt more comfortable with witnesses once he had an outline of their circumstances and his first questions were of a disarmingly friendly nature.

"Tell me about your family, Mr Khan. You have been resident in the UK for many years?"

"I wasn't born here but my parents settled in London in the eighties and sent for my brother and me soon after."

"Just the two boys?"

"There was a sister but she died. My uncle and his family run a chain of newsagents in Luton. Is this relevant, Inspector? Our residence is not in question surely?"

"No, no, of course not. I just like to have a rounded picture. Our enquiries have led to you via a woman called Miriam Crane, a dentist's receptionist. You may have known her as Mimsie."

"I've met her, yes. I first encountered the lady in August."

"Not before?"

"I never seen Miss Crane before that, sir."

"She's a pretty girl."

Khan looked confused.

"Don't you think so, Mr Khan?" Blakeney persisted.

"I suppose so." His voice was light and the accent fleeting but the phrasing was oddly out of sync as if the man had spent long hours in patient study of correct phraseology.

"You were attracted to Miss Crane."

"Not at all!"

"I only say this because Miss Crane tells us she was

frightened of you, Mr Khan. She says you accosted her outside her flat, left notes through her letterbox, made anonymous phone calls, that sort of thing."

"But I didn't force myself sexually on the young lady if that is your impression. I only wanted information."

"An odd reason to pursue her, wasn't it? She *was* alarmed, Mr Khan, and whether that was your intention or not the girl was sufficiently perturbed by your attentions to leave her job in London to take up a new position out of the city."

"She made an official complaint?"

"Not yet. But she has signed a statement which we are considering. We are more concerned about another matter. Did you know a second girl who worked at the dental surgery where you first came into contact with Miss Crane? Lynne Peters?"

He shook his head.

"This unfortunate young woman was brutally murdered on Monday evening. We shall have to ask you about your whereabouts that night. Lynne Peters was Mr Chambers's former dental nurse."

Khan hardly reacted, his quickly indrawn breath the only indication of disquiet.

"Are you fascinated by girls in nurses' uniforms, Mr Khan? You wouldn't be the first, you know. All that starched linen can be very arousing."

The man half rose from his seat, gripping the edge of the table as he leaned across.

"I'm leaving. I *don't* know this woman Peters and I hardly know the other one, Miss Crane. I don't *care* what she say but if she say I *touch* her like that, she's lying!"

"Sit down, sir. We have letters which can prove you wrote to Miss Crane on several occasions. Nasty letters. Also there is a witness, her landlord, who says he warned you off his premises. Stalking is a new term for it. But the nuisance is as old as the hills and if you are unwilling to help us in our investigation the inference will be that you have something to hide. And that would be a pity, wouldn't it? We would then be forced to call upon a very respectable lady, the dentist's sister, to confirm certain information about the criminal vandalism of the surgery in Melford Road on April the twenty-first of this year. Mrs Watson has dreadful anxieties of her own at present. Her brother suffered a breakdown as a result of this break-in and the attack on his person, and the dentist is now missing, possibly dead. She may not wish to bring charges but there could be no alternative. I'm offering you a way out, Mr Khan. I feel sure there is a great deal of information about the people who worked at Chambers's surgery which would be useful to me in my current investigation into Lynne Peters's death and so far you are the only one who can help me. You do see my dilemma, don't you, sir?"

Arif Khan slumped back, clearly devastated by Blakeney's oblique line of questioning.

Sergeant Moss's craggy features rearranged themselves into a smile which resembled nothing so much as a mugger's grimace before a brutal assault.

"Shall we start again, sir?" Moss said, taking up the running. "Let's begin with the night of April the twenty-first when it is alleged you and your brother broke into the premises at Sixteen Melford Road and tied up a defenceless man, wrecked his surgery and made threats about his future."

Arif smiled, sensing the dearth of information the police actually held, and, with considerable satisfaction, anticipating that he was about to turn the tables on these two slow-witted Englishmen.

"Ah, well, Inspector, it seems to me that you have hardly *begun* to understand the wickedness which has been undetected among the so-called professional classes in this business or you would have realised that in order to see the full picture it will be necessary to go back long before the end of April. The crime really occurred in February and the groundwork for it was laid down even before that."

Twenty-Nine

"My sister Naseem arrived in England at the beginning of February to celebrate her engagement to Ahmed Rahman, a close friend of our family who lives in London. She had never left home before. Naseem was only eighteen years old, Inspector, she spoke little English and was very, very shy. My grandmother had brought her up and the marriage was arranged after a series of meetings last summer when Ahmed visited Lahore with my brother Zulfikar and myself."

"Your sister was happy with this proposal?"

"Entirely so. She was looking forward to living near her parents at last. My grandmother is too old to give a young girl any social life and Ahmed is a very successful solicitor in Ilford, well able to offer Naseem a happy life here. The match was eminently suitable to all of us."

This last remark was spoken with a mixture of pride and regret, Khan's rigid demeanor as he sat opposite the two policemen that of a man in full command of the situation, as if it was Arif Khan, not they, who directed proceedings.

"My brother and I accompanied Naseem on the flight here in February and my sister-in-law, Khalida, welcomed her into our home and helped her to come to terms with living in London. We are greatly in favour of traditional family values, Inspector, and the formal betrothal ceremony is a very important occasion."

"And this formal engagement party took place in February?" queried Moss, leafing through the notes taken in the course of his interview with Mrs Garland.

Khan nodded. "The wedding was to be in London on March fifteenth, a very grand affair involving much organisation, much more prestigious than the register office marriages so popular in this country," he contemptuously added.

"Your sister was well acquainted with her fiancé before her arrival here?"

"Oh, yes, indeed. She was much impressed by his situation, though I must correct any misapprehension you may have that Naseem, despite being an unsophisticated girl by English standards, was an uneducated person."

"No, no, of course not," Blakeney hastened to assure him. Khan opened his wallet and produced a studio photograph of a beautiful girl with lustrous dark eyes. "Naseem," he said simply. The picture lay on the table between them like a trump card.

Khan continued, his sing-song delivery almost hypnotic.

"We introduced her to our friends in London and accepted many invitations. Unfortunately, only a few weeks after her arrival Naseem had problems with toothache. It became extremely painful and my brother telephoned and booked an urgent appointment with Mr Chambers who agreed to treat her as an emergency after the surgery closed. Zulfikar took her to the surgery but there was a long delay. He eventually had to leave her unattended in the waiting room to take his son to a private tutorial but promised to come back for Naseem at seven o'clock after confirming with the dentist that that would be the earliest time she could be expected to leave."

"And Naseem was alone in the waiting room?"

"No. There was an old woman and then another emergency was admitted, a mother with a small girl, and my brother agreed to allow the lady to go after the old woman as the child was upset. My sister was happy to wait till last and a nurse was clearly working with the dentist when Zulfikar departed although he did not see her personally."

"But no receptionist?"

"No. She had gone before they arrived. The door was open."

"Members of your family had been patients of Mr Chambers before?"

"No, never." Khan smiled, showing beautifully even white teeth. "We have never suffered from decay of that sort. Naseem, also, was unfamiliar with dental treatment – perhaps," he suggested, "in anticipation of her wedding the silly girl had been grinding her teeth at night?"

191

Blakeney irritably urged him on, failing to see what the Khan nuptials had to do with the death of Lynne Peters six months later.

"My brother fetched Naseem in his car later and although she seemed very drowsy and uncommunicative, he assumed this to be the result of the injection. She went straight to bed and refused to join the family next morning. Under questioning, her behaviour became hysterical and Khalida, my sister-in-law, got worried. She persuaded me to telephone the surgery and request some advice. We had no experience of such drugs and their effects, you see. I spoke to a woman who said she was the nurse and who questioned me closely about Naseem. She suggested we took the girl to a doctor straight away if she was in pain."

"And that was that?"

"In our family we prefer herbal medicine as a rule and Naseem was adament that her toothache was gone but I suspected she was just afraid to face more drilling."

"And this was the next morning? Your conversation with the nurse?"

"The person I spoke to was most abrupt, cut me off very quickly once she had heard what I had to say. She seemed angry – insisting I should stay away from the surgery. But being unfamiliar with dental treatment I was unsure where the responsibility for Naseem lay. She *said* her toothache was better but the effect of the drugs had changed her overnight. She refused to confide in either Khalida or our mother and the nurse had told me the right thing to do was for Naseem to consult a doctor if we were worried."

"This was the dental nurse saying this?"

"Yes, the one I spoke to, although later, when I checked with Zulfikar, I found out Miss Crane was the one who made all the appointments and normally answered the telephone."

"So what did you do?"

"We did nothing. The wedding preparations continued, Naseem behaving very quietly. Then the unthinkable occurred – Naseem had another hysterical outburst and pleaded to be allowed to go back home."

"A quarrel with the bridegroom? Cold feet?"

Khan looked severely at Blakeney, his words spoken softly

but with bitter emphasis. "The engagement celebrations had already taken place and the wedding invitations accepted, you understand. In our culture, cancelling a wedding at such a stage is *unprecedented*."

"But it *was* cancelled?"

"Postponed."

"Your sister-in-law could shed no light on Naseem's abrupt change of mind?"

"We had a family conference and agreed that the culture shock had been too great for such a quietly brought up young girl and we reluctantly decided to allow her to return to our grandmother's house and put off the wedding for two months by which time Naseem would be happy to be married from there and return to London with her new husband. Cancelling all our preparations was an enormous loss of face for the family not to mention a financial sacrifice but we feared for Naseem's health."

"So she flew home alone?"

"With Khalida. Khalida stayed with her to the end."

"Then she *was* sick?"

"In mind. In April my brother and I flew out to finalise the wedding arrangements but Naseem was much worse, refusing even to talk to Khalida or to consult our own doctor in Lahore. The situation deteriorated badly and when my brother became angry with her she finally confessed to Khalida what had happened in London. She had been raped by Chambers in the dentist's room. Naseem had remained fully awake during the assault but had been unable to move."

"Why didn't she tell the family straight away?" Moss interjected.

"Naseem was terrified, ashamed, utterly destroyed by what had happened to her. Can you not imagine her state of mind? A young girl in a foreign land, speaking hardly any English, betrothed as a virgin, the focus of a huge celebration? Khalida told her to return with us and we would report this wicked man, bring him to justice."

"And the fiancé? How did he take all this? I assume you *told* him?"

"Ahmed wanted *no* police involvement. He was willing to continue with the marriage if Naseem returned to London to a traditional wedding ceremony and so quenched the rumours which had already begun to circulate in our community. Ahmed suggested we explained Naseem's sudden illness on the English weather."

Blakeney stifled a hoot of derision, wondering how much blame could be levelled on the poor bloody climate but Khan's tragic expression brought him back to earth with a bang.

"She died."

"Abroad? Before the wedding?"

"My sister was too humiliated. She killed herself. She feared she was eternally soiled by this act and was even – so she confided in Khalida – fearful of having been impregnated by that monster! Naseem threw herself into the river. We held the funeral from my grandmother's house and came home to tell my parents what had happened. We tried to persuade them to report Mr Chambers to the police but my father refused to drag Naseem's name through the courts and, in truth, without her evidence, it would be pointless. She left no letter of explanation. We only had Khalida's word."

"Chambers acted alone?"

"We never knew. My brother was very angry – our family honour had been trampled in the dirt by that devil of a man and keeping Naseem's suffering a secret had been forced upon us. We decided on revenge. Not only for Naseem but for any other defenceless girl he might attack in the future."

"So you vandalised the surgery?"

"We rang the bell and forced ourselves in through the dentist's private entrance to his upstairs flat which is at the back, through the yard. We overcame him quite easily and bundled him into the surgery. Then we stripped off his clothes and tied him to the chair and made him witness the destruction of all his expensive equipment. We threated that if *ever* he tried to set up business again we would report him to the General Dental Council and ruin his life for ever. It was only out of respect for our parents that we had not done so already and by the time we left the man to spend the rest of the night contemplating our promises, his naked fear was self-evident. He was more scared of us than of criminal prosecution."

"You were not concerned that he would report you both to the police?"

"No, never. Chambers knew we were capable of ruining him and that even if he destroyed us too, Zulfikar and I have relatives who would never let such injustice go unpunished. Our family had been avenged."

Blakeney looked winded, mentally calculating the latent outbreaks of violence averted only by Chambers's acceptance of the brothers' threats.

"There is a possibility that your sister was not the first naive foreign girl to be attacked by this rogue dentist."

Khan looked up, vindication unfurling like a banner in his imagination.

"Asian?" he said.

"A Filipina."

Moss butted in. "Tell me, Mr Khan, why did you continue your surveillance of the Chambers set-up *after* the dentist had gone?"

"I wanted to make quite sure he was not relocating. We also needed to know about the nurse. If, in fact, Mr Chambers's sister – or the nurse I spoke to on the telephone the morning after Naseem's treatment – were as guilty as he in this rape of our lovely girl. We have long memories, Zulfikar and I. Our desire for *complete* revenge on all those involved grew with each passing day, festered in our hearts after our sister's death. Nothing would satisfy us but the sure knowledge that the man and his circle were destroyed."

"You planned to kill him?"

Khan's narrow shoulders lifted in wry dismissal. "We heard he was already dead. Had drowned. It would have been a fitting end. But we made enquiries and it seemed more likely to be an elaborate way of shaking us off. We feared he *was* planning to practise again, abroad perhaps. Or under another name? Changing one's name is a very simple matter in this country and a dentist with British qualifications can set up almost anywhere in the world."

"And Lynne Peters? The dental nurse. Where did she fit in this family feud?"

"We suspected her at first but my brother found out where she lived and discovered she had quarrelled with Chambers the very day I spoke on the phone to her about Naseem's reaction to the treatment the evening before, and left her job that same

195

morning. It was as if she guessed what had happened. She was angry, not defensive – she would not have urged me to take my sister to the doctor if she had been involved in the rape. Later I decided I had suspected the wrong person – then I started following the pretty one, Miss Crane, assuming *she* was Chambers's accomplice in all this."

"You were wrong both times, Mr Khan. Those girls were not involved in any way, not in your sister's attack at any rate. The senior one, Lynne Peters, was brought in by Chambers and his sister, Mrs Watson, to settle a complaint laid by the Filipina patient two years previously. Peters must have threatened never to help Chambers again if such an incident was repeated. I imagine she left so suddenly because having spoken to you on the telephone she guessed that your sister was another victim. Miss Peters was on your side, Mr Khan, but she had no wish to be involved in any rape case, especially if it dredged up her part in the Filapina's compensation. Now *she* is dead."

"Perhaps instead of wasting your time with me, you should be looking for Mr Chambers."

Sergeant Moss closed his eyes, knowing, too late, that he and Blakeney had been chasing the wrong cat up the wrong alley when they *should* have been setting a trap for the bloody dentist.

Thirty

P hoebe showed Mimsie into a comfortable sitting room, the sort of room set displayed in furniture exhibitions – all plush sofas, reproduction Chippendale and loopy curtains: expensive trad. Middle-Class Cosy.

Mimsie was pleased to see Phoebe restored in herself and fitting into her normal habitat like a hermit crab, safe from the billowy world outside. She made some coffee and they sat in front of the gas-fired log fire as if the sheer horror of the past few months had never existed.

Mimsie sipped her coffee, the flight bag at her feet like a time bomb ticking away, a device too obvious to ignore but which nevertheless Phoebe affected not to notice. After a preliminary skirmish around the painful business of Mr Chambers's disappearance, Mimsie ventured to dig deeper.

"I brought the flight bag back for you."

"Yes, of course." Phoebe hardly glanced at the black object sitting on her nice Indian carpet and started speaking about the wonderful show of chrysanthemums in the garden. Mimsie butted in, determined to have her say.

"He's not coming back, you know."

"I'm not a fool, Mimsie," Phoebe replied evenly. "I *know* he isn't."

"You accept he isn't coming back but do you realise he isn't dead?"

"Yes. I've had to face up to that."

"What made you change your mind?"

"He came back."

"Here?" Mimsie squeaked.

"To the bungalow at Pevensey."

"When?"

"It's a long story. After the vandalism of the surgery in

197

the spring Edward was obsessed with making a new life for himself abroad. Somewhere the Khans could not trace him. Trouble was he just did not have enough capital and Khan was threatening exposure if he tried to set up as a dentist again."

"What hold did Khan have on Mr Chambers?"

"The rape in the surgery two years ago – Lynne confided to you about that, didn't she?"

"How did you guess?"

Phoebe shrugged. "Lynne Peters renegotiated her terms on the strict understanding it never happened again."

"Did it?"

"Regrettably, yes. At the beginning of March Lynne had had a brief telephone conversation with Khan following a request for advice about his sister. Khan is a common name these days but as the patient had been treated after hours alarm bells rang in Lynne's craven little brain and she spoke to me. I poo-pooed it, of course, and naturally Edward denied it. There was a row and Lynne stormed out. Nothing further was heard from the Khans and the matter was forgotten – I assumed Lynne had made a vulgar attempt to extort extra money from my brother by her unfounded accusations. Weeks later Edward received a call from one of the Khan family saying their sister, whom he had treated, had died after flying back to their homeland and that he was responsible. He said nothing of this to me at the time but when the surgery was vandalised Edward admitted that the Khans were the perpetrators and his career was finished unless he could start again abroad."

"Did you guess he had raped another girl?"

"At first he denied it but he was in such distress the time for pretending was past. He drove off to Eastbourne to consult his psychiatrist and I followed as soon as possible."

"You've been very loyal, Phoebe. Personally, I couldn't have stuck by the man like that."

Phoebe patted her hair, stolid as ever. "Edward was ill. The breakdown was not feigned, Mimsie. He railed on about starting again – he had worked in the Middle East as a young man and harboured this longing to go back. He was being as impractical as ever, of course, not helped by hiding away in that hideously expensive clinic. My house here which we jointly own is mortgaged and linked with Edward's insurance policies, the surgery could take ages to sell and I have no income of my own. What with Lynne's increased wages and the costs of running the practice we made very little extra for a rainy day."

"There was the nestegg in his safe, of course."

"Ah, yes, of course there was that." Phoebe dismissed this awkward observation of Mimsie's as if twenty thousand pounds tucked away was a mere handful of dust.

"And then he walked out on you in Pevensey, and pretended to have committed suicide?"

"Oh no. That was my idea."

Mimsie slopped her coffee, the surface normality of their little tête-à-tête shattering like a glass wall between them. "What did you say?"

"I'm afraid so. You seem shocked. We were trapped, Mimsie. It was the only way out. I wrote the blackmail note during a visit to the clinic one afternoon and posted it myself in London. It would, in due course, substantiate the reason for Edward's apparent suicide and allow us to finance his disappearance without making me a conspirator to any fraud. While I remained the apparently innocent victim of Edward's scheme I would be safe."

"But why didn't you back him up? You did everything you could to throw doubts on his suicide."

"Mr Miller is a shrewd investigator. If I had immediately pursued an insurance claim I would have been as guilty as Edward if things went wrong. As it was, Mr Miller was on *my* side, especially after that ridiculous business of the tramp who was killed in the car crash being mistaken for Edward. That was a bizarre twist of events, something I had *not* forseen." Phoebe dabbed at the stain on Mimsie's lap with a lace-edged napkin, the flowery scent of her face powder cloying.

"Weren't you tempted, Phoebe? I mean tempted to play along at that stage? Get the claim out of the way and abandon that awful charade in Pevensey?"

"No, never! I was content to let matters take their course – get a job and wait until the seven years had elapsed if necessary. Obviously no dead body was ever going to be washed up and with half the cash from the 'blackmail' I was content to live modestly until the insurance company got tired of holding out."

"And Mr Chambers? Was he content to wait?"

"Ah, you've put your finger on it, Mimsie. That was the weakness in my plan. I should have known that a man who could not even control his sexual urges would be incapable of holding to our agreement for years if necessary. He couldn't cope on his own, you see. I packed him off to Thailand at the end of May—"

"When he had 'died' in the sea?"

Phoebe nodded. "I told Edward to lie low but being so dependent on me all these years he just hadn't the courage to get on with it. He appeared on my doorstep in the middle of August, wanting to give himself up, if you please! Abandon my long-term plans, throw aside my weeks of misery living in that wretched rathole of a bungalow, my groundwork put in with Mr Miller. I ask you! His idea was to pretend he had been suffering from amnesia, that I knew nothing of any insurance fraud, knew nothing of his weeks on the beach. But how would that sound? As I said, Mr Miller wasn't gullable, he was an experienced investigator, well able to shake down any flimsy story Edward could invent and before we knew where we were that stupid brother of mine would have confessed *my* involvement in the plan. And if Edward gave himself up, not only were we no nearer setting him up afresh in a different location but our savings had dwindled and at best we would need a good lawyer or end up being prosecuted."

"Couldn't Mr Chambers have set up a new practice in another part of England? Khan isn't exactly the CIA, Phoebe. I've met him. He's actually a pathetic little man."

Phoebe roared with laughter, an uninhibited chortle which caused her bosom to rock about like a sack of flour. "You didn't see the brother! No undernourished weakling, I assure you, Mimsie." She fingered her pearls and earnestly continued just as if she was describing a harvest festival. "The Khans were as suspicious as Mr Miller about the so-called suicide. I had heard rumours about one of them enquiring in the neighbourhood about the staff, trying to question people about Edward. At first I thought the discovery of the tramp's body would settle the Khans' vendetta but on reflection I *dare not* try to pass it off, *dare not* be the one to place myself open to prosecution if Edward did give himself up and confessed our scheme."

"You didn't trust him?"

"Edward was unstable after all those months alone. You would think living on a beach with a fluctuating population of other perverts would be his idea of heaven, wouldn't you, Mimsie? He was safe from prosecution so long as he stayed put in Thailand and if the man had had *any* gumption he might eventually have been able to set up a dental practice again. These foreigners are none too fussy about minor sexual indiscretions."

"But it wasn't minor, was it? He ruined two girl's lives and the last one died. What happened? An infection?"

"Suicide. Religious scruples of some kind her brother said."

"Even so—"

"Look, I'm only telling you all this to put your mind at rest, dear. So you know that everything is perfectly all right. There's absolutely no need to continue your silly interference with things which do not concern you. Edward will go abroad again and disappear for ever, I shall live quietly here and eventually reap my reward. There might be something in it for you, dear," she slyly added.

"Are you no longer planning to meet up with your brother when everything is settled?"

"No. In these last few months I have realised that the man is a weak fool and can only bring destruction on us both by his psychotic behaviour. He panics you see. Edward is unreliable in a crisis. I should have taken Dr Wellington's warnings more seriously."

"You mean he murdered Lynne!"

"What makes you think that? Khan will be convicted on that score. He was known to be pursuing her, blamed her for assisting Edward in his sexual deviations."

"Khan would never kill anyone, not really. He may have thought Lynne was acting *with* Mr Chambers in the rapes but he wouldn't *kill* anyone. He just wanted to protect girls like his sister being molested – he just wanted to stop Mr Chambers's horrible attacks without bringing public disgrace

201

on his family. The police have already let him go – they believe him, Phoebe, they know all about the Khan threats if he tried to set up as a dentist again. The Inspector phoned me this evening to assure me that Mr Khan was no longer a danger to me. I thought he was out to get me, really I did, but we were wrong, Phoebe."

"Well, who do *you* think murdered her? She had a boyfriend, you know, she told me so when she came down to Pevensey to fetch the account books."

"Then she must have told you he was abroad and that was how she got to borrow his car. Khan's fireproof, Phoebe."

"You didn't know Lynne as we did, dear. She was a greedy girl, took advantage of our generosity in every possible way. For all we know she tried the same tactics on her current employer, got into the way of extracting money from professional men. Or associated with unsavory partners through one of those escort agencies one reads about."

"That's rubbish! She was as poor as a church mouse, Phoebe. If she had been as grasping as you say, why did she walk out when she suspected Mr Chambers had raped a *second* girl? If Lynne had been as unprincipled as you say, she would have a double hold on you both, been in a position to milk you for evermore."

"Lynne Peters had no staying power. She was as weak as Edward in her own way. No stamina to brave it out on our side."

"Why did Lynne want the account books?"

"Presumably to try to pin us down on the undeclared treatments in Bayswater. There was no point in arousing her suspicions that I was in collusion with him over that by refusing her access to the accounts. I merely witheld the relevant receipt book. She trusted me. She thought I was Edward's victim too. The feminist angle." She snorted, immediately stifling this unladylike response in her hankie.

"But you were wrong about the account books, Phoebe. Lynne only wanted them in order to trace Khan. To *help you*, Phoebe. The poor woman really thought you were innocent. I bet she even telephoned you to say she knew how to trace Khan and was going to report the man for harassing us all in his search for Mr Chambers who Lynne thought was safely dead, out of the firing line. No scandal could affect him any more in her mind and by bringing the Khans' vendetta out into the open, you, me and Lynne would be free. You were wrong about Lynne Peters and I admit she gave me a funny impression at first. But when you got to know her, you realised she was basically a decent, honest person with a kind heart."

"People like that are dangerous."

"What?"

"I have spent all my life uselessly supporting hopeless causes. My husband was a weak man and I soon saw there was no future for me there. Edward was in the same category but he was my brother – you can't throw off flesh and blood as easily. I supported Edward for *years* but he was becoming dangerously unpredictable. Edward had the power to bring us both down. He was the sort of man who mawkishly feels contrite. Even as a boy, the essential frailty was there. He would do something frightful like the occasion when he experimentally gassed our family cat. I covered up for him and before you knew it, the stupid boy had this terrible urge to confess. *I* was the one who was punished for being *dishonest*. As if covering up a crime is as heinous as the crime itself!"

Mimsie drew back. "*Did* he kill Lynne?"

"I'm afraid he did though I don't think he intended to. I had been hiding him in that nasty bungalow for weeks and trying to persuade him to make a break for it, try to lose himself again in Brazil or in one of those North American places, Mexico or somewhere. But he was obsessed with the idea that I would abandon him. Deep down he knew I never intended to move abroad. Living in England suits me so well, you see. He had ridiculous notions of taking a new identity so we could set up together overseas but I had had my first taste of independence. It dawned on me that I need never *share* the insurance money at all. I had been the one willing to wait it out, to play my part effectively. Edward was becoming seriously unbalanced, entirely losing any ability to function alone, to think logically."

"He really was mad?"

"No, of course not. But weak people are fundamentally destructive. After Lynne had gone off with the books and

203

I tried to put his mind at rest about her intentions, he still could not accept her puny plan to contact the Khan family. Later that Sunday night, Lynne telephoned and told me she had traced Khan's address and Edward flew out of control, begged me to drive to Fulham straight away and talk her out of it. I refused, of course. But he raged on all night and there seemed no other way but to go along with his idea that a girl like Lynne Peters had been cooperative over the Filipina and would be cooperative again if we put it to her that she could share the insurance payout if she kept quiet. We had nothing else to bribe her with – we needed the twenty thousand to help us get through the long wait, but I stupidly allowed myself to be persuaded to speak to her, to try to talk her out of going to the police. There was no sense in raking over that old story even if my brother was officially dead and beyond being damaged by the scandal, just so us women could be relieved of Khan's nuisance calls and so on. We thought it best if I arrived at Ruskin Street unannounced, giving me an element of surprise."

"To see her alone? Did you intend to admit your insurance scam?"

"Confessing all was *his* idea. I didn't think it necessary. I thought I would try talking to her alone and see how she reacted. Play it by ear."

Mimsie nodded, appalled by the woman's calm insistence on what at best was a cockeyed idea of fair play and at worst, the barefaced manipulation of anyone who got in the way.

"Next evening, Monday, I knocked on the door and talked my way in, saying I had decided to move back to my house in London and needed a friend to share my troubles. Lynne wasn't a stupid girl, just not the right calibre to carry things off the way I suggested. I told her about our plan to claim the insurance money but it would take time. Would she be patient? The silly girl reacted in quite the wrong way, started shouting, and Edward, who was standing in the porch trying to curb his impatience, eventually rang the doorbell and pushed his way in. Not the way I planned it at all and obviously it gave Lynne the most awful fright seeing Edward in that fearful state, looking like a demented fool. The man upstairs was busy listening to his radio. Very loud it was. We argued

204

for hours and Lynne showed us this picture of the Filipina and said she would insist this witness returned to England and gave evidence for the Khans. Fancy keeping in touch like that! Very disloyal, don't you agree? She claimed to have traced Khan through one of the receipt books I'd given her, I can't think how, and was going to visit him next day to discuss the two cases. She wouldn't listen to reason. Not even bribery. The rest was an accident."

"*You* killed her?"

"No, of course not. Wherever do you get these ideas, Mimsie? Edward went crazy. He was still enamoured of this idea that the dental board must never find out about his goings on – as if it mattered in view of the rest! – and grabbed a pair of tights from the laundry basket on the table. She was in the middle of some ironing. At that time of night? Fancy."

"Lots of working girls have to fit in the ironing at odd hours, Phoebe," she muttered inconsequentially, dreading the affirmation of her worst fears.

Phoebe continued, unperturbed.

"He threw the tights around her neck from behind and stood at the back of her chair the way he used to when examining his patients. Suddenly I realised how excited Edward had become, sexually aroused even! He was no longer a timid little man. He towered over that girl, exerting a tremendous power – he even frightened me! I couldn't stop him. He gave the ligature a sudden twist and she slumped onto the floor."

"And you just watched?" Mimsie whispered.

"I bolted. Drove back to Pevensey like a madwoman."

"You left him there?"

"No, but there was my own self-preservation to consider, Mimsie! There was no evidence I had been there. I hadn't even taken off my gloves. I had had enough of shielding Edward from himself. If he was caught I would deny the whole thing and no one would even begin to suspect a woman who had behaved so honorably, been so steadfast in her loyalty."

"You were an accessory, Phoebe. To murder. And what about collusion with the attacks on the girls?"

"At that time Khan knew nothing about the Filipina – Lynne hadn't had a chance to have her little conference

205

with him. And I genuinely was uninvolved in the second attack on Khan's sister, you know. Edward was alone in the surgery that February evening and not a wisp of it began to circulate for weeks. He thought he was in the clear with that one. Just another simple girl, the last sort to cry havoc – but in the Khan case he had not realised she was not, unlike the little foreign maid, alone in London. He might have guessed that a girl like that would have a family, stupid man. These people stick together like glue. The wretched Khan business was like a forest fire, starting from a single spark and slowly gathering momentum. It was slow to take hold, mainly because of the intense trust these people have in their womenfolk, the enormous pride in the sanctity of an arranged marriage. Positively medieval!"

"You *can't* get away with it."

"Oh, but I have. As soon as I realised she was dead I searched the entire flat for those surgery accounts. I wished nothing to lead the police back to us and, after all, it had been six months since Lynne left our employ. But I had to give up – Edward was almost unconscious with shock. I had to get him away."

"So you did take him home?"

"For another few days. But we argued all the time and it was difficult to keep him hidden in the bungalow. There was no other way out, he knew that. So I drove him back to the quiet beach where he staged his 'suicide' before and explained what he must do. It was in the small hours and the place was deserted."

"And he accepted this?"

"Edward knew there was no more space to manoeuvre. It was high tide and we were quite alone. I watched him walk away in the darkness towards a little jetty and walk along to the end. I saw him jump. He didn't surface. In fact, he couldn't swim. His body will eventually get washed up along the coast."

Phoebe was entirely composed, her expression one of genuine regret.

"Then you can really claim the insurance?"

"Oh yes. No need to wait for years as I had anticipated."

"But what about Lynne?"

206

"There's nothing to connect me with Lynne."

"But there is. She telephoned the bungalow. Twice. It will appear on her telephone bill. The police will trace it."

"The bungalow isn't in my name."

"That won't stop them."

"I shall just say she phoned to talk about old times. You yourself gave her my phone number."

Mimsie leapt up, suddenly afraid. "What about me?"

"What do you mean?"

"Well, I know Mr Chambers killed Lynne."

"But you won't say, will you, Mimsie? Why should you get involved?"

"I knew her, Phoebe. I can't just let it go at that."

"I think you can." She picked up the tray and placed it on a side table, and positioned herself, blocking Mimsie's only exit. "You've been living from hand to mouth for *years*. Why should a girl like you get mixed up in a murder? Don't run away with the idea that you can blackmail me. I've arranged things very nicely and I don't intend to be hamstrung by another useless hanger-on for the rest of my life." Phoebe slipped the scarf from her neck and advanced, her bulky figure moving forward with the inevitability of a train in a tunnel.

"Mr Chambers didn't kill Lynne, did he?"

"No. He wasn't even there. I left him in the car. But even if he had been there he wouldn't have had the nerve. The rest is true enough. When I got home and told him the full story of how my efforts to bribe the stupid girl had failed he willingly took the course I had mapped out for him. He drowned. He really drowned, this time."

"And if you kill me, what then?"

"Girls like you get dumped in ditches every day of the week. No one knows you're here. Khan was the only person stalking you and he gave up weeks ago. I could leave your body in the park even. Why not?"

Mimsie gripped Toby's gun in the pocket of her jacket and pulled it out. The effect was electric, Phoebe reeling back, her face ashen. Mimsie moved forward, keeping both hands on the gun in the way she had seen the NYPD women on television handle their firearms, slowly backing Phoebe into a corner. She leaned against the desk where Phoebe did her accounts and without taking her eyes off her quarry, lifted the receiver and dialled 999.

Thirty-One

Mimsie managed to fit in lunch with Steve Epps at Cosmo's the following Friday, her days following the arrest of Phoebe Watson being a whirl of newspaper interviews and photocalls. Cosmo had reserved their corner table, placing a bottle of fizz on ice in recognition of his favourite customer's brush with celebrity, the muted buzz of deals filling the atmosphere like droning insects on a hot summer afternoon. It was quite like old times.

Steve was there first which was a novelty, Mimsie reflected. And he held out her chair for her too which was certainly a new twist. Mimsie looked radiant, the stress of the past weeks wiped out at a stroke. Steve filled their glasses and offered a toast.

"To Mimsie, the girl with the lethal popgun."

She laughed, slapping his hand which lay on the pink tablecloth, the waiter's eyes rolling in wry disbelief. Steve had already ordered for them both so that at least hadn't changed.

"Tell me, doll, where did it come from, this little revolver you just happened to have tucked up?"

"The replica? It was Toby's, a souvenir he brought back from the States, I think. Aileen was going to throw it out when we were sorting his stuff and I asked her if I could take it. A sort of memento really. I just slipped it in my pocket and forgot about it. Toby couldn't have left me anything more valuable."

"Still got it?"

"Yes. After a struggle. Blakeney wasn't keen but I said it was of sentimental value, a gift from an old friend."

"And it really looks the business?"

"You bet. Fooled Phoebe. It probably wouldn't have done

209

in other circumstances but the sheer shock of me suddenly producing a weapon put her off her stride long enough for me to get help."

"Whew! Wouldn't have thought you had it in you, kid."

The seafood platter arrived and Mimsie veered off the painful subject and asked Steve about the regulars still on the Chain Gang.

"Austen's got a part in a panto in Wolverhampton. Wangled a spot for Bobby an'all which was lousy of him. Means I'll be short over Christmas just when I really need someone on the gate to keep an eye on them villains."

"Bit downmarket for Austen, isn't it?"

"He's not proud. And Bobby's over the moon."

"We *must* go and see it, Steve."

He quickly changed the subject, Wolverhampton hardly lighting any flares in his imagination. He rattled on, fascinated by the Chambers affair, unable to leave it alone.

"What's going to happen? To Phoebe and the brother I mean? Let's face it, Mims, without that silly old sod Chambers backing you up you'd have been right in the shit, gun or no gun."

She laughed. "I was due for a stroke of luck." Then, sobering, she admitted, "But you're right. Phoebe Watson was the most fantastic liar. I was completely taken in right to the end. Who would have believed a boring old bag like that could so nearly pull it off? Hatching that insurance scam, setting up the phony blackmail, not to mention—"

"Hang about! You mean there *was* no blackmail?"

"No, never. Phoebe wrote the note, posted it in London, collected the money from the safe in the surgery and never needed to go through that nonsense of leaving the cash under a table in the supermarket cafe at all. It was brilliant the way she tied us all up in knots, leading everyone to assume she was Chambers's dupe."

"Blimey, Austen could take a few tips from her when it comes to putting it over. Amazing."

"That was it. Not only did she look distressed and ill after all those months in the bungalow but she kept changing her lines, admitting things which, oddly enough, only made us believe her story even more. It was only right at the end, when she knew I wasn't going to play along with it, that she turned on me and came out with something *like* the truth and even then I wasn't sure. She'll probably trot out *another* story when it comes to court, you see."

"*He* had the last laugh though, you've got to hand it to the guy."

"Mr Chambers? When I think how close I got to disaster it makes my flesh creep. I'd certainly been completely taken in by Phoebe's story about his 'real' suicide by drowning, so I was totally flabbergasted when he turned up – she would have convinced Blakeney I had flipped, you know. All she had to do was deny everything. I hadn't a single bit of proof."

"Did he drive to Fulham with her to see the Peters girl that night?"

"Yes. That's why dealing with Phoebe's lies was so impossible. A lot of what she said *was* right. He did browbeat her into confronting Lynne but he stayed outside in the car the whole time. He only learned about the murder when Phoebe cannonballed out of there and drove them both back to the coast. I'm sure she hadn't intended to kill her but then Phoebe couldn't accept that I wouldn't play ball either. She misjudged both of us."

"And his *second* 'suicide'. *That* was her idea?"

"So Chambers told the police. She had controlled the man all his life, of course. That much she admitted and, looking back, you can see it, though when *I* knew him he didn't strike me as a wimp. Basically, he had a conscience, that was the trouble. Phoebe recognised that this fatal flaw of his was the weak spot in the insurance fraud. Once she told him she had been forced to murder Lynne to save them, he fell apart. Suggesting he *really* killed himself this time must have seemed a happy release for a man in a frail psychological state faced with being shackled with a homicidal harpy for the rest of time. Problem was he couldn't swim."

"Mimsie! That's the whole *point* of drowning!"

She delicately wiped her mouth on her napkin, leaning back to allow the waiter to remove the platter of fish debris from the table. "If Phoebe had offered him a syringe filled with one of his druggy concoctions the man would have taken it, no messing. But sending him out to jump off the end of a jetty in the pitch dark was really not on. He was *afraid* of the sea, poor man."

"He waded ashore?"

"No, he was too frightened to strike out for the beach and too frightened to let go of the jetty when he surfaced. He apparently clung to the girders underneath until an angler turned up hours later at dawn to set up his rods and things. He heard poor old Chambers bleating and splashing about under the jetty, got hold of a rowing boat and eventually reeled him in. He was frozen stiff and too far gone to say anything. Lay unconscious in hospital for hours. He had no identification on him and when he did come round refused to utter a word. They thought he was a harmless nutter and transferred him to a psychiatric unit. Later his lifesaving angler visited him as a friend – he was some sort of lay preacher apparently – and Chambers broke down and spilled the beans. The police got the rest out of him and luckily it matched my story so I was finally off the hook myself."

"Blakeney didn't believe you?"

"Not at first, no. Honestly, Steve, Phoebe was absolutely credible. Talk about being calm under pressure! She flatly denied the whole thing and, let's face it, she doesn't *look* like Lady Macbeth, does she?"

"Well hardly!"

"Never mind. One good thing came out of it though. Mr Miller's offered me a job."

"The insurance inspector?"

"Yes. He was *very* impressed by my performance. He believed Phoebe, too, at first. I wasn't the only mug."

"And what's the job? His secretary?"

"Have a heart! He's asked me to train as his assistant. A sort of detective. How about that? Lots of foreign travel. Masses of expenses. Nice clothes. The business!"

"And he pays you as well as shelling out for all this globetrotting?"

"More than *you* ever did, Steve Epps. *And* every month. I'll even get to keep the Rolex on a regular basis for a change."

Steve looked crestfallen, like a man watching his dreamboat disappear over the horizon. She blew him a kiss before tucking into her steak.

212

"And what happens to the new boyfriend while you're raking it in with this new racket?"

"Alex?" She paused, her fork in mid-air, wary as an alley cat. "Who told you about Alex?"

Steve shrugged, still mulish.

"Well, if you must know, we've come to a little arrangement. I keep on my flat at Mr Phidias's place and Alex and I play it by ear."

"In bloody Esher? With a poncy *solicitor*?" His response was not encouraging, his experience of lawyers far from rosy and Suburbia clearly off the edge of the world in his book.

"I need my own space," she retorted, a key phrase she had latched onto from reading *Cosmopolitan* which seemed to cover most exigencies. Steve looked slightly mollified and as a makeweight Mimsie rushed in with, "And I haven't forgotten the thousand I owe you. Mr Miller might be able to get me some sort of reward from the insurance company for my part in nailing Phoebe."

"Great." He didn't sound enthusiastic. "And does the poor bloody angler get a wedge for fishing Chambers out of the soup? And the Khans? What about them?"

Mimsie stared at her plate, caught up in the ramifications of the whole wretched business. "There will be a prosecution of some sort but Blakeney thinks they'll get off lightly. In view of their cooperation with the police, he said."

"Well, I never!" Steve's cynical response threatened to cloud the celebration but Mimsie plunged on, dispersing his blues at a stroke.

"What about Toby's house? Did you and Jerry Logan pull it off with Rita? Persuade her to put her inheritance your way?"

Steve grinned, the old chirpy chappy rising above the small change of winning and losing.

"Yeah. Even Rita ain't immune to my charm for ever, babe. You wait, chasing iffy suicides round the fleshpots of the living dead'll soon seem a bit of a drag. And when it does, Mimsie Crane will be back on her knees, begging to work for Epps Building Services, just see if she don't."

213

Mimsie laughed. "Dream on, boyo."

But somewhere in the back of her mind a small doubt no bigger than a spark flickered in response.

* * *